# Until Now...

Denise Skelton

Library of Congress control number 2009936834



First Chance Publishing books may be ordered through booksellers or by contacting

First Chance Publishing
4725 Dorsey Hall Dr. Ste A 404
Ellicott City, MD 21042
443-739-6571

ISBN-13: 978-0-9790877-3-8 (pbk)
ISBN-13: 978-0-9790877-8-3 (ebk)
ISBN-10: 0-9790877-3-2 (pbk)

Cover art by Bookadesing.com
Printed in the United States of America

# Acknowledgements

To my friends, new and old.
Because of my writing, I have been blessed with meeting an array of wonderful new friends in the last few years. This book is dedicated to them. Lorna R, and Linda B, who always encourage me with their great emails. Theirdre C. who just graduated with a GPA 3.9, Kathy H., and Laura K., whose strength is second to none. And, to the rest of my kind and loving friends, that have supported me along the way.

Love ya all,
Denise

A special thanks to Robin L. of Saskatchewan Canada. Robin's suggestion, *Until Now...* was the winning title entry in the contest to help name this book.

# Chapter 1

"Oooh, lord," Terry Meyers Wilkerson said, letting out a long slow moan. Sucking in a deep breath, she gingerly slid the pillow over her head, hoping to block the glare of the early morning sunlight shining through the bedroom window. "Oh crap," she whispered, and cringed from the echo of what seemed to be an unbelievably loud and constant drip-drip of water that leaked from the showerhead in the adjacent bathroom.

Shifting slightly, she finally noticed the arm thrown across her left shoulder and the leg across her left hip. She groaned, pushing the arm and leg away as she rolled on to her back and pushed her hair from her face. Her head was pounding, her mouth was as dry as sand, and it tasted like she had licked something too revolting to be identified.

*The margaritas*, she thought, and groaned again, then tried to burrow her way into the mattress.

The shift of movement from the opposite side of the bed made her groan again. Terry had been sleeping alone for almost two years. Her husband had left her and their two sons. Well, more like abandoned them for his new woman, his new child, and his new life. Terry had grown accustomed to sleeping alone, and she wasn't sure she wanted to share her bed with anyone; at least not for more than a few hours here and there. She especially didn't want to wake to find that a testosterone-based mammal had spent the night in her bed.

"Hey." She nudged the warm body beside her. "Hey. Wake up. What are you doing in here?"

"You said I could," came a groggy reply.

Frowning, Terry let her mind trace the previous evening's events. She'd had gone out for drinks and dancing at Jillian's. She'd met someone. What was his name? Ethan, Elton, Erin? That was it, Erin. Erin was fine, with long lean legs and a killer smile. He'd spent most of the evening with Terry, listening attentively, laughing in all the right places, and gazing at her as if she had hung the stars. Until she mentioned her sons; at that point, Erin headed for the hills.

*The prick.*

He had told Terry that he was going to the men's room. Twenty minutes later, Terry saw him whispering sweet nothings in another woman's ear.

Terry had hoped to go out to dinner a few times with Erin, maybe get intimate. She wasn't expecting a vow of love or even a promise ring. But, damn! After Erin found a new woman, Terry spent the remainder of the evening sucking down margaritas, hoping to drown her misery as she complained about how all men were the scum of the earth.

"God, I hate men," she complained. "All of you. Pigs!"

"That's pretty harsh," Ben, Terry's cousin, Dee's husband, said as he raised his hand to get the waitress's attention.

Terry glanced up at him, and gave a sharp nod of her head. "Harsh. But true."

"Terry, I believe you just keep picking the wrong type of men," Dee said. "Maybe you need to look deeper; look for substance instead of outward appearances."

## Chapter 1

Terry looked around the padded booth at her family and friends. Ben was smiling lovingly at his wife. With her hair piled on her head and soft ringlets hanging around her neck, Dee looked much younger than her thirty-five years. Ben reached out, stroking his wife's cheek with her flawless cocoa complexion, his emerald green eyes shining with love and admiration. On the opposite side of the booth, Terry and Dee's best friend, Holly, sat with her back against Tyler, her fiancé's, chest while his left arm draped across her left shoulder. Holly, a police detective, had the fiery red hair and green eyes of her Irish ancestors.

"David wasn't the wrong kind of man," Terry reminded Dee. "He had substance; he wanted to get married, have a family, and settle down. He wanted all the things that women think makes a good husband."

"Well," Tyler said, after placing another drink order. "Call me crazy, but from where I'm sitting, there seems to be a bit of a problem. David may have wanted to settle down and have a family; he just wanted to do it with more than one woman."

Terry glared at him. "Why, thank you, Sunshine. Thank you for reminding me that my ex- husband is a lowlife adulterer." Tyler grinned apologetically, showing perfectly even, white teeth and deep dimples. His skin looked like smooth milk chocolate, and in the last few months he had started sporting a beard, which only added to his extraordinary good looks. Terry let out an unattractive snort. "Scum, all of you. That's it," she said, banging her fist on the tabletop, startling everyone. "That's it, I'm through. No more men for me. I'm swearing off men. No dating, no sex, no nothing, for the next, one…uh, two... Uh, no, better make that one year."

Holly picked up her drink, and grinned at Terry. "You, Terry Ann Meyers, with no man in your life for a year? I don't see that happening."

"David and I have been separated for nearly two years, and I haven't been seeing anyone."

"Not for the lack of trying," Holly reminded her. "Terry, you've gone out on a couple of dates over the last two years."

"One date does not imply seeing someone. I went to dinner a few times."

"What about that guy with the big head. What was his name? William?" Dee asked. "You went out with him a few times."

"Three times, and only because he said he was a plumber and would fix the drain in the downstairs bathroom. Unfortunately, the only elbows that he knew about were his crusty-ass elbows. They hadn't seen an ounce of lotion in the last ten years."

"So, you used this guy so you could get free plumbing work done?" Tyler said in the midst of Dee and Holly's laughter. "That ain't even right."

"Please, I got three free meals, and he got the pleasure of enjoying my company during those dinners. Through the entire evening, all he wanted to talk about was how nice his apartment was, and how large his big screen television was. Too bad his apartment was in his mama's basement." Terry grunted. "Hell, the way I see it, he owes me a whole new bathroom."

Dee shook her head. "I agree with Holly; I don't know if you can go that long without dating."

"Well, you know what? I can, and I will. You just watch. No men for me." Terry folded her arms and nodded like a child as she made her declaration.

"Hmm, how long did you say?" Dee asked.

"A month," Holly injected, and Dee laughed.

## Chapter 1

"Nope, a year," Terry said, pursing her lips, giving her head a quick nod and then she paused. "Um...okay one. One whole year; no relationships for me," she declared again.

"Um hm," Both Dee and Holly said, eyeing Terry. "You'll see."

After her pledge, Terry sat grudgingly and watched as Dee made goo-goo eyes at her man, and Holly made out with hers. After another hour of such unbearable torture, Terry conceded and caught a cab home.

Terry glanced to her left. She definitely didn't remember extending an invitation to share her bed. "You can't come creeping in here in the middle of the night."

Keith leaned across the small space towards her. "But-"

"Woo hoo, that morning breath," Terry howled, covered her nose, and pushed him back.

He grinned at her. "I didn't even brush my teeth yet."

"No smooches until you brush those stank teeth," Terry said fanning a hand in front of her face.

"Okay Mommy," six-year-old Keith Wilkerson said before sliding from the bed and racing from the room.

Glancing at the clock, Terry saw that it was 6:40 AM. Grimacing, she pushed back the covers, crawled from the bed and headed to the bathroom for a quick shower before leaving for work. *Damn,* she thought, she should have skipped that last margarita. When she entered the bathroom she switched on the light, the almost blinding glare emanating from the light bulb made her wince, and she quickly switched it off. Groaning again, the thought came to her that, if she was lucky, she'd slip, fall, and drown in the shower, thus relieving her hangover.

Twenty-five minutes later, Terry walked from her bedroom dressed in a crisp white blouse, pleated gray slacks and black loafers. She wore her dark brown hair pulled back into a loose ponytail and her chestnut complexion was void of any makeup. She banged on her eldest son, DJ's bedroom door.

"Breakfast in five minutes," Terry called as she walked past, and then paused. Grinning she took three steps backwards and quickly opened the door. "Didn't you hear me?"

At fourteen, DJ was already just over five and a half feet tall, five inches taller than his mother, and close to a hundred and fifty pounds. He jumped, hearing the door open, and quickly pulled his pants up, tumbling and almost falling to the floor. "Mom!"

Terry laughed and snorted at the same time. "Boy, you ain't got nothing there that I haven't seen. I said breakfast would be ready in five minutes."

Closing the door, she grinned and headed down to the kitchen with a little more bounce in her step. When she entered the kitchen, Keith was already there, sitting at the counter watching *Arthur*. Terry picked up the television remote, turning the channel to the morning news.

"Mommy, I was watching that."

"Yesterday was your day, tomorrow is DJ's, and today is mine. You know the rules. We all take turns watching what we want in the morning."

Terry took three bowls from the cabinet, filled them with Cheerios, and plucked up a banana.

"But, it's so boring," Keith whined.

"Boy, you're not old enough to be bored."

"Please, Mommy!" Keith whined again.

"Nope."

# Chapter 1

Pealing the banana, she cut it into very thin slices, putting five slices over each of the bowls of cereal. She poured milk into each, and was setting the bowls on the counter when DJ entered the kitchen.

"Mom, can we have sausage and eggs this morning?" DJ asked sliding into the stool next to his younger brother.

"You know we can only have sausage and eggs on Sundays. Right now, it's not in the budget."

"We didn't have sausage and eggs this past Sunday."

"Well then, we'll just have extra sausage next time." *I hope.*

"Mommy, these are nasty. I hate Cheerios, " Keith mumbled.

"So do I," Terry said, sniffing the spoonful of cereal she was about to put in her mouth, and then scrunched up her nose. "But, it can't be helped; this is what's in the budget."

Actually, it was a generic brand, and they tasted so bad that Terry was surprised that the grocery store didn't offer customers a dollar a bag just to take them off their hands. She had to agree with Keith; they were nasty, but it was better than nothing.

Keith looked at the bowl Terry had placed in front of him with disdain. "You can tell Daddy, tell him we don't like Cheerios."

"No, she can't," DJ glared at his brother.

"DJ," Terry warned.

Sure, she could tell their father that his sons were tired of eating repulsive generic cereal every morning and hot dogs three nights a week. But he already knew that they were in financial trouble. He knew their situation; he just didn't seem to care. But she didn't want to tell Keith that. At first, when his father left, Terry had told Keith that his daddy had gone on a business trip; and she'd stuck to that story for two weeks. Eventually she'd had to tell him the truth. He had been devastated; he didn't understand why his daddy wanted to live with a stranger and not them. Terry could tell him that his father didn't give a damn about living with his children, and that he couldn't care less if they ate at all, but why make Keith suffer more then he already was?

"Well you can't," DJ said to his mother, and then, dropping his eyes, he stabbed his spoon in his bowl. "He doesn't care about us eating Cheerios every day; he doesn't care if we eat at all."

"He does too!" Keith immediately said, defending his father.

"DJ," Terry warned again.

"Tell him, Mommy!" Keith said, looking at his mother for confirmation.

"I bet Shareese doesn't have to eat Cheerios every day," DJ complained.

"Okay, that's enough," Terry said, rose, and gathered the bowls from the counter. Crossing the kitchen, she ran the cereal down the drain, clicked on the garbage disposal, and rinsed the bowls. "Go get your things together. We'll stop by McDonald's and grab you guys a sausage biscuit."

"Yippee!" Keith yelled as he jumped from the counter and rushed from the kitchen.

DJ followed at a much slower pace. "Sorry, Mom."

Terry sighed, stroking his cheek as he passed her. "Don't worry about it, buddy."

Twenty-two months ago, their lives had changed. They went instantly from a happy family of four to a confused and struggling family of three. Twenty-two months since her ex-husband had come home from work and told her that he wasn't in love with her anymore.

# Chapter 1

That he had met someone else, and she was going to have his baby. Five years before that day, Terry would have chased him from their home with a baseball bat, and she would have made both of them rue the day they had crossed her. But, she'd changed, she'd grown, she'd evolved…for the most part.

Now it was just her and her boys. She had a mortgage for a house that she couldn't afford, a car that stayed broken almost as much as it worked, and a teenage son who had shot up five inches in six months. David had promised to pay half of the mortgage, but hadn't paid his share in almost a year. He hadn't paid her the agreed amount of child support in the last few months. Things had been hard, and it didn't look like it would be getting any easier any time soon. The hours at her job as a customer service representative at the mall were being cut because of the economy, and that couldn't have come at a worse time. For the past six months, she'd borrowed half the money for the mortgage payment from her cousin Dee. She didn't complain about it, and Terry promised herself that she'd pay back every cent, but it seemed that all she was doing was getting deeper and deeper in debt. She didn't want to sell the house; the boys had had a hard enough time with their father abandoning them, they didn't need to lose their home too, but she was running out of options.

Digging inside her purse, she pulled out her wallet, checking her cash. "Seven dollars and thirty-five cents; great," she sighed.

She could get two sausage biscuits and an orange juice for the boys to share. On her way to work, she could stop at the grocery store and grab a Cup of Noodles for lunch. If she were lucky, she'd have enough to buy a small box of that sweet cereal for the boys to have in the morning. Sighing again, she grabbed her purse from the table and headed for the front door.

***

Walking up the apartment building steps, Wade Nelson shifted the box that he held to one hand as he used his free hand to open the door to the apartment he'd moved into five days back. The door to his right opened and two women came bouncing into the hallway.

"Hi neighbor," the first woman, a blond with eyes as blue as marbles said.

"Oooh, hey sexy," the second woman, a brunette, said allowing her fingers to trail down his arm as she passed him.

"Hey," Wade grinned in amusement and did a three-sixty, watching the women sashay to the end of the hallway and down the stairs. Wade initially had had reservations about moving into the complex, knowing that it wasn't in the best neighborhood. But, if these women were anything like the neighbors he'd have, he was going to definitely enjoy it here. "Oh yeah, I'm liking this move already," he muttered.

Walking into the apartment, he closed the door with his foot and dropped the box and his keys on a tall narrow table next to the door. The living-dining room combination was simple, with eggshell-colored walls and slightly plush tan carpet. It was sparsely furnished, with a dark blue sofa and blue and white striped ottoman. A forty-eight-inch television sat across from the sofa, and next to the television was a three foot bookshelf that held various comedy DVD's. On the other side of the room was a black metal desk that he'd purchased at the second-hand store, which held a state-of-the-art computer. The room was well lit, with a sliding glass door, void of window dressing.

Going into the kitchen, Wade grabbed a mug from the counter top. He scowled at the dried coffee at the bottom of the cup, and then stepped to the sink to run water in the mug and give it a quick rinse. He filled the mug with fresh water, popping it into the microwave for two minutes, and then scooped a spoonful of instant coffee into it. Taking the steaming mug with him, he crossed the room to his desk.

Sitting down, he leaned back in his chair with his elbows propped on the armrests and the mug clasped between both hands as he contemplated his move from Boston to Chicago. He'd given his family a few weeks' notice before he packed up his belongings and moved, and they were asking a lot of questions that he couldn't answer yet. He had two weeks to review additional information that he'd received, make contact with crucial people, and gather more data on parties of interest before he started his assignment as the new English teacher at Thomas Jefferson High. He had just enough time to meet and check out the staff, get a feel of the place, and go over the curriculum before the first day of class. Wade was confident about everything in his life, his family and relationships, and his choice of occupation. But, as confident as he was in his ability to teach, he wasn't as sure about his ability to deal with teenagers. He'd dealt with many unsavory characters, ruthless, violent people. At the moment, he felt, if given half a chance, these teens would eat him alive, and that scared the hell out of him. Setting his cup down, he removed a stack of files from one of the desk drawers, and scanned the folders, trying to see if there was something in the notes that he had missed, something that the other agent who had worked the case had missed. Something was going on at Thomas Jefferson High, and it was his job to find out who was behind it and to put a stop to it.

He moved his cup to the floor next to his chair, pulled his keys from the front pocket of his jeans, and opened the top locked drawer of his desk to remove another stack of files. Before closing the drawer, he grabbed a handful of peanut M&M candies from a bag that had been tucked at the back. He pulled them from the drawer and plopped them next to the mouse as he booted up the computer. Scanning a few of the files while he waited for the desktop to display on the monitor, he memorized what he could about different members of the faculty at Thomas Jefferson.

The ringing of the phone jarred Wade's attention from the document he was reading. With a glance at the phone, he decided to let it go to the answering machine.

"Hello, Khair. Where are you?" His grandmother asked in her native Malay tongue, using his Malaysian name.

Wade smiled when he heard her voice. He'd lived in Boston for the last six years, and even though he talked to his family a few times a month and visited on holidays, he still missed them; especially his mother, who, no matter what, always believed in him, and his grandmother, with her insistence that he not forget his Malaysian roots. Yet, there was also her desire to find him the perfect wife. Thinking about his grandmother's need for matchmaking, he grunted, shaking his head.

Wade had spent his first twelve years in Malaysia, before his Chicago born Dutch-Irish father and his Malaysian mother moved to the US. At that time, it was like an adventure moving to America and experiencing a new culture. But things weren't as easy as he thought they would be. Sometimes he felt as if he didn't belong anywhere. At the beginning, he felt awkward with his father's family, not wanting to say or do the wrong thing. When he went to school, the awkwardness grew. He had inherited his father's height, surpassing him by two inches when he topped out at six foot three as a rather tall twelve-year-old. He also inherited his father's steel-gray eyes, but that was as far as the resemblance went; everything else he inherited from his mother. From her glossy dark brown hair, to her beautiful olive complexion, he'd gone through high school hearing how tall he was to be an Asian, how he should play basketball, and other stereotypes. By the time he turned sixteen he had outgrown his awkwardness and developed a tough outer shell that he donned when he needed it, which was a handy characteristic in his line of work.

He listened to his grandmother tell him that she'd found the perfect woman for him, someone who would make a good wife and mother. Someone who did not run around the country showing everyone her body like his friend, Jennifer, did. Wade had tried to explain to his grandmother that Jennifer was a model and that he and Jennifer were not dating but just friends. His grandmother kept on insisting that Jennifer was looking for a husband and that her handsome grandson was just the man who "that woman", wanted.

Then she moved on to ask him why he'd moved from Boston. In the last twelve years, he had lived in California, Atlanta, and Boston. She needed to know why he'd just left Boston all of a sudden.

"Khair, Khair, are you there?"

Wade dropped the folders on the floor next to the coffee mug and logged onto the internet. He continued to tap at the keyboard as he listened to his grandmother.

"Khair," she began, alternating her speech between Malay and English, "if you don't talk to me, I will have Adli bring me to your house," she said, referring to his brother Adam. She paused. "What you doing so important that you can't talk to your…"

The answering machine clicked off in the middle of his grandmother's inquisition. Within thirty seconds, the phone rang again. "Khair!" His grandmother demanded.

"Damn," Wade muttered reaching for the phone. "Nenek," he said using the Malaysian term for grandmother. "I have to go grocery shopping; I'll be there once I'm done."

"Where were you? What are you doing?"

"I'm working, Nenek, I'm sorry; I couldn't get to the phone."

His grandmother paused, obviously lost in thought. "Are you working with that girl? You're not bringing her? I don't like her."

"No, Nenek, I'm not bringing Jennifer. She's not even here in Chicago." Wade hadn't bothered to tell his grandmother that Jennifer had a condo in Chicago as well as California, and New York, or that Jennifer would probably be in Chicago before the holidays. That would just start a whole new rant about how "that woman" was a stalker, and how he needed to call the authorities so that they could deal with the problem. "I'm coming alone, Nenek. I'll be there shortly."

"Good, because she's not a nice girl, running around the world half naked," she said with a click of her tongue. "If you had a nice wife you…"

"Nenek, I love you, I have to go now."

"…would not have to go to the store."

"I'll see you soon." Wade hung up before his grandmother had a chance to say anything else.

# Chapter 2

"It's been five months, David. Five months at $450 is $2,250. That's how much you owe me in child support," Terry said leaning against the maple-colored counter that separated the mall employees from the waiting customers at the Customer Service Center.

"Terry, I know how to count."

"The kids need things, they need food."

"I know that too."

"Well damn it, you sure don't act as if you know it. David, I can't do this alone. You promised to help with the mortgage payment, and it's been almost a year since you've done that as well."

"No, Terry, I gave up all rights to the house during the divorce, so that's not my problem," David interrupted her. "The mortgage, that's your problem."

"No, not *my* problem, *our* problem. You said that I get to keep the house, and that you would help with the payment so the boys wouldn't have to move. You haven't kept your word; now you don't even want to pay the agreed amount for child support."

David paused only a moment before he changed his tone from challenging to slightly pleading. "Come on, Terry, we're having a hard time."

"Bullshit!" Terry snapped. On the other side of the counter, a tight-lipped woman with an even tighter bun glared at Terry. She smiled, holding up a finger gesturing that she would only be another moment. “David, you forget who you’re talking to. I know how much you bring home every two weeks.”

“This is customer service?” The tight-lipped woman said in a way that made Terry wonder if what she’d just said was a question or a statement. The sarcasm did not get past Terry, who gave the woman a dry stare and then pointed up indicating the sign that read Customer Service. For her effort, Terry received a glare followed by a grunt of disgust.

“I’m sorry, ma’am; just give me one more minute,” Terry said and then into the phone added, “DJ has outgrown nearly all of his pants, he’ll be starting school in a few weeks, and he needs clothes. I also need to get some things for Keith.”

“His name is David, not DJ,” Terry heard from across the telephone line. “David, not DJ, damn it.”

“He wants to be called DJ. He’s trying to find himself, and he didn’t want to go by his middle name, some kid on the basketball team’s name is Jerome, so he chose to use his first and middle initials. I don’t see where it’s a problem.”

“I know this is your doing, first you tell him everything that goes on between us, and now he wants to go by a different name. I know your game; you’re trying to turn my son against me.”

Terry shook her head. No matter how many times she heard it, it still amazed her how David could turn his deteriorating relationship with his sons around and make her the bad guy. What David didn’t want to believe was that when he and his new girlfriend had confronted Terry with their plans to be together, DJ was home. David thought that the boy was out playing basketball with his friends, but DJ had come home to change his shoes.

## Chapter 2

While he was on his way down stairs, he heard his father telling Terry that he found someone else and that he was leaving them to be with her.

"This is completely appalling," The customer complained.

Terry glanced at the other woman, and then gesturing to the phone with her free hand. "I know, right. Men are such jerks." And, to David she said, "Oh yes, that was precisely my plan, I thought to myself, what can I do to drive a wedge between David and his son? Hmm… let me think, I know, if only I could get little David to change his name, it would just drive his father out of his mind. He'll be so distraught; he'll go to work and fling himself from the top of the building." Terry snorted. "Can't you just imagine me rocking back and forth, plotting, and twiddling my thumbs?" She paused. "You're such an idiot. That's absolutely ridiculous. Besides, you're doing a fine job of turning DJ against you yourself. I don't have to do anything, just sit back and let you piss your relationship to hell."

"Whatever, Terry. What about Keith? Are you still going to meet me later so he can spend the night with me or has he turned against me too?"

"Miss," Tight-lipped said indignantly.

"Um, I'm on the phone here!" Terry snapped at the other woman, rolling her eyes and turning her attention back to the phone call. "David, you're such an asshole. But I guess I learned that the hard way two years ago, huh?"

"Like I said, Terry, whatever. Are you going to bring Keith or what?"

"Sure, I'll meet you after work, and you'll have a check for me, right?" He was silent. "David!" Terry yelled.

"Yeah, I'll have a check for you," David barked back before hanging up.

***

"Damn it, David," Terry hissed into her cellphone as she paced behind her car. She had left work and raced to the sitter's to pick up Keith. After retrieving him and heading home, she'd had him take what had to be the quickest bath in history, and he was dressed, packed and out the door in fifteen minutes flat. Now she was standing in a strip mall parking lot where she had waited forty-five minutes past the time David had said he would meet her before placing the call to see what was keeping him. She looked into the back seat of the car, seeing Keith open his backpack for what was probably the tenth time to make sure that he had his favorite action figures. Terry had made sure he wore one of his Sunday shirts and a pair of khaki pants, and he wore a smile of excitement at the idea of spending the night with his father.

"Terry, Shareese has Lamaze class. I can't disappoint her."

"Oh please, save the excuses. What about disappointing your son? Wait a minute, what do you mean Lamaze class?"

"Shareese is pregnant."

"Didn't she just have the baby? What, wasn't it like, last week?"

"Terry, he's almost one."

"Geez, David, that girl has had two babies in less than two years, and now she's going to have another one? What the hell is wrong with you?"

"What can I say? I'm fertile."

## Chapter 2

"Have the two of you not heard of…ah… birth control?"

"Come on, Terry, give me a damn break."

"You know what, David, I don't give a shit about that. What I care about is that you keep your promise to Keith. You have other children, not just the ones you happen to make with her."

"Terry, I'm trying to make this work, right now Shareese needs me."

"And DJ and Keith don't?"

"Terry, I'll make it up to Keith, look just tell him…"

"No, David, you won't make it up to him!" Moving quickly from yelling to almost screaming, Terry walked a few yards away from the car. "You said that the last time, and the time before that and the time before that!" People passed her walking toward the stores, several turning to glance in the direction of Terry's raised voice. She glared at one couple who stopped walking to watch her. "What?" She asked the couple heatedly, and they turned and kept walking towards the store.

"Come on, Terry. Shit!"

"No, David, I'm tired of your bullshit. I'm tired of trying to do everything by myself, I'm tired of making up excuses to Keith for why his sorry ass daddy can't spend time with him, and I'm tired of your bitch ass!" Terry paused long enough to hear David hurl a string of curses at her. "David, kiss my ass!" Terry screamed, snapping the cell shut. Closing her eyes, it took everything in her not to jump up and down screaming and cursing. She walked in a circle trying to calm down, and after a few moments, she dropped her cellphone into her purse and walked to the side of the car, and opened the door. "Come on, Keith."

"Mommy, what time are we meeting Daddy?"

Terry ignored Keith's question as she towed him across the parking lot and in to the grocery store. The breeze from the air conditioner hit her as she stepped through the door, cooling her down from the ninety-eight degrees outside, but instead of making her feel better, it just pissed her off more.

"Mommy?"

Terry walked toward the two rows of shopping carts, dropping Keith's hand, and grabbing a cart. She pulled. It didn't move; she pulled again. Nothing. She stepped to the next row and pulled.

"Mommy, when are we meeting Daddy?"

"Keith, please," Terry murmured, blinking back tears and yanked the unmoving cart. Still nothing.

***

Wade did not want to go to the supermarket; he hated shopping for groceries, or cooking or doing anything domestic. Not that he couldn't, he could clean just as well if not better than a lot of women. He was a pretty good cook; he even knew how to mend a hole in a sweater or pair of socks. He knew all of these things, he just detested doing them, and he shunned them whenever the unpleasant tasks presented themselves. Against his nenek's wishes, his mother made sure that he and his brother knew everything that was necessary for a single man to survive.

He drove to the end of the mall parking lot, pulling his silver pickup into a parking spot. He locked the doors and walked briskly across the lot toward the row of stores. He passed behind a dark blue SUV backing out of a parking space. The driver pulled out without looking over her shoulder, and Wade backed up several steps as she kept backing up in his direction.

## Chapter 2

"Hey!" he angrily yelled, thumping on the back window.

Slamming on the brakes, the driver looked in the rearview mirror, startled, and then mouthed, "Oh, sorry." She waved and chuckled as she shook her head. Wade glowered at her, grunted, and walked around the vehicle and continued into the supermarket.

When he entered the store, Wade saw that there were only a few carts left, and it pissed him off even more than that twit who thought it was funny to come within inches of maiming him. Now he had to deal with crowded aisles, long lines, and testy customers. *Oh goodie.* He stopped behind a woman blocking the last two rows of carts. She seemed to be having a hard time dislodging the shopping cart that she'd been tugging on. It seemed as though she was not going to give up anytime soon. Great, now he was probably going to have to fight some woman for a cart. Wade watched as she snatched and pulled at the carts. She was a rather small and slight woman, maybe two inches over five feet, and certainly not more than 125 lbs. Her dark brown hair was in a loose ponytail and wisps of hair hung around her slender neck. His eyes traveled down her body to her curvaceous hips clad in gray slacks. *Nice.* Wade looked around, impatiently waiting. He turned back to the woman in front of him and sighed. *Okay, that's enough.* He reached around the woman, grasping the cart with the intention of pulling it free for her.

***

A hand reached around her, grasping the handle of the shopping cart.

"Excuse me!" Terry growled, glaring over her shoulder.

The man behind her raised his hands in submission, taking a retreating step back. Turning her attention back to the object of her immediate anger, she shook the row of carts; the sound of metal clattered and rang through the entrance of the store. Trembling from aggravation and anger, she couldn't stop the sob that escaped from her throat and the tears that ran down her cheeks. She looked down at Keith, seeing his lip trembling as he tried to control his tears.

Leaving the carts, Terry squatted in front of her son, gathering him into her arms. "I'm sorry, honey."

"He's not coming to get me, is he?"

"I'm sorry," Terry whispered brushing the tears from Keith's small, round cheeks.

"It's okay, Mommy."

At that moment, the only thing Terry wanted was to be standing in front of her ex-husband; if she were, she would knee him in the groin so hard his testicles would be lodged in his chest.

***

Wade watched the woman draw her child into her arms. He listened as she comforted him, brushing tears from his cheeks. He felt awkward and strangely angry. Some men were just assholes. How could this guy, whoever he was, be such a jerk to cause this woman and child such heartache? He took a step closer and then paused. What could he do? He didn't know these people; how could he help? Glancing around, he spotted a vending machine. He walked to it, deposited some change, and selected two bottles of water. On top of the machine, he saw a roll of paper towels next to a bottle of window cleaner. He tore off two sheets and walked back to the woman and her child.

He dislodged one of the carts, pulling it free. "Here you go, ma'am."

***

Terry glanced up at the man standing behind her; he had freed one of the carts and was offering it to her, along with bottled water and paper towels.

"Hey," she said straightening. "I'm sorry for snapping at you."

She bit her lip, fighting to stop the tears streaming down her cheeks.

"Don't worry about it, we all get upset from time to time." he hesitated, and then asked, "Are you all right… I mean…is there something that I can do to help?"

Terry hesitated. "Do you know of a quick way to get rid of a dead body?"

"Ah…What?"

"Just kidding," Terry said, and then lowering her voice, she added, "Sort of."

# Chapter 3

Getting out of his pickup, Wade picked up the two garbage cans sitting next to the curb, and walked up the driveway and around to the back yard. He placed the cans in the bin at the far end of the yard before going to the back door, and tapping on the window. A moment later, a barely five foot tall, stout Malaysian woman walked in from another part of the house. Whcn she spotted Wade, a huge smile spread across her face. Her waist-length braid swung from side to side as she hurried across the kitchen and opened the French door.

"Khair," Nur-Erlina Chui greeted him, pulling her grandson down into a tight bear hug that she was so famous for.

Wade faked a groan, the same way he used to do when he was a boy. He whispered the one thing he would always say to her during one of her infamous hugs, "Your hugs are so fierce that they could make a teddy bear scream for mercy."

She pulled back, grinning up at him and playfully pinched his arm. Wade laughed and hugged his grandmother again, kissing her cheek.

"Hello, Nenek. How are you?"

"What took you so long? I talked to you hours ago, and you said you were coming then."

## Chapter 3

"Nenek, I had some work that I needed to take care of. After that, I went grocery shopping." Wade saw the look his grandmother was giving him, and quickly asked, "Where's Mamma? Is she home from work yet?"

"She's upstairs changing. They, Nurjahan and your father, want to take us out for dinner. I told them, 'Why waste money going out to eat when I can make dinner?' I tell them that you like my *Sambal Udang,* but they said that they wanted to go to dinner and that I may cook dinner on Sunday." She grunted waving her hand. "Foolish, always wasting money."

"Look who's here?" came a voice from Wade's right.

The man walking down the hall was just over six feet, with light brown hair that had turned mostly gray since the last time Wade had seen him. He was also thin, much thinner than Wade remembered. His father's face seemed narrower and marred by an abundance of wrinkles from time, worry, and excessive drinking. His dark blue dress shirt was unbuttoned and rolled up at the sleeves, and his black slacks had a sharp crease. Leaning heavily on his cane for support, he limped down the hall.

"Hey, dad," Wade greeted his father, giving him a slight nod and stepped closer to the elder man extending his right hand.

Wade Sr. regarded his son for a moment. "Is that how you greet your old-man?"

Before Wade could respond, his father clasped the offered hand, quickly pulling Wade into a hug. Wade's spine stiffened instinctively as Wade Sr. held him tight. The faint odor of stale cigarette smoke and day-old beer clung to the man, bringing back an array of memories that Wade wished he could forget as he forced himself not to push his father away.

After a moment, he awkwardly reached up and patted his father's back. "How have you been, Dad?"

"Good, son, good," Wade Sr. released his son before stepping back. "You look well."

"Thanks. So do you."

"So," Wade Sr. said leaning on his cane again. "How long are you home for?"

Wade slipped his hands into the front pockets of his jeans and leaned against the counter. "I don't know yet."

His father regarded him for a moment, suspicion written across his face. "Don't know. What do you mean you don't know?"

"Where's Mamma?" Wade asked, ignoring the question.

"She's upstairs getting dressed," Wade Sr. answered. "What do you mean by you don't know how long you'll be staying?"

"I told Wade that you and Nurjahan don't want me to cook *Sambal Udang* for him," Nenek said. "That you'd rather waste money than let me cook."

"Now, Erlina," Wade Sr. said to his mother-in-law. "You know that that isn't true. We thought that you might like a break from cooking all of the time."

Wade noted the ever-present tone of slight condescension in his father's voice.

"I don't need a break," Erlina replied. "It's only cooking."

"I think it would be wonderful if Nenek cooks," Wade said. "I haven't had a good meal in a while, and I miss it." He smiled as his grandmother beamed proudly at him.

"Your mother and I have already made reservations," Wade Sr. said, keeping his voice low, but with a slight edge that Wade didn't miss.

## Chapter 3

Wade glanced at his father, seeing the cold sharpness in the eyes that watched his grandmother. Wade looked at his grandmother and noted that she shifted nervously from one foot to the other. But, as nervous as she appeared, his grandmother never broke eye contact with his father. Wade's blood began to simmer as he looked back in his father's direction and his father's gaze instantly met Wade's. The two men watched each other for what seemed like minutes but which was only seconds.

An instant later, his grandmother said, "Jahan says that Shalan and Aldi and their families will come over later for dessert."

Shalan was Wade's older sister and Aldi, Adam, was Wade's younger brother.

"That will be good," she continued. "I made banana fritters. I made extra, some for you to take home with you," she said, walking past Wade and patting him not too lightly on the belly.

"Wade!" came a voice he knew and loved.

Wade turned at the sound of his mother's voice, and then rushed across the room, sweeping her off her feet and hugging her tightly.

"Mamma!"

Wade stood like that for a few moments, just holding his mother, her soft hair brushing his cheek. He inhaled the faint hint of gardenia, reminding him of the better part of his childhood.

"Wade, you need to put your mother down. You're hurting her," Wade Sr. all but demanded.

"Hush, he's doing no such thing," Nurjahan Nelson told her husband.

"I've missed you, mamma," Wade whispered for her ears only.

"I've missed you, too," she whispered just as softly.

Wade placed her back on her feet, and looked down and into her warm chocolate eyes. “How are you, really?”

“I’m good, perfect even, now that you’re home.”

# Chapter 4

Wade rolled onto his back, reaching for his bedside clock. Turning it slightly towards him, he checked the time: 6:27 AM. He turned back over, pulling the pillow over his head, hoping to block out the sounds of what he had learned was his neighbor Hugo's new exercise regimen.

For the last four days, Wade had been treated to an hour-long constant *thump thump thump* coming from the apartment above. It usually started between 6:00 and 6:10 am. The first time it had happened, Wade had bolted upright, thinking that he was still in California and that he was in the midst of an earthquake. On the second day, he'd had enough and was headed up to confront his neighbor when a man of about twenty-five emerged from the apartment. Wade met the man on the landing and introduced himself, and the neighbor promptly introduced himself as Hugo Wilder. He rambled on about how he was ten minutes late leaving his apartment, as he quickly skirted Wade, and this being the second time this week and he didn't want to give his supervisor another reason to write him up.

When Wade had returned home that evening, Hugo had just left Wade's door and was heading up to his own apartment. Hugo was a big man, close to three hundred pounds, and only a few inches over five and a half feet tall – and a pastry chef, which explained a lot. He said that he'd come by to officially welcome Wade to the community and was bearing gifts: two cups of Starbucks coffee and a few samples of the desserts that he'd prepared at work that day.

Five minutes after Wade had invited Hugo into the apartment, they were leaning on the counter, sipping coffee, and eating the best coconut caramel crunch cake Wade had ever tasted. He watched Hugo, who had expressive eyes and an infectious smile, as he told Wade about his desire to lose seventy pounds. Hugo said he needed to lose the weight before Christmas so that he could invite the new hostess at his job, whom he proclaimed himself to be madly in love with, out for New Year's Eve. Hugo said he woke up every morning at 5:50 and started his exercise regimen, which consisted of an aerobic program for an hour. After that, he would go down to the lake and take a two-mile walk, come home, shower and get ready for his nine-and-a-half hour shift at work.

Wade groaned, pulling a second pillow over his head. Hugo seemed like such a good guy that Wade didn't say anything about being jolted awake by the loud thumping. Hell, who was he to try to hinder a man from reaching his goal of obtaining who he thought was the love of his life? Another series of thuds echoed through the room and Wade snatched the pillows off of his head, punching them with his fist. Maybe he was going to have to reevaluate his position on Hugo being a good guy.

After another ten minutes, Wade realized he wasn't going to get any more sleep and got up to go to the bathroom. After relieving himself, washing his face, and brushing his teeth, he went to the closet and selected some dark blue sweat shorts and a white tee shirt. He quickly dressed before putting on his socks and running shoes. Grabbing his keys, he headed from the apartment down to the park for a jog.

***

Grunting, Terry threw the sofa cushions over her shoulder. *Ninety-eight cents, who the hell has a sofa that didn't have at least a few bucks trapped inside?*

Kneeling in front of the cinnamon-colored living room sofa, Terry blew the hair from her face, dropping back on her calves. It was only 7:30 am, but if today was going to be anything like yesterday, she knew that her Saturday was not going to be good. If finding only ninety-eight cents when she needed almost three dollars in order to get a half gallon of milk was any indication, she knew that this was going to be a great start to another shitty day.

Yesterday, before leaving work, her boss had called her into the human resources office and told her that things were not working out and that he was sorry, and that he was going to have to let her go. Terry tried to convince him that he was mistaken and that she was doing a bang-up job. That was, until he reminded her that her using the telephone for personal use, especially when she had a customer waiting, was not acceptable. As Terry had guessed, old tight-lips went running straight to Human Resources as soon as Terry got around to completing her transaction. All she wanted was a fifty-dollar mall gift certificate for crying out loud, it wasn't like she couldn't wait a few minutes. *The bitch.*

Then that asshole, David, blowing Terry off, and not making good on the much-needed money that he'd promised. The melt down at the grocery store in front of a total stranger. And the icing on the cake, going to the check-out line with thirty-four dollars in groceries inside her shopping cart, only to find out that she had a whopping seventeen dollars and seventy-three cents in the bank. Wonderful.

At least the man that she'd yelled at next to the shopping carts had been understanding. After he had given her the paper towels and bottled water, he squatted down in front of Terry, opened the second bottle of water, and gave it to Keith, and then the two of them spoke quietly. Terry didn't pay complete attention to what they were saying; it sounded like something about the new Batman from what small tidbits she caught. She half listened to him, looking out for indecent comments as she tried to pull herself together. When she finally calmed down and focused on their conversation, she heard Dark Knight, Battle Cape, and Electro Strike, and she realized that they were talking about Batman action figures. Then she realized that the man was engaging Keith in conversation to give her a minute to get herself together.

As he squatted next to Terry, she had a chance to get a good look at him. He was of Asian descent, with thick hair that was a rich dark brown. It looked as soft as satin and was neatly trimmed. He was tall, she couldn't tell how tall, but he had a least eight or nine inches on her. He had broad shoulders, and strong looking forearms that rested on equally strong-looking thighs. But, what she noticed most about him was his piercing steel-gray eyes, eyes that held intelligence, compassion and deep emotions, eyes that probably didn't miss much of anything. Terry wasn't afraid to say that he possibly had the most beautiful eyes she'd ever seen on a man.

She'd offered to pay him for the water, but he refused, which was a good thing since she knew that she didn't have enough change hiding at the bottom of her purse to repay him. She thanked the stranger and he bid her farewell, telling Terry it was nice to meet her, before grabbing one of the shopping carts and sauntering away, giving Terry the opportunity to check out just how muscular his body was, including his great butt.

She had raced through the market after that, making sure to pick up just the necessities: bread, hot dogs, the cheap ones, cereal, also the cheap brand, and a few other things. While in the dairy department, she searched the egg cartons and found one with three broken eggs. She took it to the clerk in the dairy department hoping he would give her a discount.

When Terry asked if he could give her something off the price, he'd looked at her as if he was confused by her question, and she had to repeat it before he said, "Um… no." Then he took the carton from her hands and gave her a new one. "Here you go."

"But," Terry said, "I want those." she reached for the eggs that the clerk held in a near death-grip. "So, if I take those, I can get a discount, right?"

"We can't sell you a damaged carton," the younger man said, pulling the eggs back from Terry.

Terry watched him put the carton inside of a shopping cart that he was working from, which held boxes and tubs of butter and margarine he was restocking.

"Well," she asked slowly. "What will you guys do with them?"

He looked at her as if, in that short time, he had already forgotten what they were talking about, and Terry had to force herself not to roll her eyes.

"The broken eggs, I mean!"

"Oh, we'll throw them away."

She bit her lip, looking at the eggs again. "So, can you give them to me?"

"No, I can't."

"Why not? You're just going to throw them away. You said so yourself."

"I can't give them to you. If I did, I could lose my job. It's against company policy."

"That's ridiculous and a total waste." Terry looked around and then stepped closer to the younger man, lowering her voice. "Tell you what, we can just pretend that I'm the garbage woman, I'll dump them when I get outside."

Terry grinned at him and gave him her 'baby, you know you want to do this for me' smile, which, to her utter dismay, did not work.

"Sorry, ma'am. Those are the rules."

*Ma'am*, Terry bristled. No way was she old enough to be called ma'am. She eyed the clerk, who was now giving her a red-cheeked blush. Heaving a weighty sigh, Terry looked down at the eggs she held. "You guys wouldn't happen to sell eggs by the half dozen?"

He shook his head. "Sorry."

Terry rolled her eyes then and, placing the dozen eggs in her cart, made her way to the register; only to be totally embarrassed when her debit card declined her thirty-three seventy-four purchase. Terry glanced around at the people standing in line and made a big production of how banks were always messing up people's accounts. She got quite a few nods and murmurs of agreements before she pushed the cart to the side and went to the ATM to check her account balance. When she saw her measly seventeen-and-change balance, she wanted to curse. And then she wanted to drive over to David's house, knock on his door, and when he answered, punch him right in the mouth.

She stood at the ATM for a moment, fantasizing about the dazed looked on David's face when she knocked him on his ass, until Keith's tugging on her slacks brought her attention back to the problem at hand. She sighed, took out fifteen dollars, and went back to the cashier, selecting a few items that, fate among fates, cost fifteen forty-one. Luckily, the person in line behind her was Randy, a guy she'd dated a few months before she and her dirt-bag-slash-ex-husband, David, made their relationship official. When they were outside of the grocery store, Randy had asked her about getting together that evening. She'd told him that she didn't know if she could, she had to see about getting a babysitter. He'd looked down at Keith with a surprised expression, like it was the first time he'd noticed the child.

"Oh," he had said. "I thought you had an older kid."

"We haven't seen each other in eight years! DJ is fourteen; this is my other son, Keith. Keith, this is an old friend of mommy's, Mr. Randy."

Terry smiled shyly at Randy when he looked down at her son. Randy nodded, and then looked back up at Terry. At that moment, she remembered her oath not to get involved with any men; her instinct told her to walk away, to take her ass home, take a cold shower and watch television with the boys. But she ignored it, thinking that something positive had to happen today.

After exchanging numbers with Randy, she drove home with a smiling Keith clutching a Lunchable, which she'd let him select at the grocery store to make amends for his father not keeping his word. The Lunchable cost four dollars, which took from the necessities that they needed, but after seeing the smile on Keith's face, she thought it was well worth it.

Pushing the previous day's events to the back of her mind, Terry rose from her spot in front of the sofa. She straightened the sofa cushions, and then raced upstairs to her bedroom. Searching the pile of clothes that she had folded and laid on the foot of her bed, she slipped a dark blue sweatshirt over her pajamas. Grabbing her keys, she headed out the front door. She unlocked the door and slid behind the steering wheel, starting the car. Whispering a silent prayer, Terry heard the car stall for a moment before coming to life. She couldn't believe she was going to use a buck-fifty in gas to drive down to the convenience store to buy a dollar pint of milk for the boys' cereal. Did they even sell pints of milk anymore? If she were slick enough, maybe she could mix a little water in with the milk and make it stretch before the kids could see her. As she drove, her memories drifted back to yesterday again.

After making baked beans and hot dogs, she asked DJ if he'd mind keeping an eye on Keith for a couple hours and told him that she would bring him something back for his efforts.

She showered and slipped on a white dress with red flowers and red sandals and was off to meet Randy. It took her an extra twenty-five minutes to locate his apartment complex. After the first ten minutes of being lost, she almost gave up and went home, but she finally found it and parked. Once he'd buzzed her inside his apartment building, and she reached the third floor, she felt better about the evening.

"Hey," he said pulling Terry into his arms and kissing her as soon as he opened the door.

At first, Terry leaned into him, accepting the kiss, and then she backed up a bit, breaking the kiss and smiled up at him.

"Hey." She looked around the apartment when he let his arms drop from her hips. "Nice place."

## Chapter 4

"Yeah, I like it," he said, never taking his eyes from her. "Go ahead and have a seat while I go jump in the shower."

"Where are we going?" Terry asked, as he headed toward the back of the apartment.

He turned back to her. "I thought we'd just hang out here, maybe watch a movie, order some takeout." His pink tongue slipped from his mouth brushing his lower lip, as his eyes roamed over Terry's body, lingering on her breasts, never traveling back to her face to make eye contact, and then he turned and headed toward the back of the apartment. "Oh," he called over his shoulder. "You can't use the powder room while I'm in the shower; if you flush the toilet it changes the water temperature if someone's in the shower."

Terry watched him disappear down the hall, then looked around the well-maintained room. The room was tastefully decorated. The off-white carpet and curtains looked fresh and complemented the chocolate sofa and armchair. On both sides of the sofa were end tables and next to them were tall cream-colored vases that held dried bamboo. Terry walked to one of the tables, examining the African figure and bowl of crystal eggs. The room was beautifully decorated. It didn't look like something a bachelor would put together; it definitely had a woman's touch. Terry quickly looked around the room again, and then walked to the back of the apartment in the direction Randy had vanished. She glanced around the room. The comforter had a yellow floral print with scalloped edges and there were at least half-dozen throw pillows on the bed. Terry scanned the room quickly, seeing Randy's wallet on the dresser. She walked to the dresser, picking it up. She opened it, finding two credit cards, a debit card, and other miscellaneous cards in the credit card slots. On the inside, she found a few pictures and five dollars.

"Five dollars! That's all the hell you have, five dollars? Sorry ass bum."

She took that to give to DJ for keeping an eye on Keith. Stepping closer to the window, using the sunlight in order to see, she sifted through the pictures; there were three of them, all of the same woman. In the first picture, she was with three other women, and it looked like they were at a nightclub. The second was a picture of her alone, sitting sideways on a chair with a purple background. The third was of her and Randy together, he in a black tuxedo, and the woman wearing a wedding dress!

The phone rang, and the answering machine immediately picked up. "Hey, baby, I'm just calling to let you know that I was able to get an earlier flight home, and I'll be landing tomorrow afternoon at three instead of tomorrow night. I love you. And Tina says hi."

Terry glared in the direction of the bathroom door, hearing a happy Randy singing away in the shower. "You no-good bastard," She muttered and then picked up his cellphone, which lay next to his wallet, and took it and the wallet with her.

She grabbed her purse from the table and went into the powder room. Raising the toilet seat, she dropped the contents from his wallet into the toilet, dropping the wallet on the floor. Then, flipping the phone open, she scanned the phone numbers searching for female names.

The first number went directly to an answering machine; the second was answered by a cheerful, "Hi, baby."

Terry quickly told the other woman, who had demanded to know why Terry was calling her from her husband's phone, that she was with Randy, that she didn't know that he was married and that she just wanted the other woman to know what sort of man her husband was. Then Terry snapped the phone in two and dropped it into the toilet with the other items, and then flushed. She waited for Randy's scream, and grinned in satisfaction before she left the apartment for home.

And, to add the final touch in making her Friday evening just perfect, Terry's maternal grandmother had called her and practically begged Terry to allow her cousin LaKeisha to stay with her and the boys for the upcoming school year. When her grandmother suggested it, Terry immediately shot down the idea.

"No, no, no," she had said, before her grandmother could even finish her question. "Nope, can't do it, not gonna happen. Nooo."

Terry did not want any of her crazy, country family coming to stay with her and the boys, and she especially didn't want her cousin Keisha staying with them.

Terry got out of the car, running into the Royal Farms, and found that she had just enough to get a quart of milk. Well she had enough after she took seventeen cents from the need-a-penny-leave-a-penny container next to the register. She left the store, jumped into her car, and headed home.

# Chapter 5

"Gran, please," Terry tried to plead with her maternal grandmother for the third time in as many days. "I can do a lot of things, almost anything you ask, but not this. Let me see if I can find an apartment for Keisha, or someone who's looking for a roommate. I think that would work out much better for the both of us."

Terry remained silent as she listened to her grandmother who seemed to go on, with no sign of stopping. Yesterday her grandmother had tried to use scare tactics, saying that Terry and the boys shouldn't be in that big scary house all alone. "For heaven's sakes," she had said. "What if a madman broke into the house? At least with Keisha there you would have another adult to help you." Never mind that with the way things had been going over the last couple of years, Terry had so much pent-up rage that if someone dared enter their home uninvited she would probably stomp a mud-hole in their ass and walk it dry.

The day before that, her grandmother had used the guilt approach. "Terry, what if something happened to poor innocent Keisha? You know you would never forgive yourself. I mean, just think of it, you would be so heartbroken knowing that you could have prevented such an awful thing from happening to poor Keisha by simply letting her come stay with you. And it's such a small thing."

Today her grandmother was breaking out the big guns. Guilt and need were her weapons of choice.

"Terry, you know you need the money," her grandmother was saying. "And Keisha doesn't have anyone else to stay with; I don't want her staying with strangers. Before you say it, I don't feel comfortable with her staying on campus, so many things can happen there. You know how she is, if anything were to happen to her. You know how much I'd worry about her if she were to stay on campus. I'd nearly worry myself to death. She's so…so gullible."

Terry heaved a weighty sigh. "Yeah, I know Gran, but-"

"Terry, she can help you, while you help her. She can pay her own way from the housing stipend that she gets from her scholarship and help with the children. It will be good for the both of you. Keisha will have someone to watch out for her, which she desperately needs, and you know you can use the money, and…"

Terry loved her cousin, she really did, and the girl was smart, probably one of the smartest people in their family. The problem was that, as smart as Keisha was, she often had the common sense of a peanut, and it drove Terry insane.

Terry remembered the last time that she went to visit her grandmother in Atlanta. She'd asked Terry to take Keisha to the Motor Vehicles Department to take her driving test. Her grandmother had said that she'd been having problems seeing during the evenings, suffering from night blindness, and that it would be a big help if Keisha had her driver's license. Terry rose the following morning and drove a solemn-looking Keisha to the

DMV. Once she had finished the driving test, Terry was so proud of her that she jumped up and down, whooping and hollering as a grinning Keisha walked toward her.

"Congratulations," the examiner had said, giving Keisha the necessary papers. "You just go through those doors and have your photo taken for your license, and you're all done."

Keisha had frowned at the man, a puzzled look on her face. "Picture taken for what?"

The examiner paused and looked from Keisha to Terry, who only hunched her shoulders, and then back at Keisha. "You need to have your picture taken to get your driver's license."

Keisha looked appalled. "Oh, I can't have my picture taken. I have to go home first and take my curlers out."

Terry looked up at Keisha's hair, not really paying much attention when they had left the house. Her family from Atlanta sometimes went out like that, even though she would never do it, she tried not to let it bother her when they did.

She took a step toward Keisha, reaching for her hair, "Just take them out…"

"No!" Keisha took a step back, her hands flying protectively to her hair. "My hair is still wet; I can't get my picture taken right now." She turned to the examiner. "I'm just going to go home, do my hair, and change my clothes, and I'll be right back. I live right over there; you can almost see my house from here."

Terry looked in the direction that Keisha had pointed. Yeah, you could see her house all right. If you looked across the parking lot, that was almost the width of a football field, a six-lane highway, and three miles of dense woods, why, you could almost make out their grandmother's back porch. Terry then turned to look at her cousin and was so bewildered that the only thing she could do was stare for a moment before shaking her head and walking away.

Terry massaged her brow and drew in a deep breath. "Okay, Gran."

"And the boys will love to have Keisha staying with you all. She can help them with their…"

"Okay, Gran." Her grandmother paused, listening to Terry. "She can come and stay with us, but the first time she calls me Terry Ann, her simple butt is going to be on the first thing smoking back to Georgia."

"Terry, that is so good of you, I promise you, won't be sorry. Keisha's going to be a big help to you. Just you wait and see."

Terry could only grunt at that. "So, when will she be coming?"

"Well," Her grandmother hedged, taking a long pause before she spoke again. "Um, she left last night around 11 pm, her bus is supposed to arrive at 3 pm this afternoon."

"What?"

"She has your address," her grandmother added quickly. "She should be arriving any minute."

"See, that ain't even right," Terry said, listening to her grandmother laugh on the other end of the line.

"Give the boys my love," her grandmother said, before Terry could start ranting. "And watch out for your cousin."

Terry heard the line go dead. "Son of a bitch!" She cursed before turning off the phone and laying her forehead against the cool table.

Terry didn't have much family in Chicago, only her cousin Dee, Dee's husband Ben, and their twenty-month old twin boys. And, because of her reckless and wild ways, Terry had almost ruined her relationship with Dee. It had been almost ten years since she had nearly made almost irreparable damages in her and Dee's relationship; anyone else would have written Terry off, but not her cousin. Dee had forgiven Terry. It took more than a year, but eventually things returned to normal between the cousins.

Terry rose from the table and crossed the room to the sink, filling a glass full of water and taking a small sip before she returned to her seat at the table. She didn't like to think about the things that she had done in the past. Not that she was a saint now, far from it. She was human, but she still tried to do the right thing in most cases. Now she guessed the right thing was to let Keisha spend the next nine or ten months with her and the kids. She could do this; she could live with her cousin for a few months. She could get Keisha settled and once Keisha made a few friends, maybe they would decide to get a place together.

"Yeah, I can do this. It's like having a tenant, like renting out the spare bedroom." Placing the glass on the table and dropping her face in her hands. Terry moaned. *Who the hell am I trying to fool?*

It had taken time for her to get used to living with David, once they had gotten married. And living with the boys wasn't a picnic, with all the whining and bickering. Not to mention the mess they left in their wake, with DJ's dirty dishes in the sink and Keith's toys everywhere. She loved them, they were her life, but half the time they drove her crazy. Terry heard the doorbell ring, but didn't have the energy to get up and answer it.

A moment later DJ called her from the living room. "Mom! Guess who's here?"

"A pain in my ass," Terry muttered, getting up and heading toward the living room.

## Chapter 5

Standing just inside the front door was a twenty-year-old woman with long, thick brown braids highlighted in various shades of blond and gold. She had a small round face with a complexion the color of creamy caramel and a narrow, long nose, which looked out of proportion to her five and a half foot, just over two hundred pound rounded body. But the only things that Terry noticed were the bright red jeans that looked to be three sizes too small and the equally tight bright yellow top.

With her arms spread wide and a big grin on her face, Terry's cousin, Keisha Johnson squealed, "Terry Ann!"

"Oh, good lord," Terry muttered throwing her hands in the air, before she turned and headed back into the kitchen.

# Chapter 6

"I really appreciate you doing this for me, Leon," Terry said to her neighbor Leon Marshall.

He nodded, giving her a shy smile; his smooth fawn complexion showed signs of a blush and his hazel eyes, which were only slightly darker than her own, sparkled. He grabbed the supply line hose for the washing machine, moved the washer further from the wall, and wiggled behind it.

Terry's morning had started out good. She had risen at 5:30 AM, gone downstairs, and put a load of clothes in the washer. Then she ran up to her bedroom, changed into her workout clothes, went to the living room, and popped in her cardio dance aerobics DVD. Half an hour later, she turned off the television and headed to the kitchen to get a drink of water. When she walked past the door that led to the basement, she saw movement out of the corner of her eye and turned to see one of Keith's balls floating past.

"What the hell?"

She walked halfway down the steps. That was when she noticed the water on the floor. She'd rushed the rest of the way downstairs and run into the laundry room, seeing water running from an unknown place under the washer. Terry rushed across the room and turned off the washer, water, and everything else she could think of that would overload, short out or blow up in the basement. After that, she went upstairs to wake up Keisha, DJ and Keith, grabbed almost every towel in the house, and spent the next hour and a half mopping up the mess. At 9 AM, she went to see her neighbor Leon, who lived two doors down, and asked him if he knew anything about plumbing. She was grateful that he offered to come take a look at the washer, and he said he was sure that he could fix whatever was wrong.

Luckily, it only took Leon a matter of minutes to find out that the problem was a minor one. He said that the hot water supply line had burst and that it was an easy enough fix. He even went to the hardware store, bought the line, and was now replacing the old one.

Terry leaned to the side, trying to see what Leon was doing to remove the supply line. She wasn't really interested in what he was doing – actually, she couldn't have cared less - but anything was better than looking at Leon's plumber's crack. She thought it funny that he had a plumber's crack, considering he wasn't a plumber, was only five foot six, and weighed somewhere on the north side of two hundred and fifty pounds. Not to mention his nasty teeth. Terry suppressed a shudder. His top teeth were yellow and orange, reminding her of Halloween and candy corn, and not in a good way. His bottom teeth were brown with a little band of green near the gum line to add just the right amount of yuck.

"So, Terry, I was thinking," Leon said, he shifted trying to get closer to his work, and as he did so, he wiggled his butt, causing his pants to edge down another inch. Terry flinched, cringed, and turned away, taking a few steps out of the laundry room. "Since I'm here, maybe we could set a time to get together. I'm thinking,

I could fix you dinner, we could have a little wine, some music, a little dancing. Get to know each other better."

Terry snorted, "Not in this lifetime, buddy." She murmured under her breath.

"What?"

Terry looked back at Leon, who was peering over his shoulder at her. Seeing the look on Leon's face, her brows rose, and she laughed nervously. "Um, did I say that out loud?"

"Yes!" Leon snapped.

He wiggled from side to side, scooting backwards out of the tight spot between the washer and dryer. He stood, picking up his tools, and angrily shoved them inside a brown leather pouch that he had brought with him. He turned and stormed out of the laundry room.

Terry ran in front of him, blocking his path. "Leon, I'm sorry, I didn't mean it, seriously. You know you can't count the things that people say to themselves as them really saying them out loud. Haven't you ever heard that, it's like a private conversation…No, it's like? Like a joke. Yeah. You know a joke. Sike." Leon pushed past her, heading for the steps. "I was only joking, Leon." Terry called, practically running behind him. "Come on, don't be like that." she followed him up the steps and to the back door. "Sike, sike. I said sike damn it."

"Forget you!" Leon threw over his shoulder, as he lumbered down the steps. "And you owe me twelve bucks!"

Terry sighed, watching him hike his pants up as he stomped across the yard. "Yeah well, forget you too, idiot," she mumbled, and then sighed, closing the door on the sight of Leon hiking his pants up again.

## Chapter 6

After four tries and three hours, two of them spent cleaning what seemed like a never-ending river of water off the floor, Terry had finally figured out how to properly attach the water line to the washing machine. By 8:30 PM, she felt pretty good. She'd fixed the washer, had all of the laundry done, had Keith ready for bed without any fuss, procured twenty-four dollars for DJ's school gym uniform, and had even managed not to kill Keisha for calling her Terry Ann at least twenty times. She figured things were starting to look up.

# Chapter 7

"I heard about the job you did in Reno a few years back," Raymond Foster, one of the agents at the Chicago FBI, said.

He was referring to a case where Wade went undercover in order to catch a child predator. He had convinced the perp that he wanted to buy pictures of little boys and set up a meeting. When Wade arrived at the destination for the meeting, the perp had hundreds of photos of young boys ages four to eleven. Wade had felt ill as he sat and looked through the pictures. It took everything in him not to grab the sick bastard and choke the life out of him. After their fifth meeting, the perp asked Wade if he wanted to see the real thing, and that was all Wade needed. They followed through, and six people were arrested in connection with the sting.

Those were the cases that Wade worked most often, the ones where he caught sexual predators and put an end to the abuse of children and women.

Wade regarded the other man for a moment and then gave him a slight nod.

"So, Nelson, what do you have for us?"

"Nothing more than your guy did so far," Wade replied. "Since it's the beginning of the school year, we haven't had much movement. The records show that by this time last year, there were six handguns recovered from various students. So far this year, there haven't been any. Either they haven't started supplying them yet, or the distributor has gotten better at hiding them. Two students were apprehended with cocaine, but both are playing dumb."

Forster massaged his neck. "The school board wants to bring in metal detectors."

"Right. The problem with the metal detector is, it may stop the students for bringing guns into the building, but it won't keep them from hiding them outside and then picking them up after school. If guns and drugs are being sold at the school, that's the best place to catch whoever is supplying them." Wade was thoughtful for a moment. "Do you think they could provide more security? Maybe we can provide a few bodies; that way, at least we can have added protection for the students."

"I'll get right on that," Foster said, before leaving the room.

***

Terry dropped the newspaper on the coffee table along with the ink pen. She massaged her brow trying to ease the barely noticeable throb from the headache she felt coming on, while she listened to Keith run down the stairs with DJ in hot pursuit. Keith jumped on the sofa, sliding close to his mother as DJ rounded the archway.

"Mommy, DJ's going to hit me," Keith squealed.

"He keeps messing with me, Mom," DJ said, glaring at his younger brother.

Terry looked from one boy to the other. "All right, what's going on?"

"He keeps messing with me," DJ said again.

Keith wedged himself closer to his mother. "No, I'm not."

“Messing with you how?” Terry asked DJ.

“He keeps coming in my room and switching the lights on and off.”

“No, I don’t.”

“You didn’t turn off my light?” DJ asked, placing his hands on his hips.

Keith shifted his eyes in his mother’s direction and back before he answered. “Mommy, I only did it one time.”

“Twice! And you keep opening my door.”

“Keith, why are you purposely annoying DJ?” Terry asked. Keith dropped his head and hunched his narrow shoulders. “But you were annoying him, right?” Keith paused, clearly thinking about what his mother had said, before his head bobbed up and down. “What if I told you that the next time you went into DJ’s room with the sole purpose of annoying him that you would have to give him one of your mornings of TV watching? Would you like that?”

Keith’s head snapped up at that. “I wouldn’t like that.”

“And, DJ doesn’t like your annoying him. So, if you do it again, that’s what’s going to happen. The next time you feel particularly bored and decide that it would be entertaining to annoy your brother, you’ll have to give up your next television day to him as compensation.”

Keith looked up at his mother confused. “Huh?”

“Compensation is payment, Keith,” she said.

Keith’s mouth dropped open, “But-”

“No buts. Now go upstairs and brush your teeth, it’s almost time for bed.”

Keith scurried from the sofa, making a wide berth around his brother as DJ pretended he was lunging for him.

## Chapter 7

"DJ!" Terry admonished, bringing the boy's attention back to her.

"Huh?" He turned back to his mother and grinned sheepishly.

"What are you doing in your room other than changing your clothes that you need to have the door closed?"

DJ shifted from one foot to the other. "Nothing."

"Then you need to leave the door open," she said firmly.

"But, it's my room; I should be able to close the door when I want to."

"No, it's my room. I'm just letting you use it until you move out," Terry said, folding her arms across her chest. "And I'd like for you to leave the door open, unless you're changing your clothes."

DJ sighed and dropped his shoulders, and then reluctantly mumbled, "Okay."

Once DJ left the living room, Terry picked up the newspaper, scanning the remainder of the help wanted section. After another ten minutes of not finding anything of interest, she folded the paper, dropping it next to her on the sofa. Laying her head back and closing her eyes, Terry sighed. The kids only had two weeks left before school started and she still hadn't spoken to David about helping her gather the things the kids needed to start. She had been offered two jobs in the past few weeks. Unfortunately, both were part-time, and the pay was barely more than minimum wages. After paying childcare for Keith, there would be enough to pay only a portion of the mortgage. Maybe she could take in more boarders. She could move Keith in with her and rent out his room. And she could rent out the basement. She groaned, remembering two mornings ago when Keisha came down to the kitchen in a hurry to get over to the financial aid office. She had a Pop Tart and popped it into the microwave. Terry thought nothing of it, until she saw the small sparks and realized that Keisha had put the Pop Tart in the microwave still in the foil wrapping.

"Maybe taking in boarders is not the right answer," she mumbled to herself.

She was so deep in thought that she barely heard the front door open.

"Hey, Terry Ann!"

Terry groaned. "Why is it so hard for you to call me Terry? Its only two syllables, as opposed to three; Terry, say it with me, Ter-ry."

"Terry," Keisha said with a roll of her eyes.

"Good," Terry said dropping her head against the back of the sofa again.

"What are you doing?" Keisha asked sitting on the sofa and picking up the paper.

"Searching for a job."

"Any luck?"

"Nope, nothing."

"But, guess what, I found a job. Part-time, of course, but it's something."

"Congratulations," Terry said, without emotion.

"Thanks. I'll be one of the hostesses at this new restaurant. It's only a few evenings a week, but it's something. With the housing allowance from my financial aid and the scholarship, I figure I should have enough to help you and still have some spending money."

"And how did registration go?"

"Good, I was able to get all the classes that I wanted. Since I took all of my prerequisite classes last year, I was able to sign up for five classes that I wanted, including Principles of Financial Management. I have a friend back home, Reese, whose father owns three hotels. Last year, he started an investment brokerage firm. She's sure she can get me in as a Financial Analyst at an entry level. She says they start out at around $40,000."

Terry lifted her head, glancing in Keisha's direction. "Really?"

"Yep. Reese talked to her father about it in the past. We've known each other forever, and they know how good I am with numbers."

Terry looked at Keisha. Her brown eyes lit up at the thought of her future, of the career that she would have. And she would do it, of that Terry had no doubt. Keisha was smart, she was always an A student and had always been in advanced classes.

"I think it's real important to do something that you like, and I'm lucky to have a friend whose father is in a position to offer me the opportunity." Keisha tilted her head, watching Terry for a moment. "Have you thought about going back to school?"

Terry snorted. "Keisha, I can't afford to go back to school. I can't even afford to be out of work for the weeks that I have been."

"You're a single mom; you can get grants and loans."

"I can't get money from the government to pay the mortgage. If I can't pay the mortgage, I lose the house, if I lose the house, we live on the street. I'm pretty sure that one of the criteria for getting any sort of loan is that you may not be homeless. So no, I can't go back to school."

"Well then, maybe you can find a job that you like and make it a career. Maybe you can ask Ben for a job."

Terry shook her head. "No, I wouldn't feel right asking him."

"Why not? Ben's a great guy; I know he'll help you."

"Yeah, he's a great guy." Terry sighed. "Look, Keisha, it's a long story." And one that Terry didn't want to go into with her cousin. Terry didn't want to tell Keisha or anyone about how, when Ben and Dee had first started dating, that she set out to win Ben away from Dee.

*Well*, Terry thought to herself, *steal was more accurate.*

She'd set out to steal Ben from Dee by pursuing him behind Dee's back. Once she got Ben's attention, they began dating. She was young and oh so self-absorbed that she'd convinced herself that she was justified in doing whatever she deemed necessary to get what she wanted, even losing the love and respect of her family. In the end, she learned that the man that she was dating was not Ben Harrison, millionaire executive, but Ben's personal driver, Mike Kellam. Terry was so sure that she had won the hand of Ben that she arranged to have her family meet at a restaurant with the intention of bringing her and Ben's relationship out in the open and rubbing Dee's face in it at the same time. But things didn't go as she had planned, and in the middle of a crowded restaurant she had blatantly sabotaged her family life for a mistaken identity, dishonesty, and greed.

Dee had forgiven Terry eventually. Ben was careful. And even Holly had come to terms with what Terry had done to both Dee and herself. Terry winced, thinking about the terrible things that she had done to Holly. It had taken many more years and plenty of abuse and groveling for Holly to forgive: the abuse from Holly, and the groveling from Terry.

"Nope, I don't think I'll be asking Ben for a job. Besides, I don't even know what they do over at Harrison."

Keisha reached for Terry's hand, giving it a gentle squeeze, before rising from the couch. "I'm sure you'll come up with something. You're really smart; and there are so many things that you can do. Try looking to the people that you know for suggestions, maybe Holly or Dee." She turned and headed towards the steps. "Night."

"Night, Keisha." Terry rose from the sofa, taking the newspaper and pen with her, and walked into the kitchen.

She dropped the paper into the recycle bin and put the pen in one of the kitchen drawers before heading up to bed herself.

# Chapter 8

Reaching for the ringing phone and nearly knocking it from the nightstand, Terry grabbed it just before it toppled over the edge and to the floor.

"Shit," She mumbled, almost wasting the cup of tea she held in her other hand. As soon as Terry brought the phone to her ear she said, "This had better be good."

"Hey, it's me," Holly answered.

"You do know what time it is, don't you?"

Holly sighed. "Yeah, yeah, I know. But this is important."

"It can't be more important than Patrick."

Terry had taken a hot shower and then dressed in her pink-and-white Betty Boop pajamas. Now she was settled under the blankets, with a cup of hot tea, three chocolate chip cookies, and the remote control, all set to watch her favorite television show, *Gray's Anatomy*. She openly lusted over her fantasy future husband, Patrick Dempsey.

"Somebody had better be dead or dying."

"Terry, Dee's here, and she's upset."

Terry paused, the cup halfway to her lips. "Upset about what?"

"That's the problem. She's been here for fifteen minutes, and she's been crying the whole time. I can't get her to calm down enough for her to tell me what's going on."

Terry threw the covers back, this time spilling tea down the side of the bed. She ignored the spill and used the remote to click off the television set. "I'm on my way."

Twenty minutes later, Terry burst into the kitchen wearing faded blue jeans with a hole in the right knee, red and white tennis shoes and a bright red tee shirt that read: *A good friend will bail you out of jail. A great friend will be sitting in the cell next to you saying, 'Oh shit, we fucked up!'*

"All right," Terry demanded, her mouth pressed into a tight line. "Whose ass are we going to kick?"

"This French chick named Bianca," Dee said, her chin trembling slightly.

Terry's teeth clinched and her nostrils flared. "Come on," she said, turning toward the door. "Let's go."

"Hey, wait a minute. You don't even know what's going on." Holly jumped up from her seat at the table to grab Terry's arm and lead her to Dee's side.

"Dee said she needed my help. That's all I need to hear."

"But you don't know why she needs your help."

"Doesn't matter," Terry said as she shook her head, wiggled free from Holly's grasp and walked back toward the door. "Let's go."

"No!" Holly raced across the room quickly, grabbed Terry's arm again, and tugged her back to the table. "Listen to the story first." She looked down at Dee. "Dee, tell Terry what you just told me."

Dee blinked back tears and in a low tormented voice said, "Ben is having an affair."

Terry looked at Dee for a long moment with her mouth agape, and then she busted out laughing.

Holly took Dee's hand. "You see how ridiculous that sounds? Even the woman who believes that all men are the scum of the earth thinks that's hilarious."

"I can't believe you. You got me out of my bed and away from Patrick for this? Ain't this some shit." Terry glared at Holly, and then to Dee said, "Where the hell did you get a crazy-ass idea like that?"

"This woman Bianca, she's new at Harrison, and she's beautiful and sophisticated."

"So? What are you, the ugly step-sister?" Terry asked indignantly.

Tears welled at the rim of Dee's eyes. "She's gorgeous, and she's always hanging around when I go to the office. She's so sweet and friendly, I hate her."

Terry and Holly looked at each other.

"Honey," Holly said. "That's ridiculous. She works there; of course she's going to be there when you go to the office."

"But she's always in Ben's office when I go to see him," Dee tried to reason.

Terry folded her arms across her breasts. "Okay, let's start from the beginning. What does this Bianca chick do at Harrison?"

"She's Ben's new assistant."

Holly and Terry looked at each other again, and Terry shook her head.

"Sweetie," Holly said hesitantly, "Are you pregnant?"

"What? No! And if I were, what difference would that make? It wouldn't change the fact that Ben is having an affair!" Dee said in desperation.

"Dee, there's nothing to worry about, I agree with Red," Terry said, using Holly's nickname. "Ben loves you; I've never seen a man that loves his woman more than Ben loves you." She glanced at Holly, "Well, other than Tyler. God, you wenches make me sick." Terry muttered and walked over to one of the free chairs to flop down.

"What's going on with you?" Holly said, and followed Terry's lead, sitting in the other chair.

"Nothing," Terry said, letting out a huge sigh. Holly watched her intently. "Really, it's nothing. I guess I'm just feeling sorry for myself. I mean, you guys have the perfect lives with the perfect mates, and I'm just trying to make it from one day to the next."

"Do you need any help?" Holly offered. "Tyler and I can-"

"No, I appreciate you offering; but I'm sure everything will be okay. I'm just blowing off steam, I guess."

"Hey!" Dee yelled, waving her arms frantically. "What about me? Have I suddenly become invisible here? I'm having a crisis, for God sakes!"

"Stop being dramatic, you don't have a crisis," Holly said, laughing and shaking her head.

Dee frowned at her, folded her arms, and pouted.

Holly looked at her closely and then grinned broadly. "Oh my goodness, you are pregnant!"

"Uh..." Terry turned around, looking at Dee.

"She's pregnant," Holly said again.

"What makes you say that?" Dee asked, placing her hand on her abdomen.

"You are!" Terry said accusingly.

Dee sighed. "All right, I don't know for sure."

"Oh, you are so knocked up," Terry said. "Hence, the idea that Ben is having an affair."

"Believe me," Dee said. "Something's going on."

"Honey, Ben is not having an affair," Holly said. "It's the hormones making you think that. You remember the last time you were pregnant? Your emotions were all over the place."

"Yeah, I know. But…" Dee started.

"Does Ben know?" Terry asked.

"No, I haven't told him yet. He's been working so many hours; it's like I hardly see him."

"Is it him working long hours or you?" Holly asked.

"Yeah, you can't work long hours anymore now that you're expecting," Terry injected.

"I don't work long hours, not always. I just work one night a week, and that evening Ben is with the boys."

"I don't mean doing surveillances," Holly said. "I mean working in the office, going over reports, making calls to clients from home. Even though you're at home you're still working."

"Well," Dee said slowly.

"She makes such a cute prego," Terry said watching Dee with her head tilted.

"Don't call me prego," Dee snapped, rolling her eyes.

"I bet 'Schlock' never looked that good pregnant. I bet she looks like a walrus." Terry looked from Dee to Holly then back. "Oh, I didn't tell you? She's pregnant…again. None of the kids are over the age of two, and she's having another one. Hell, the youngest one can't be more than five or six months old."

Dee looked thoughtful for a moment. "Hasn't it been longer? Isn't he almost one?"

"I guess the concept of birth control escapes them," Terry went on, ignoring Dee's question.

"But..." Dee started to say, and then obviously changed her mind.

"How are DJ and Keith taking it? Do they know yet?" Holly asked.

## Chapter 8

"Nope, I haven't told them," Terry said, shaking her head. And I don't think I will. It's hard enough knowing that they can't get much time with their father because he's spending it with his new family. This…this will all but stop any time he spends with the boys."

# Chapter 9

"Thanks, dad," Wade said, accepting the beer from his father.

Wade Sr. sat in the vacant Adirondack chair next to Wade as Wade looked around the yard at his family. It had been several years since he'd been home to visit for more than a day. The last time he had visited was the previous Thanksgiving and then he'd just stayed overnight. Now that he was back in Chicago indefinitely, he realized how much he had really missed living so close to them. His brother Adam's son, Jack, was eight and his daughter, April, was twelve. They had grown a lot since his last visit, and their sister Shalan's daughter, Chelsea, was only twenty-one and already engaged.

When the family met at his parents' house for dessert a couple weeks ago, Shalan had told Wade about Chelsea's engagement, but Wade hadn't had a chance to meet Chelsea's fiancé yet. Shalan had said that Jason was from a rather wealthy family. He was a bank manager. Chelsea had moved into his condominium with him sometime around the beginning of the year. Wade gathered from Cliff, Shalan's husband that neither he nor Shalan cared much for Jason.

The next day, Wade did a little checking on Jason Bleeker and found that he'd had a few run-ins with the law: a few juvenile offenses, trespassing, shoplifting, and under-aged drinking. At eighteen, he was arrested for DUI and at twenty, disorderly conduct, but nothing in the past four years. Wade watched Chelsea as she stood next to her fiancé. Jason slowly ran his hand up and down her arm. She looked up at him, and Wade saw the look of uncertainty flash in her eyes and disappear almost as soon as it had appeared.

"So how's everything been, really?" His father asked. "I know you didn't just decide to up and leave your home and job to move back here."

Wade had expected this question. It had just taken longer than he'd anticipated for his father to corner him. During the past weeks that he'd been back in Chicago, he'd visited his parents' home a few times, and he'd expected that question to be the first thing his father had said to him when he walked in, or at least the second, following close behind, "What do you want?"

"Everything's good," Wade answered keeping his eyes on the young couple across the yard.

"So, your decision to leave your last position," His father said, and then paused, "Whatever that might have been…was your own?" His father regarded him suspiciously again. "You weren't asked to leave, I hope?"

Wade sniffed, weighing his answer. Regardless of what he told his father, Wade knew his father wouldn't believe him. Wade believed that if his father witnessed a total stranger committing a heinous crime, and that person said that he was innocent and that Wade had committed the crime, his father would believe Wade was the culprit.

*The sad part*, Wade thought, *was that when I was a child,my father and I were close.*

When they were in Malaysia, he and his father didn't spend a lot of time together, but when they did, it was good. When his father had a day off from work, he would seek out his sons and take them fishing or hiking. Sometimes they would do something that seemed trivial to their father, like sleep overnight in the tent in the back yard. It didn't seem like much to Wade Sr. but it had meant a lot to Wade and Adam. When they moved to the States, their father seemed to change to a different person, someone none of them recognized. He spent most of his time away from home, and when he was home, he didn't want any of his children around.

When their second year in Chicago rolled around, Wade Sr. was drinking weekly. By the third year, he was drinking almost daily. During their second year in Chicago, Shalan was a senior in high school and preparing for college. With school, friends and her part-time job, she spent very little time at home, so she didn't experience some of the things that Wade and Adam had. Wade was fourteen, and he had learned quickly that the best thing for him to do was to stay as far away from their father as possible. Wade did his best to take eleven-year-old Adam with him whenever he could. Wade knew that being gone was the best thing for both Adam and him; he knew that their father didn't need any provocation to attack his brother or him.

"If I tell you that I decided that I needed a change instead of being asked to leave, would you really believe me?"

His father looked down at his thumb as he ran it along the edge of his beer can. "I'd like to think I would." Wade doubted that, but did not say as much. "Look, son, I'm glad you're home, for whatever reason, and I want to rebuild our relationship. Lord knows, it's been too long."

Wade doubted that as well. Looking across the yard, he saw the happy smile his mother gave him at seeing Wade Sr. sitting next to him. Wade could practically hear his mother's voice as she said, "Wade, your father is trying. He wants to make amends. Can you at least try? Please?"

At seeing the look on his mother's face, Wade knew that he *would* make an effort. He would not do it for the man sitting next to him. He didn't deserve it, nor would he ever deserve it. Wade would do it for the one woman that he loved more than life itself.

"So how have you been, Dad?" Wade asked, trying to shift the conversation from himself. "How's the leg feeling?"

"Good," Wade Sr. answered. "I've been meaning to ask you. What did you do in Boston?" Wade met his father's piercing gaze. "I mean, you never told me and your mamma what kind of work you did." his father's tone turned accusing. "Whenever we asked, we never got a straight answer. It's like you had something to hide."

His father's gaze was penetrating, and Wade could tell he was looking for any hint of trouble. His tone said that he hoped he would find some. Keeping his voice even, Wade said, "I taught English in Boston, Dad, I've been teaching for a few years now."

His father's brows rose, and then he narrowed his eyes suspiciously. "Since when? How did you get to be a teacher? You didn't go to school for it."

Wade took a swallow from his beer. He wanted to ask his father how he would know what Wade went to school for. After Wade turned eighteen and left home, he went to Indianapolis. He didn't know anyone and his only possessions were his duffle bag full of clothes and $600 dollars that he'd saved. He rented a room in a boarding house, where most of his clothes were stolen the week after moving in. He'd learned that the landlord's son was the culprit, but instead of stomping the crap out of the guy like he wanted to do, he packed up what little he had left and moved on. He worked odd jobs, sometimes two or three at a time for a year, until he had a few thousand dollars saved, and then he applied to attend Indiana University. It took him almost six years of going to school while he worked, but he got his BA in Criminal Justice. He never talked to anyone about the things he did or what he wanted from life, his career goals or dreams. He didn't tell his mother or grandmother, because he knew anything that he said would be more fodder in his father's arsenal; the only person he'd ever felt he could confide in was Jennifer.

When Wade brought the bottle down from his lips, he squeezed it, while trying to maintain his composure.

"Well?" his father asked. "Are you legally a teacher or will we have the authorities on our doorstep looking for you?"

Wade scoffed sardonically, shaking his head. It was funny that his father would ask him about the authorities coming in search of him. The only person in their family that the police had ever visited their home for was his father, when he was on one of his drunken binges.

"I'm really sorry to disappoint you, Dad, but it's completely legal."

Wade Sir's face immediately reddened and his eyes narrowed as he assessed Wade. "Boy, you ain't changed one bit, have you? You've still got that haughty attitude."

Wade sat totally still, his expression stony as he continued to watch the movement in the yard. His eyes met Shalan's. She spoke to her mother and grandmother, and then crossed the yard. She stood between Wade and her father's chairs as she looked out at their family gathered round in the yard.

Wade's brother Adam was helping Jack and April fix the flat tire on April's bike. His mother and grandmother were having a debate on if it were best to cook the chicken or the burgers on the grill first, and who would be manning the fire. Cliff, Chelsea, Chelsea's fiancé, Jason, and Adam's wife, Leslie sat at the picnic table playing a game of Yahtzee.

Wade Sr. looked over at his wife and mother-in-law for a few minutes in silence. "Hump, looks like I'd better get over there, or we'll never get anything to eat today."

He scooted to the edge of his seat, and with his daughter's help, he pushed himself up from the chair and, using his cane, limped across the yard.

Shalan took the seat her father had just vacated. "Hey, little brother, how are you?"

"I'm good, how about yourself?"

"Good." she took a sip of her iced tea. "How are things going with you and dad?" Wade didn't answer. "Mamma's really happy that you're home."

"Yeah, I know."

"We all really missed you, even Daddy."

"You know, I find that just a little hard to believe." He glanced at her and, seeing the pained looked in her eyes, said, "Look, Shalan, I know what you're trying to do."

She looked away for a moment and then smiled innocently at him. "What are you talking about?"

Wade had to laughed, "Shay, you are so transparent. You've always tried to be the peacemaker. I understand your need to do that, and I appreciate it. But please don't. I don't need you to mend fences with me and dad."

"Wade, someone has to."

"The only people who can bring us together are Dad and I, and I honestly don't know if that's even possible."

She leaned forward, and tilted her head to the side, regarding him closely. "I think it is." She paused and then glanced at their parents standing across the yard, before turning back to him. "Can you at least try, please?"

Wade looked at his sister, seeing the need to make things better in her eyes. Shalan got that from their mother, always the diplomat, and the person who wanted everyone's life to be as good, if not better, than her own. At the beginning, when their father would get into one of his moods, Shalan would try to use her position as daddy's little girl to calm him and make things better for Wade and Adam. As time progressed, their father became more hostile. When Shalan started spending less time at home and eventually moved to Pennsylvania to go to college, she seemed to forget the beast that often resided in their home. Now Wade could see that she was still ever the peacemaker. She was also blind. She didn't seem to notice the way Adam sometimes became angry or was short with their father. She didn't see the way Adam watched his children with their grandfather, looking for any signs of anger or hostility. He looked across the yard at his mother who laughed as she shooed his grandmother away from the grill and passed her husband the pair of tongs. He didn't want to tell his sister that he knew that things would never be right between them; not now, not ever. Even if he did, she would never understand. No one would.

"Okay, Shay, I'll give it a try," he finally said. "So, how have Cliff and Chelsea been?"

Shalan smiled as she looked across the yard at her family and nodded. The smile was there, but it didn't reach her eyes. Wade looked in the direction that Shalan was looking. His niece Chelsea and her fiancé Jason now stood a few feet away from the picnic table, talking. The young man reached up to brush the hair from Chelsea's face, and she flinched. Wade's brow furrowed and his jaw clinched. Jason took a step closer to Chelsea, leaned close, and whispered something in her ear.

"They grow up so fast," Shalan said, heaving a heavy sigh.

"You say everything is okay, but I get the feeling that there's something going on that you're not telling me," Wade said, still watching the couple from across the yard.

Shalan glanced at him. "Yeah, there was some trouble for a while there."

"What sort of trouble?"

"Fighting, arguing. She's called us a few times. Once Chelsea and Jason had an argument, Chelsea said that Jason got so upset that he pushed her. Cliff and I went over to the apartment. When we arrived, she told us that it was a misunderstanding and that she didn't need us. Cliff was livid. He was close to punching Jason out, and he demanded that Chelsea come home with us, but she wouldn't hear any of it. A few months later, she called me as I was heading out to work. She was frantic and said that Jason was so angry and aggressive that she thought that he might strike her. Cliff had already left for work, so I called him and the police. Cliff arrived at the apartment just as I did. When we went inside, the police said that Chelsea told them that they just had an argument and that everything was fine. They had gotten a little loud was all. Cliff and I tried to convince her to leave with us, but she still refused. As far as I know, there haven't been any other problems. Though, at this point, I don't even know if she would tell us if anything was wrong."

Wade ran his free hand through his hair. "Shay, why didn't you tell me?"

"Why, Wade? You lived in Boston, what could you possibly have done?"

*A hell of a lot more than you think.* Wade thought to himself.

"I've tried talking to her," Shalan continued. "I've even asked Mamma and Nenek to speak with her, but no one seems to be able to get through to her, so there's nothing that you could have said."

Wade felt his left eye twitch as he watched Jason lean close and whisper in Chelsea's ear again. He saw her smile falter, then she met Jason's gaze and dropped her eyes, biting her lip nervously.

When Shalan spoke again, her voice was sad and distant. "I know I can't choose the man who Chelsea decides to spend her life with, even though as parents we sometimes wish we could. I only want her to be happy." Her voiced lowered a little more. "I only want her to be safe."

# Chapter 10

Sunlight caressed the landscape of the sixteen-acre Eden-like lot that Dee and Ben called their back yard. Whenever Terry walked into this yard during the spring or summer, it made her think of paradise. The path that led from the main part of the yard had flowerbeds on both sides with vibrant purples, pink and white flowers. The path led down to a basketball and tennis court, as well as an Olympic-sized pool. The area closest to the house, which Dee called the main yard, housed a fourteen-foot circular Koi pond with a ten-foot tall fountain in the center. They had already fed the children, and the twins were inside taking a nap while their part-time nanny looked on. DJ was down at the basketball court shooting hoops with his friend Terrell, and Abby and Keith were entertaining themselves at the Koi pond.

After the adults dished food onto their plates and sat down at the table, Terry decided that this would be the perfect time to bring up her business ideas. "You know what, guys? I've been thinking."

"Oh lord," Holly groaned.

Terry glared at her, and Holly laughed. "I was thinking that maybe I could go into the PI business with Dee."

Dee coughed and sputtered, choking on her drink. Ben quickly reached behind her, patting her back.

"Yeah, it would be great. We could work together in the family business."

Dee shook her head, her eyes watering as she pushed her husband's hand away.

"Just think of it," Terry went on. "The Meyers women conquer the investigative world."

"No!" Dee finally managed to say.

Terry threw a malevolent look at Dee. "What, why not?"

Dee leaned across the table toward her cousin. "Do you remember the last time I took you to work with me?"

"I can't be held responsible for that, I was emotional. I was under duress," Terry said quickly.

She heard Tyler and Holly snicker, and she cut her eyes in their direction before looking back at Dee.

"You were crazy," Dee snapped. "You threw coffee on my subject's white dress, blowing my case to hell."

Terry raised her hands in surrender. "See, in my defense, she deserved it. She was a skank ho who was cheating on her husband. Besides," Terry said, raising her chin high, "the coffee was cold."

"Doesn't matter if she was a skank or not, you blew my case. Oh yeah, and let's not forget the restaurant incident."

"See, that was over two years ago. Why you gotta be bringing up old stuff? And you said yourself that you had all of the information you needed when I confronted Mr. Home Wrecker."

"That's not the point."

Terry sucked her teeth and rolled her eyes. She immediately realized what she had done. She needed a different approach to make Dee see things her way; she smiled sincerely. "Come on, Dee, I need to do this." She raised her hand as if to take an oath. "I promise to behave this time, I swear. Scouts honor."

"Didn't you get kicked out of the girl scouts for..?" Holly added, devilment shining in her eyes.

"That was so long ago, and has nothing to do with this," Terry snapped at Holly, who only grinned. Ben and Tyler laughed, and Terry glared at the both of them before turning back to Dee. "Please!" She tried giving Dee her lost puppy look.

"Nope."

"Pretty please?"

"Nope, absolutely not, no way, no how."

"Fine; be that way," Terry grumbled, picked up her fork, and pushed macaroni salad around on her plate as she waited a few moments.

She watched Dee out of the corner of her eye to see if she would at least give her idea some thought. Dee turned to whisper something to Ben. He laughed and brushed the hair from her cheek. When Dee didn't seem to be giving Terry's idea the slightest bit of consideration, Terry sucked her teeth again, dropping her fork on her plate.

"Geez, fine, whatever," she grunted dramatically. "Well, there's something else that I've been thinking about doing. What do you think of me starting a child-care?"

"Hmm..." Dee steepled her hands under her chin. "You know, I think that's a great idea."

"Really?" Holly, Ben, Tyler, and even Terry all asked simultaneously.

"Yeah," Dee said. "You took early child psychology in college."

"Yeah..." Terry said, hesitantly at first and then with more pride added. "Well, yes, I did."

“That was only a few credits,” Holly said. “A few credits does not a child expert make.”

“No, I have more than a few credits, thank you very much,” Terry said smugly.

“She’s very good with the kids,” Dee added. “And they love her.”

“That’s because she’s like one of them. They’re practically playmates,” Holly reminded Dee.

“Girl, I can relate to them, they love me.” Terry grinned.

“Oh boy,” Holly groaned playfully. “I can just see it. The parents of Chicago are in deep trouble. We’ll have a city full of roguish, potty-mouthed, seven-year-olds. ”

Terry laughed, throwing her napkin across the table at Holly, who caught it and threw it back.

“I think it’s a great idea, you’d make a perfect childcare provider,” Dee said after a moment.

“Thanks. I was thinking that I could fix up the basement, make it a playroom, and if you guys have some toys that the kids are not using, I can take them off your hands.”

“Abby has some old toys that I can give you, and we’ll help any way we can,” Holly said, before taking a bite from her burger.

“I know a couple guys who might be willing to lend a hand,” Tyler said. “I think we can get a day’s work out of them. Maybe we could build a wall to separate the area where you plan on having the kids take naps from the play area, and design an area to prepare snacks.”

“And Ben and I’ll donate the paint, and a few other items to decorate,” Dee said, and Ben nodded in agreement. “And, we’ll even be your first customers.”

This time it was Ben who sputtered and coughed. “What?”

## Chapter 10

"Sure, it'll be great! Terry can take care of the twins."

"I don't know; I sort of wanted to do the business part on my own," Terry said. "I want to know that I can make a go of it. You know what I'm saying?"

"I totally agree with you," Ben said quickly, addressing Terry. "You'll know that you're achieving everything on your own. It'll give you a great sense of accomplishment."

"Don't be silly, baby, she'll be achieving things on her own," Dee said to her husband, and then turned back to Terry. "It'll be all about business, you can write a contract and Ben and I will sign it. We'll pay the same fee as everyone else and follow all of the rules. We'll make everything strictly business, and we'll know that the boys are with someone who loves them. And when we have the new baby…"

"Sweetheart, can we talk about this later?" Ben whispered, then glanced in Holly's direction when he heard her snicker.

"Okay, let's do it," Terry said.

Just then, Keith ran across the yard to his mother holding his knee. "Mommy," he cried.

"We can paint the rooms bright colors, maybe yellow or blue. I saw this really nice green on television last week," Terry said.

"Mommy!"

"Yeah," Dee added, "that'll work, or you can paint it a couple of colors. Maybe a soft blue and a green."

"And I can decorate it with alphabets and cartoon characters," Terry grinned eagerly.

"Mommy," Keith wailed, nearly jumping up and down.

"What?" Terry finally asked impatiently.

"I bumped my knee, and it hurts."

Terry leaned forward, checking Keith's knee. She didn't see anything, not a scratch, bump or mark. Terry shook her head slightly; Keith was going through a phase that she was praying would pass quickly. He would cry about everything. He cried when he didn't get his way, and he cried when she reprimanded him. He even cried when she told him it was time to turn off the television to take his bath.

"You'll be okay, go walk it off," Terry said, physically turning him back in the direction of the open yard and giving him a slight push. "You know," she said turning back to Dee. "I have a good feeling about this. I'm going to make this a success."

Ben looked at Keith and then at Terry, appalled. "Um, sweetheart, I don't know about this. I think it may be best if we give Terry help in another way. We could give her money, lots of money." Ben's face said it all; he was searching his mind for an idea, something, anything. "Maybe she'd like to try some other business. I can see her opening a store or a restaurant." He nodded, looking across the table at Terry. "Yeah, a restaurant sounds really good."

"And maybe you can keep Abby too?" Dee continued, as if she hadn't heard a thing her husband had said.

Holly opened her mouth to speak, and then paused, all eyes immediately focused on her. Everyone, that is, except Ben, who was looking at his wife as if she had morphed into a three-headed snake. Holly looked at Terry, and then at her daughter, who was standing in the middle of the yard looking up toward the top of the water fountain. Her head was tilted to the side, and she had an angelic look on her face as fine wisps of her sandy brown hair blew in the slight breeze. Abby bit her lip as if she was in deep thought, and then her angelic look turned sly as she glanced at Keith. At that moment, Terry knew that whatever the ‘monster child’ had planned would end in Keith crying. She looked at Holly, who sighed and shook her head slightly.

“I guess you can keep Abby,” Holly said. “It’s not like she’s completely normal, after hanging out with you lunatics anyway.”

Terry clapped her hands excitedly. “Great!”

# Chapter 11

As the evening came to an end, Wade, his brother, and brother-in-law, and even his father busied themselves helping the women carry all of the food into the house. Jason sat on one of the lounge chairs, his eyes closed as he nursed a beer. Wade watched him for a moment, as his nine-year-old nephew, Jack slipped by him, carrying a platter into the house that was nearly as wide as he was tall. Crossing the yard, Wade kicked the bottom of Jason's sandal and he bolted upright, wasting beer down the front of his shirt.

"Hey, man, you made me waste my beer!" Jason glowered up at Wade.

"If you haven't noticed," Wade said tightly. "We all pitch in around here. I think you need to move your ass and help with the clean-up."

"At my parents' house, we usually leave those things for the women to take care of."

"Well, boy, you ain't in Kansas anymore. Now, move your ass."

"Wade," his mother called from the doorway. "Let him be. It's no big deal; we're all done here anyway."

Jason smiled smugly up at Wade. His smile wavered and then died once he saw a look in Wade's eyes that caused him to visibly tremble.

## Chapter 11

Once he pushed the grill to the far corner of the yard, Wade slipped the cover over it and strolled across the grass towards the house. He glanced inside, seeing everyone gathered in the kitchen, either sitting around the table, or helping to put the food away, everyone except Jason. Wade watched as Jason reclined on the lounge chair, tapping his feet to music that only he could hear. Opening his eyes, Jason smiled to himself, holding up the beer bottle, tilting it at an angle to check the contents before he drained the last of it. He closed his eyes for an instant, as if savoring the last swallow, and then rose and casually crossed the yard, bypassing the garbage can and setting the beer bottle on the picnic table before he stepped on the patio to enter the house. Wade took three long steps, blocking Jason's path into the kitchen.

"Hey, man, what's up?" Jason gave Wade a quick once over, his blond brows raised in question.

Looking over his shoulder, Wade watched his niece for a moment before turning back to the younger man, who instantly grinned at him. Wade took a step closer, looming over the other man, who inhaled a sharp breath. His grin slid from his face, and he shuffled back several feet.

"Take a good look at me, you bastard," Wade said in a low and menacing voice. "Do I really look like the sort of man you wanna fuck with?"

The calm look in Wade's eyes was more frightening than his menacing tone, and alarm quickly took the place of the smug expression that Jason wore. When he tried to speak, his mouth opened and closed like a fish, and the only thing he managed to mutter was, "Uh..."

"My niece is a good girl, and I don't want to see her hurt or upset. That's the only reason I'm not shoving a shish kebob skewer up your ass and roasting you on the grill. But," Wade closed the space that separated them, "If I even get the slightest inkling that you put your hands on her again…" Wade studied Jason's face, while his own face held an unfathomable expression. He watched as perspiration beaded on the other man's upper lip and temples. "Well," Wade finally said, "let's just say that you would gladly welcome having a sharp object impale you and roast you over an open fire, as opposed to what I would do to you then! Do we understand each other?"

Jason only nodded.

Wade turned his head slightly, leaning closer, his ear only inches from Jason's nose.

"I'm sorry. I didn't catch that."

"Yes, sir," came a barely audible reply.

Wade glared at him again and gave a slight nod. "Good."

He held Jason's eyes for a moment more before letting Jason slip by him. Jason waited a heartbeat before he forced his feet to move, and he did his best not to touch Wade as he eased passed him and entered the house.

# Chapter 12

To Terry's dismay, she learned that it took a lot longer than a few weeks to obtain a child-care license in the state of Illinois. She completed and submitted her application, and set up a date for the home inspection, which was a little more than a month away. She closed the booklet that she was reading, *Illinois Child Care for Family Home Providers*, and dropped it on the table. At this rate, she wouldn't have a license until October. After talking to Rose Mitchell, another child care provider, to see what she could learn and what to expect, she'd given up any hopes of getting her license early. Rose only knew of one person who'd gotten her license in less than three months, but that license was issued on the second day of the three-month wait.

Terry groaned. No job or income of any kind. And, that jerk, David, was ducking out, hiding from her at every turn. When she called his cell, it immediately went to the voicemail, or if she called from another number, he'd instantly hang up on her. He wouldn't take her calls at work, so she knew that if she visited him there, he wouldn't see her. She didn't want to take him to court to make him pay child support, even though she couldn't stand him. In fact, if the earth was flat and he walked to the edge to get a peek, she would probably find great joy in pushing him over the edge. But he was DJ and

Keith's father, and they had enough to deal with without their father using her going through the courts to force him to support his children.

Terry glanced up at the clock: 2:17 PM. When she and David were still together, they would visit David's mother on Sunday afternoons, following Mass. Knowing David, he still visited his momma and had dinner with her every Sunday. Terry debated calling her ex-mother-in-law's home. David's mother, Grace Wilkerson, never liked Terry. Terry knew it was because when she was young, she was wild and did a lot of things that she was now ashamed of. She'd tried to manipulate David and everyone else to get what she thought she deserved. She even cheated on him. That was years ago, and she had done everything she could to make up for it. Terry did what she could to be a good wife, mother, and daughter-in-law. At the drop of a dime, she would race to Grace's house and take her wherever she wanted to go. Terry would run errands for Grace, and sometimes clean her house or do her laundry, but Grace never had a thank-you or a kind word to say.

Terry could imagine David sitting across the table from his mother and smiling with pride, as she told Terry, "No, David's not here. And I haven't seen him in weeks. By the way, have you seen the new baby? Oh, he's absolutely adorable."

Heaving a heavy sigh, Terry picked up the phone, and dialed David's mother's phone number. After the third ring, Terry heard "Hello."

"Hello, Grace, how are you?"

"I'm fine. Who's calling?"

Terry's jaw locked to keep in the rude reply that was on the tip of her tongue. *Oh bitch, please, you know who this is*. "Grace, this is Terry, your daughter-in-law."

"Oh, Terry, honey, how are you?"

"I'm good…"

"And the boys?"

"They're good as well. Grace, I'm trying to locate David. He wouldn't happen to be there, would he?"

"As a matter of fact, he is. Hold on a second."

Terry was so shocked that she glanced at the phone to make sure it wasn't a figment of her imagination.

"What's up?" David asked once he came on the phone.

"David, this has gone far enough. I need your help, I can't do this alone."

"Terry, what do you want me to do?"

"I want you to take care of your obligations."

"I am taking care of my obligations. Shareese and I are buying a new house and my finances are stretched to the limit. Now with another baby on the way, things are very hard for us."

"David, I didn't call you for any excuses, I don't want to hear any of them. The only thing I want to hear from you is: the check is in the mail."

"Terry, you need to stop being so bitchy."

"I don't know, call me dumb, but I tend to get a little bitchy when the electric company threatens to cut the lights off, and the kids are constantly crying about being hungry. It tends to get on your nerves, if you know what I mean."

"You don't have to be nasty."

"I am *so* not being nasty. You wanna see nasty? How about if I dress DJ and Keith in their worst clothes and come to your job begging for money for food so that everyone can see what a wonderful daddy you are?"

"I don't even know why I'm wasting my time talking to you. I'm trying to tell you that I just can't do everything."

"David, you're not doing everything. You're not doing *anything* for DJ and Keith at all. You know what, I am so tired of your shit, I advise you to do whatever you have to do to make your child support payments, or you will rue the day you ever laid eyes on me!"

"Is that a threat?"

"Uh, Yeah!"

Terry heard rustling on the other end of the phone and then Shareese's shrill voice yelled. "Who do you think you're talking to?"

"Great. Just perfect," Terry said in monotone. "I don't have time to play your game, little girl."

"You don't call my mother-in-law's house and harass my man, bitch."

Terry dropped her face in her hands. She was *so* not in the mood for this. "Look Shaley…"

"Shareese, my name is Shareese, damn it."

"Yeah, whatever, Shareese, right."

Terry knew what her name was. She would have to be deaf not to know the woman's name, since she'd heard David say it at least a million times over the last two years. At first, Terry didn't want to remember Shareese's name. What woman wanted to remember the name of the whore who had stolen her husband? But now, Terry didn't care; she wasn't even upset about it anymore. Hell, as far as Terry was concerned, Shareese did her a favor. She showed Terry what an unworthy sorry dirt bag David truly was. Terry figured that if it hadn't been Shareese, it would have probably been some other woman.

Plus, Terry felt rather sorry for the little nitwit. Not long before David had told Terry that he was leaving her, they had celebrated their eight-year wedding anniversary. David had sent her a dozen red roses and made arrangements for DJ and Keith to spend the night with his mother while he took Terry out for dinner and dancing. While David held her close and spun her around the dance floor, he sang along with Will Downing, pledging his undying loved to her. It was just one month, one month before leaving her, that David was telling her how much he loved her.

And now he was probably telling Shareese the same thing. How long would it be before he got tired of her? How did Shareese know that he was not planning the same thing for her? Did she think that, since David wasn't faithful to his wife, he wouldn't cheat on her? If it were Terry, that's what she'd think. Hell, he could be thinking of dumping Shareese for a newer model with less mileage before she gave birth to their third child.

Nope. Terry would not show sympathy for Shareese; just like she wouldn't address her by name. She would rather run butt-assed naked through Time Square, during the height of tourist season, in a hundred and twenty degree heat, dipped in honey with a swarm of killer bees hot on her ass.

"This is between me and David; you need to stop putting yourself in the middle of all of this. Why don't you go play with your baby dolls and leave this mess for the grown folks to handle? David has responsibilities and-"

"Yes, David does have responsibilities, and they are to me and our children."

"DJ and Keith didn't just disappear when David crawled between your thighs, stupid!" Terry said, her anger rapidly building. "They are his children as well, and he's going to damn well take care of them."

"Terry," Grace said calmly through the phone.

Terry took a deep breath. "Yeah, Grace?"

"I don't like the way this thing with you and David has been going."

“Neither do I-”

“Let me finish. David is starting a new life with Shareese, and you need to understand that.”

*What the hell?* Terry thought.

Grace continued, “And I think you need to move on with your life and leave David and Shareese alone.”

“What do you mean, leave them alone?”

“I mean, stop harassing them, stop with your tricks to get David back. We know your tricks, and they won’t work.”

“What! Are you people insane?”

“And David will not be giving you any more money, until you establish paternity for those children. I honestly don’t think that the children are his and he agrees, so you need to let the court handle this.”

“Now you’re trying to tell me that you don’t think that DJ and Keith are David’s?” Terry said in a low and menacing voice. “You bitch. You’re going to do this to your grandsons, you’re going to hurt them just because you hate me?

“That is our decision,” Grace said, “and we will let the courts decide how to handle things.”

Then there was a click and the line went dead. Terry hung up the phone and dropped her face into her hands. She turned the phone back on and dialed Holly’s number.

“Hey," she said, once Holly answered the phone. “Do you think Keith can stay there for a few more hours?”

Once Holly okayed her request, Terry went up to her bedroom, removed her clothes down to her underwear, crawled under the covers, and had a two-hour cry.

# Chapter 13

The first few weeks of school went a lot smoother than Wade had expected. Much to his delight, and moreover relief, the students seemed to like him. The boys, who weren't afraid of him, thought he was cool, and the girls thought he was neat and, from what some of the faculty had told him, hot.

It was just past 3 PM and Wade was tired, edgy, and pissed off. They were barely into the third week of the school year, and there always seemed to be something going on. On any given day, there were kids making out in the stairwell, smoking in the bathroom, or trying to exit the building when they were supposed to be in class. Earlier in the day, some knucklehead decided that it would be fun to set off a stink bomb in one of the science classrooms, and they had to evacuate the building until the fire department gave the okay for them to return to their classrooms.

When the fire department gave the green light and everyone started to reenter the building, Wade noticed six boys slipping around the side of the building. He waited a moment before following them. He recognized the boys as kids from his homeroom class. The one boy who stood out was Micah Hennock. Micah was a funny, bright, charismatic boy. He was also trouble. Wade knew Micah was a known marijuana dealer. As far as

Wade could tell, he hadn't set up shop yet. He usually waited a few weeks after the school year started, but Wade knew it was only a matter of time. Micah was small-time, and not who Wade wanted; he wanted Micah's supplier. When he rounded the corner, Wade spotted Micah run to a row of hedges and step behind them. When he emerged a moment later, his hands were empty and his backpack was gone. He ran to catch up with his friends, two of whom were lighting up cigarettes. Wade had reached them just as they were about to leave school property.

"Hey, guys, what's going on?" Wade said.

The boys nearly jumped out of their skins, spinning around and facing Wade. One of the boys dropped his cigarette, shoving his hands into his pocket. One of the others took a long drag from his, eyeing Wade as if he dared him to say something. Wade stepped close to him, popping the cigarette from his fingers and plucked it away.

"What are you guys doing?" Wade said, his voice louder and stronger than his first enquiry.

"Nothing," Micah said. "We were just about to go back inside the building."

"It looked like you were heading away from the building instead of toward it." Wade glanced over his shoulder to the bush where Micah had stashed his backpack. He took a few steps backwards into the grass, not taking his eyes from the boys. Bending quickly, he scooped up the backpack and stepped back on the path. He unzipped the front pocket, and found a cigar and a lighter.

"Hey, that's personal property," Micah complained, stepping toward Wade. "You can't do that."

## Chapter 13

"Actually, I can," Wade murmured. He unzipped the top of the pack and rummaged inside, until he found a bag of marijuana.

"Hey," Micah said, raising his hands. "That's not mine!"

Wade shook his head. "Boys, it seems that we have a problem."

Wade massaged his brow. Damn, he was tired. He should have just taken these boys to the office and let them handle this, but he needed them here. He needed them at school, not suspended, or expelled. These were the boys that Micah had been with since the beginning of the school year; they seemed inseparable. These boys could lead Wade to Micah's supplier. He massaged his tired eyes.

He had been going to his parents' house every few days to check on his mother and grandmother. Last evening, while he was visiting, his grandmother walked behind his chair, giving him a brief hug from behind. She had felt something in his shirt pocket and plucked it out, wanting to see what it was. Of all the things for her to find, would have to be a packet of Top papers that he had taken from one of the students earlier that day.

"What is this?" She had asked. Without even thinking, Wade had told her what it was. When she asked what it was for he explained that as well. "Ooh my lord, you're taking the dope?"

Wade had given her an open-mouthed stare and then laughed. "Nenek, I'm not-"

"Wade, Nurjahan," She yelled. "Come, look at your son. He's taking the dope."

"Oh hell," Wade's laugh turned into a groan. "Nenek, I took that from one of the kids at school."

Wade Sr. limped into the kitchen and stopped in the doorway, leaning on his cane. He watched as his mother-in-law ranted and fluttered around, trying to pull Wade from his seat, all the while going on and on about rehab. Wade looked at his father, seeing what could only be described as a satisfied look on his face.

"He's taking the dope, Wade," as Nenek went on and on. "He's taking the dope. We have to drive him to rehab. Come on, we have to go now."

Wade could only laugh as he dropped his face into his hands, whispering, "Ah shit."

His grandmother had nearly lost her mind, and it had taken almost an hour before Wade could convince her that he was not a drug addict.

After he returned the boys to the school building, he escorted them to the office, where the police were called. While the police were in one of the other offices dealing with the six teens, Wade and the principal were having a conference call with the superintendent. The superintendent had told the principal who Wade was. They'd discussed the situation with the boys, and Wade stated that he'd like to figure out a way to keep the boys at school. Wade was able to come up with a plan to have the boys punished for their indiscretion and still kept in school. Micah admitted to carrying the marijuana. He claimed the other boys didn't know anything about it, but that was all he said. When asked where he got it, he said he found it, then quickly clammed up.

As the parents entered the classroom, Wade rose from behind his desk to introduce himself and explain that he wanted to wait for all the parents to arrive before they discussed the meeting. The parents found seats near their sons, asking them what was going on. Some of the boys just hunched their shoulders. A few, Wade suspected, tried to tell a colorful version of the truth before he had time to tell their parents what had happened.

Wade stood and walked to the front of the classroom, picking up the eraser and wiping the dry-erase board. Wade noticed a familiar face entering the classroom. He turned to watch her as she crossed the room. It was the woman he'd met at the grocery store a few weeks ago. She wore a teal-colored scooped neck blouse that showed what Wade thought was an extremely impressive and mouthwatering amount of cleavage, and a pair of jeans that hugged her luscious hips like a second skin. He eyed her as she walked down the aisle of desks. Her hips swayed gently from side to side as she walked, heightening his appreciation for her tight jeans. The first thing that sprang into Wade's mind was *sexy*.

Wade made a sound of approval and heard male laughter coming from his right. In the front row of desk were three parents with their sons, one male and two females. The looks that the females gave him were of total disapproval. The male, on the other hand, had that knowing grin that many men shared from time to time that said, "*Yeah man, you're right, she's hot*."

"How's it going?" Wade said, giving the trio a quick nod before turning his attention back to the sexy creature that was now hovering over one of the boys.

She wore her brown hair down around her shoulders. She stood over her son, DJ, with her hands on her hips, glaring down at him. Wade couldn't hear what she was saying, but her son looked up at her, grinned sheepishly, and hunched his shoulders. When she pulled out the chair and bent to place her purse on the floor next to it, a lock of hair fell forwards, and she flipped it back over her shoulder. The movement gave Wade a better view of her delicious cleavage, and he absentmindedly licked his lips.

Once all of the parents were seated next to their children Wade said, "I'm sorry to have to call you in for this meeting."

"Then why did you?" One of the fathers demanded.

Wade met the man's glare, and then glanced at his son, Roderick, who only dropped his eyes. The door opened as the principal walked in, closing the door behind him. He introduced himself to the parents, and then proceeded to tell them what had transpired earlier in the day. There were gasps and outrage from the parents. Wade stood next to the door, watching the reactions of the students. His eyes zoomed in on DJ's mother. While the principal continued to talk, DJ's mother shot DJ a murderous glare.

"None of your sons will be charged with possession of an illegal substance. Micah has confessed that it was his and that none of the boys knew that he had it, but there is still the matter of possession of tobacco on school property and attempting to leave school grounds." He reached inside his breast pocket, producing several sheets of paper. "The school is going to go out on a limb and assume that this is the first time that you guys have pulled this." All the boys quickly nodded. Wade figured half of them were lying. "So, the first thing you're going to do is sign up for the Smoking Cessation class." He gestured toward Wade, who passed out information, and then returned to his spot next to the door.

One of the parents raised her hand. "What is a Smoking Cessation class?"

"It's a class that teaches the risks of smoking and provides educational information that will help them quit smoking, if they choose to do so," The principal explained.

## Chapter 13

"Is that it?" Roderick's father asked, rising from his seat and gesturing for his son to do the same.

"No," Wade said as he moved to stand in front of the room next to the principal.

After introducing himself, he addressed the parents. The principal had made a phone call to the elementary school in the same zone, one within walking distance of the high school. He spoke to the principal and told her that he had five students who were interested in tutoring some of the fifth-graders in math. She told him that they had a program, but that it didn't start until November. He assured her that these students were eager to help and that they would be available when the program began. Wade told the boys and their parents that he would be in charge of the tutoring program. He would make sure that they would be there for each and every session.

"And if you're not there when you're supposed to be, I will hunt you down, and drag you there kicking and screaming," Wade said. "And you won't like me very much if I have to come searching for you."

The boys groaned, some of the parents looked pleased, and a couple looked disturbed.

Roderick's father looked at his son with a huge grin on his face. "You're gonna have this guy," he nodded his head in Wade's direction, "up ya ass if you don't tow the row." he looked at Wade and chuckled. "That'll teach ya the next time you decide to skip out of school early," he said, grinning and then asked. "That it?"

Wade glanced to his right at the principal, who nodded. Roderick's father was the first to rise from his seat. Walking to the front of the class, he nodded a greeting to the principal and then engulfed Wade's hand in his larger, meatier hand.

"Nice meeting you, Mr. Nelson."

***

Terry's jaw ached from grinding it so much. She stayed seated with her fist balled tight, fighting to hold on to her temper. If she didn't, she was afraid she would shake DJ until his teeth rattled. What the hell was he thinking? Cutting, smoking, and drugs? She glared at DJ.

"Mom?"

"Zip it," she muttered. "I don't want to hear from you until we get home."

When the last parent left the room, Terry rose and walked to the front of the classroom. She didn't look back, knowing DJ would follow. Wade nodded to DJ, who stood quietly behind his mother with his hands shoved deep in his pocket and his head hung low.

"I'm sorry our second meeting has to be under such circumstances, Mrs. Wilkerson."

"Meyers," Terry corrected. "Ms. Terry Meyers." Terry looked over her shoulder at DJ, and then back at Wade. "I… thanks again. You know, for the thing at the grocery store. Um, I don't usually break down like that."

Wade nodded. "How is your son?"

"Keith? He's good." Terry watched him closely for a moment, his steel grey eyes penetrating hers, and then she looked away. "Not a quarter into the school year and I'm already being summoned in for a meeting." She paused and sighed. "I'm sorry about this mess."

Wade glanced over Terry's shoulder at DJ, who was fidgeting nervously. He adjusted his backpack, and cleared his throat before he inched next to his mother. "Mr. Nelson…"

Terry didn't know what pissed her off more, the stunt that DJ pulled at school, or him asking Wade Nelson if he thought the police could send him to a juvenile detention center. He cut a fearful eye in his mother's direction and asked how long Wade thought he would have to stay there, if they locked him up. Terry knew what he was implying. He'd rather be locked up than go home with his crazed mother. And, evidently, Wade had known what DJ had meant too, because he had laughed saying, "Nope, that won't protect you."

Terry had bristled at his statement and stormed from the classroom, DJ reluctantly followed her down the hall.

"I'm sorry, Mom," DJ said as soon as they entered the house.

Terry dropped her purse on the sofa and wheeled on her son, "What in the world were you thinking?"

"I don't know. I wasn't thinking."

"Obviously. Cutting school, smoking, drugs!"

"Mom, they weren't mine."

"DJ, you were there with him, you saw him hiding his book bag."

"But, the weed wasn't mine," he said, his voice taking on a sharp tone. Terry's brows rose. DJ looked at her sheepishly and whispered, "Sorry."

"You knew that Micah had the drugs in his bag, didn't you?" When DJ did not respond right away, Terry had her answer. "God, DJ!"

"I didn't have it."

"But you knew about them. What if Micah had told the principal and the police that you were aware of the drugs, where do you think you'd be right now?"

"But I didn't know about the drugs," he suddenly said.

"DJ, don't lie." He just stood in front of her with his hands shoved deep in his pockets. Terry shook her head. "All right then, let's just say that you didn't know about the drugs, which I am not buying, but let's just say for the sake of saying it that you didn't. What about trying to skip out of school; what about the cigarettes?"

"It wasn't my cigarette either; I was holding it for Roderick."

"Boy, do I have 'idiot' tattooed across my forehead?"

He opened his mouth and then paused, snapping it shut. Terry took a menacing step toward him gritting her teeth.

She closed her eyes and took a deep breath. *Lord, help me. If I lay my hands on this child, I swear I'll kill him.* She opened her eyes, looking at her child, who just a few weeks ago was her baby, but who was turning into a stranger.

"You're grounded. For a month, and for that month, you will be washing the dinner dishes every weeknight, as well as the breakfast and lunch dishes during the weekend. And for lying, you will lose your computer for a month. The only time that you can use it is for school work, and I will be there monitoring your use."

# Chapter 14

"Hi Wade."

Wade looked up from the file that he was reviewing. "Hey, Emma."

"Mac just made some fresh coffee," she said, slipping her jacket off and hanging it on the back of one of the chairs that surrounded the conference room table.

"Sure. Thanks." Wade said, turning his attention back to his task.

Emma Patel walked back inside the conference room, setting down some of the cups that she'd carried in front of Wade. She sat in one of the seats on the other side of the table. "So, how's the case coming along?"

Wade sighed, dropping the file that he was reading on the table and picked up a cup. "It's not. I don't get it. Foster was been on this case for four months, before I came on board, and we've come up with nothing since I started at that school."

Emma's blond brows rose. "No leads at all?"

"No, nothing; we had one kid with a cigar and some weed, and that's it." Wade sighed. "Something's going on. I know Foster, and he's thorough and carful. Something's not right."

"Maybe he did something to give himself away. Made the dealer suspicious."

"No, I've known this guy for years. He can adapt to any situation and blend in anywhere. If he hasn't come up with anything, it's because someone talked."

"Not many people knew that he was working undercover: just the superintendent, the principal, vice principal, and the head of security."

"I'm thinking that was four people too many." Wade sat back in his seat, looking up at the ceiling. "Of course, the superintendent knows that I'm at Jefferson. Now the principal knows. I've asked them not to inform anyone else."

"What about that kid that you nabbed; ah… what's his name, Micah?"

"Juvenile, first offence, and even though it's his first offence, he knows the ropes. He's not talking. The little dumb ass thinks that not snitching's going to win him some prize, I guess." Wade shook his head and sat forward. "I have one teacher here," he nudged the files with an index finger. "Amanda Westwood. Her boyfriend, Tim Rutland, was busted a while back for distribution. He was released last January; however, as far as I can tell, he hasn't been at Jefferson. Not even to pick up Westwood." Wade dropped the file back on the table. "I'm missing something."

He leaned back in his seat again to stare at the ceiling.

"No one saying anything? No gossip?"

"Nothing."

"I'm surprised. There's always gossip."

Wade stared at the ceiling for a few more minutes and then dropped his feet on the floor. "Good idea."

"What? What idea?"

"Gossip. If there's none going around, we'll just have to start some and see what pops up."

# Chapter 15

Terry paced an aimless circle around the asphalt behind her car. The intense late September sun blazed down on her and the exhaust from passing cars, along with the knowledge that here was another job that she wasn't going to get, made her slightly nauseous.

She forced a casual calmness into her voice that she just didn't feel and said, "Good afternoon, my name is Terry Meyers, I have an appointment with Mr. Wroth for 2:30, and I'm running a little late. Is it possible for us to reschedule my appointment for later this afternoon?"

Terry held her breath, and crossed her fingers. When she'd talked to Mr. Wroth earlier during the week, she had a preliminary interview over the phone, and he seemed impressed. Now all she needed to do was get in front of him, impress him with her charm, and the job would be hers.

"I'm sorry, but Mr. Wroth has a very busy schedule, he doesn't have any other openings."

"Ms… um?"

"Spencer."

"Yes, Ms. Spencer, I have a job interview with Mr. Wroth and my car just broke down, I'm trying to reach AAA, and they keep giving me the runaround. I'm going to be honest with you; I really, really, need this job. I have two sons that I'm raising alone, a mortgage payment that's months delinquent, and a car that is truly on its last leg. Could you please help me out here?"

Ms. Spencer paused and then said in a much lower voice, "Ma'am, I wish I could help, but Mr. Wroth is a real stickler about missed appointments. Even if it isn't your fault, it won't matter to him. I honestly wish that there were something I could do. Really, I'm sorry."

Terry's shoulders dropped, dejected, and she sighed. "I understand. Thank you anyway."

She snapped the phone shut and dropped her face in her hands. After a moment, she opened the phone. She dialed the number to AAA again. After listening to the prompts, and punching the appropriate numbers she was finally connected to a live body.

"Hi, I'm trying to get my car towed."

"I'll need your account number," The voice on the other end said. Terry read the numbers from the card she'd pulled from the glove compartment. "Can I get your name, ma'am?"

"Terry M…" she paused. "Terry Wilkerson."

"Ma'am, there's no Terry listed on that account."

"That's what the other person said when I called earlier, but there's a mistake, there has to be. Can you check again, please?"

"Ma'am, your name was removed from the account a few months ago." The other woman said hesitantly.

"No, that's not possible. This can't be happening. What am I supposed to do?" Terry asked the woman.

"I don't know, ma'am."

"I'm standing next to my car in the middle of a busy road. People are flying past me at fifty miles per hour, yelling, and giving me obscene gestures."

"I'm sorry, ma'am, but there's nothing I can do."

Snapping the phone closed, Terry felt a surge of rage course through her. Without thinking, and she threw the phone to the asphalt, raised her foot, and brought it down hard. She stomped several times before she sagged against the car. After a moment, she looked down at her demolished phone and moaned. "Wonderful." Her shoulders dropped, and she looked skywards as cars continued to speed by giving her not so friendly waves and gestures.

She got into the car, sat back, and sighed. To hell with it, she would just wait here until the police came and towed her car away, with her in it. She reached across the seat and rolled the passenger window down so she wouldn't die from a heat stroke, but she rolled up the driver's window with the hope of filtering the blaring horns and exhaust from the passing vehicles. Bringing her left leg up, she braced her knee against the door, and rested her elbow on her knee as she covered her face. She listened to the car horns blaring as they passed her.

"Stupid assholes," she muttered. "They act as if I looked around and said to myself, 'Well shit, this looks like the perfect place to break down. Let me just stop the car right here.' Freaking jerks."

Terry had paid Saundra Henson, the childcare provider that she used when she worked, to pick Keith up from school, and keep him until she returned from her interview. She had used money that she could ill afford, but she was positive that she would get this position. Terry put the car in auxiliary mode to check the time. 2:17 PM. She was supposed to pick Keith up at 5 PM. If the cops took their sweet time about coming to tow her car away, there would be no telling how long she'd be waiting. She also had to pick DJ up at his track practice on the other side of town. Maybe she could call one of the other parents to ask if they would mind dropping him off.

"I wonder if I can convince the cops to give me a ride over to the school to pick up DJ, and then take the both of us home? Hmm…"

This was not good, she didn't have the resources to get her car fixed, she owed Dee and Ben a ton of money, and she couldn't borrow more from them. Even with Keisha staying with them, she could barely keep the lights on and buy groceries, and now this.

Terry groaned. "Great, simply marvelous; just when I'm at my lowest. Just when I think things can't possibly get any worse, the fates creep right up on me just to kick me in the ass." She snorted, slouching further in the seat. "The bitches."

After about twenty minutes of grumbling and complaining, Terry heard a light tap on the driver's side window. Without looking to see whom it was, she lifted her left hand from her face, flipped off whoever had the audacity to interrupt her during her pity party, and covered her face again. She heard male laughter and another tap on the window. Looking to her left, she looked up and into the gray eyes of DJ's English teacher, Mr. Nelson.

# Chapter 16

When Wade walked to the driver's side of the broken-down car, he paused before tapping on the window. He was surprised to see that the woman sitting behind the steering wheel was the mother of David Wilkerson, but it didn't surprise him when she flipped him off. Laughing, he looked around at the passing cars before he tapped on the window a second time.

"Pop the hood," Wade said, once she finally looked up.

She watched him for a moment, her beautiful hazel eyes seemed to draw him in. Wade felt his gut tighten and he scowled. Turning, he gestured toward the front of the car. When he heard the thump of the hood being released, he opened it and leaned forward, wiggling the battery cable to make sure that it was tight. He pulled the oil dipstick out, and using two fingers wiped off the excess oil, stuck the stick back into the well and pulled it out once again. Seeing that the oil level was good and that the oil was fairly clean, he replaced the stick. He moved to the other side of the car and wiggled the fan belt. Walking to the front of the car again, he removed the cap from the radiator.

***

Terry's gaze followed Wade's wide shoulders as he ambled to the front of the car. When he stopped in front of the car, Terry watched as sunlight shimmered off his silky chestnut hair. Her eyes traveled quickly to his heart-stopping, beautiful eyes and lips that look like they were made for nibbling. A deep sexual hunger started in her midsection traveling south. He opened the hood, and she slid down in her seat, watching from under the crack in the hood.

He walked to the passenger side of the car, still searching under the hood. Leaning over as far as she could, without actually lying in the passenger seat, Terry tried to get a better look at his muscular body. She couldn't really get a good look at him, but what she did see was…"Mmm, baby. He is so hot," She whispered.

He moved back to the front of the car and Terry resumed her slouched position, and continued to peek under the crack of the hood. His leather jacket hid most of his torso, but what she could see was well-defined and oh so scrumptious. She groaned, nibbling her lips. The next instant the hood dropped down, and Terry felt as if she were caught doing something wrong. Her cheeks felt flush, and were growing hotter by the second. He lifted one dark brow, and a smug grin spread across his face. A moment later, he sauntered around the car to the driver's side door.

"Looks like you won't be going anywhere anytime soon."

"Na ah, the hell you say," Terry said dryly.

He laughed. "You're overheated. Looks like you have a hole in your radiator."

Terry gave him a once over and grunted. *Over heated? You have no idea.* "I'm guessing there's nothing that I can do to at least get the car home?"

"Nope, not if you mean to drive it, there isn't. Do you have triple-A?"

She gave a weary shrug. "Unfortunately, no."

"If you want, I can call a tow truck."

Terry sighed looking away from him. "No, that's not an option either."

Out of the corner of her eye, she could see Wade watch her intently for a moment, then he looked to his right at the traffic flying by. Taking a quick glance around them, he eyed a construction jobsite across the street.

"Well, the least that I can do is move your car out of traffic. Sit tight."

Terry watched as Wade walked briskly across the street to a man standing on the sidewalk in front of the construction site. The construction worker held a hard-hat in one hand and was leaning against a lamppost talking on a cellphone. When Wade approached him, Wade waited a few moments until the other man finished his phone call, and then they spoke briefly before Wade pointed across the street in the direction of her car. After he finished talking to the man, Wade crossed the street stopping at her door saying, "Be right back."

Terry watched in the side view mirror as he walked back to his motorcycle. He threw his muscular jean-clad leg over the body of the bike, straddling it, before putting the key in the ignition. The bike roared to life and Wade pulled it around her car and into the parking lot. When he rose from the bike, he removed his jacket, putting it inside a compartment under the seat along with his gloves, and locked it. He made it back to her car as three men walked across the street to meet him.

Wade turned to Terry. "Put the car in neutral, and pull it into that parking lot," he directed, and indicated the parking lot he'd parked his motorcycle in.

In less than five minutes, Wade and the other three men had her car out of the street and into one of the parking spaces on the lot. Wade thanked the other men before they crossed the street back to their jobs.

Terry got out of the car as Wade reached her door. "Thank you, Mr. Nelson, you don't know how much I appreciate this."

"I'm Wade, Mr. Nelson is my father. And it's no problem."

"Wade. I'm Terry. Thanks, Wade."

He gave her a quick nod. "Your car should be safe here until tomorrow. I wouldn't leave it much longer than that."

Terry glanced back at her car, and she hoped that a total look of uncertainty wasn't flashing across her face. "Ah… yeah, right. So… I'll…"

"Look, I have this friend who drives a tow truck," he said quickly. "I'm sure he wouldn't mind towing your car home for you."

Terry paused and then sighed. "I really don't have the money to…"

"This guy's cool, and he owes me a favor. I'm sure he'll do it at no cost. Give me a few minutes."

Wade left Terry standing next to her car as he removed his cellphone from his pocket and walked about ten feet away, placing a phone call. Ten minutes later, he returned to her side.

"How about we go get a cup of coffee and wait for the tow truck?" he suggested.

Terry nodded and they made their way across the parking lot to a Panera Bread restaurant. Once inside, Wade asked Terry what she wanted. When she told him coffee with cream and sugar, he suggested that she go find a table, while he placed their order.

## Chapter 16

Finding a table next to the window, Terry slid into one of the chairs, placing her purse on the window ledge. She glanced around at the other customers, who were either chatting with their companions, reading, or working on laptops. They all seemed to have something going on in their lives, something that probably didn't consist of a broken car or an ex with a twit of a bimbo knocked-up – again – wife who seemed intent on crushing her at every turn.

Terry turned to look out the window. David was an asshole, but he wouldn't have removed her from the AAA membership; not that it wasn't something that he would do, he just wouldn't remember it. He would get the bill, pay it and that would be that. No, this was Shareese's doing. Terry bit her lip staring across the lot at her car. Shareese made sure that everything that Terry and David had in both of their names had been replaced with her own. If it was something that was Terry's responsibility, than David's name was no longer associated with it. That meant no health insurance for her, no AAA, nothing. She looked at Wade standing at the counter. He seemed like a decent guy. Well, as decent as most of them seem when you first meet them. This guy had to be married, or at least he had a girlfriend. Terry didn't see a ring, but she knew that didn't mean anything.

Wade approached the table a short while later with two coffees and a pecan roll sliced in half. Sitting down he said, "I hope you're not allergic to pecans."

"No. Thanks." Terry gratefully took the slice that Wade placed in front of her. "So, how's DJ doing in your class?"

"He's doing fine. He's a good kid."

"Yeah, he is."

"I'm a little concerned about some of the kids that he hangs with. Sometimes he seems a little distracted, and I've noticed a couple times that he displayed exaggerated anger."

Terry placed the fork on the plate resting her left elbow on the table and ran her hand through her hair. "He hasn't been acting up in class, has he?"

"No more than any other kids. He seems as if he would be more even-keeled."

Terry nodded. "He usually is. He's just going through a hard time." Terry dropped her head for a moment and then looked back up, meeting his gaze. "My ex-husband and I went through a divorce recently."

"I'm sorry. That has to be difficult."

"Sorry about the divorce? Don't be, he's a sorry sack of dog shit," Terry said without a thought. The left side of Wade's mouth twitched as he obviously tried to suppress a smile. "Anyway, the kids are the ones that are suffering, and even though DJ seems to be handling things well enough, he's taking it pretty hard; maybe even harder than Keith. Combine that with the fact that their father puts his new wife above all else…Well, you know what I mean."

Wade gave her a sympathetic look, and she fidgeted under his gaze before turning and looking out the window. After a moment, she glanced down at her wrist, checking the time, and then reached into the pocket of her jacket. Searching for her cellphone, she immediately remembered the misfortune that it met between her foot and the asphalt.

"Do you mind if I use your phone? Mine broke."

"It wouldn't happen to have been the one I saw lying next to your car?" Terry remained silent, just watching him with her hand outstretched. Wade raised an amused brow, and gave her a sexy half smile. "Hmm, I thought so."

***

He passed the phone to her and watched her as she placed her call. She fingered a loose tendril of hair on her neck, with slim delicate fingers. Wade watched her fingers twirl the hair at the nape of her neck, and then his eyes dropped from her fingers to her shoulder and traveled down to her breasts. He watched the rise and fall of her breasts, mesmerized by the swell of her creamy, smooth skin. He wanted to reach across the short distance separating them and touch her. He wanted to feel the softness of her silky skin with his fingers, with his tongue. Groaning, Wade picked up his cup and hastily looked away as he took a big gulp of coffee.

"Keisha, are you busy? I need you to go to Ms. Sandra's and pick Keith up for me." Pause. "Yes, I know it's more than eight blocks away, but I can't make it in time." Pause. "Keisha, it won't take you that long to walk to her house." Turning away from the table, she said in almost a whisper. "I had to pay her twenty-five bucks to pick him up from school and keep him for a couple of hours, I don't have the money to pay her for keeping Keith for an extra hour, let alone two." Another pause. "Come on, Keisha, don't be like that." She waited another moment and then snapped, "Do you see my car in the driveway?" Pause. "Then how the hell are you going to drive it?"

Snapping the phone shut, she turned back to Wade, grinned sheepishly, and then said, "Thanks."

Wade shifted in his chair trying to control the desire that shot straight from his brain to his groin. "You're welcome."

They talked about Wade's new position and some of the things the kids did, as they ate the pecan roll and drank their coffees, while Wade worked to keep his eyes from sliding from her beautiful face downwards. Thirty-five minutes after entering Panera's, the tow truck pulled into the parking lot. They cleaned the table and left the shop, heading back to Terry's car.

When they approached the tow truck driver, he said, "Wade Nelson?" Wade nodded. "I'm gonna need your proof of ownership before I can tow the car."

"No problem," Wade said before turning to Terry. She was frowning up at him, her hazel eyes peering at him intently. It made him think of floating on warm honey. He grinned. "What?"

"A friend, huh?"

"Hey, a stranger is just a friend that you haven't met yet. He's going to need to see your license and registration."

"Uh-huh," Terry eyed him for a moment before she walked to the car.

# Chapter 17

In less than fifteen minutes, the car was loaded on the tow truck, and the driver was preparing to leave.

"Would you like a ride home, or would you rather ride in the tow truck?" Wade asked before the driver started the truck.

*Ride on a fast moving vehicle with my arms wrapped around the hottest guy I've seen in years. Hell yeah!* "I haven't ridden on a motorcycle in years. I guess that would be sort of cool," Terry said as casually as she could muster, but cringed when she heard the slightly high-pitched squeak of her own voice.

Wade glanced in her direction and gave her a lop-sided grin. Terry felt her belly flip-flop. He turned, and she followed him to his bike, where he opened the compartment, removing a jacket and held it up for her. She stepped closer, and he held it as she slipped it on. It smelled of leather, sweet spice, and man, and Terry fought the urge to close her eyes and take a big whiff. He picked up his helmet and stepped in front of her to slip it over her head. He squatted down a bit to fasten the chin strap and Terry watched his movements, his long fingers moving gracefully. She instantly wondered what those fingers would feel like gently stroking the tips of her nipples and traveling down her body.

*Whew, calm down girl.*

Wade helped Terry to stow her purse in the compartment. Then, he put his keys between his teeth, holding them while he slipped on fingerless leather gloves. With his leg over the bike, he settled into the seat before starting it.

He glanced at Terry. "Hop on."

Looking over his shoulder Wade watched as Terry made two attempts to jump on the motorcycle. Before she gave it a third try, he leaned to his right and reached behind. His hand brushed her hip as he helped her onto the bike. Terry's eyes met his and she smiled as she settled onto the bike. Wade slipped on his sunglasses. Terry moved closer to him, putting her arms around his waist.

"You might want to hold on tighter than that," he said, before pulling off.

***

She jerked slightly and tightened her grip, pressing her nose into his back. *God, he smells good*, she thought. She closed her eyes and rested her head against his back.

It took about twenty minutes to get Terry home, but to her, it seemed as if it was only five. She unfastened the helmet and slid from the motorcycle.

"I know a little about cars," Wade said as Terry pulled the jacket off and handed him both the helmet and jacket. "I could come by tomorrow and fix it for you."

Terry looked up at the house and saw Keisha peek out the living room window, before the front door swung open.

"Terry Ann," Keisha said as she hustled down the steps to Terry's side. "What happened to your car?"

## Chapter 17

Terry's eyes narrowed at hearing Keisha call her Terry Ann, and then she sighed. "It broke down, Keisha."

Keisha wore an aqua baby doll top and jeans. She wore her hair piled on top of her head with a few braids framing her face. Terry thought she looked pretty. And then she sighed again. If only Keisha's blouse weren't so small that it looked as if her breasts would pop from the tiny cups of her bra and put someone's eyes out. The seams that held the small top together were stretched so tight that if they were to rip, it would instantly send little pieces of thread flying through the neighborhood like kamikaze mosquitoes attacking everyone in sight.

"Wade, this is my cousin Keisha; Keisha, this is DJ's English teacher, Wade Nelson."

"Nice to meet you, Keisha," Wade said.

"Hi," Keisha said before turning to Terry. "I'm glad you're home, I'm meeting Deion in a little while. We're going to the movies to see that new horror movie, the one where-"

"Okay, Keisha, that's great. You did pick up Keith?"

"Yep, all done. He's safe and sound," Keisha said with exaggerated cheer. "And, um… I ordered pizza for DJ and Keith."

"Wow." Terry's brows rose in surprise. "Thank you."

Keisha hung her thumbs from the back pockets of her jeans and smiled nervously at Terry. "I left the money on the table, I even left the tip."

Terry's surprise quickly turned to suspicion, and she narrowed her eyes slightly. "Uh, okay. Thanks again."

"Um… and… um…"

"All right, Keisha, spit it out."

"I," she looked at Wade, and then back at Terry. "Um… remember that I told you that I was supposed to get some money this week? Well, I sort of don't have it right now. I know you needed it for the electric," Keisha rushed on. "But, an emergency came up and now… I… have… to…" Keisha paused, obviously seeing the murderous look in Terry's eyes. "Um… give it to you, um… later," she said the last word with a squeak.

Terry ground her teeth until she literally heard her jaw pop. She glared at Keisha. "Keisha, go in the house, I'll talk to you when I come inside."

Keisha looked at Wade and then back at Terry. "But Deion…"

"Go in the house," Terry said in a voice so low it sounded more like a growl.

Keisha's eyes grew large, and she spun and scurried into the house. Terry let her head drop forwards for a moment before raising it and turning back to Wade, giving him the biggest, phoniest smile he'd ever seen.

"Sorry about that," She said, slowly bringing her temper under control.

Wade nodded. "No problem."

"Uh… thanks for the ride, and your help with the car," she said, as the tow truck pulled up and backed into the driveway.

"I'm glad I could help."

"About fixing my car tomorrow, I don't think…"

"It won't be a problem. It'll just take me an hour or so, and it'll hardly cost anything, just a few bucks. Most of it will be labor."

Terry looked back up at the house and saw the living room curtains drop back into place, no doubt Keisha. "That would be great. About the tow, I don't know when I'll be able to repay you."

"Not to worry. Really, I have AAA, and I called them. I'm paying for it, so why not use it? And if my sister or my mother were in the same predicament, I'd like to think that someone would help them." Terry's smile turned genuine, and it made Wade's chest rise and fall quickly. Had his heart just skipped a beat? Did his palms suddenly feel clammy? *Aw, hell.*

"Okay," she said. "Thank you."

Wade slid back on his motorcycle. "I'll be over tomorrow morning, early."

Terry nodded again. "See you tomorrow, early."

After watching Wade roar off, Terry walked into the house with a purpose. When she entered, she barely caught a glimpse of Keisha hitting the top step and scampering down the hall to her room. DJ was sitting on the sofa, staring at the television and didn't acknowledge Terry when she entered.

She stopped next to the sofa, and looked down at him. "Hi, mom,". She said, in just a slightly mocking tone.

DJ looked up at his mother and mumbled a barely audible, "Hi."

She dropped her purse on the sofa. "Where's your brother?" DJ hunched his shoulders. "How was track practice?" another hunch was all the answer she received. Terry sat on the arm of the sofa. "All right, what's going on?"

"Nothing," DJ answered, still looking at the television.

Terry reached over, plucking the remote from his hand, and turned off the television. DJ rose for the sofa and headed to the stairs.

"Freeze," she snapped. "What is going on?"

DJ returned to the sofa and dropped back down. "Why is everything like this?"

"Like what, DJ?"

"Like this," he waved his arms, encompassing the room. "Why don't we have any food, and why don't we have cable TV anymore? Why can't I get new shoes and pants that fit me?"

"DJ, I'm doing the best I can. I know you wish things could be the way they were. And I know you miss your father."

"No, I don't."

"Yes, you do. There's nothing wrong with you missing your dad, and I wish I could make things better for you. Just give me time, I'll get things together."

She stood, watching him, and waiting for a response. When he did nothing but slouch further down into the sofa, Terry turned and left the room.

Walking into the kitchen, Terry crossed the room, searching her utility drawer for a pad and a pen. She pulled a chair from the table and sat down. On the top of the pad, she scratched the words, 'Things to Do'.

Tapping the pen against the pad, Terry muttered. "Okay," Dee didn't think she had it in her to be a PI. "Fine," she whispered. What she had to do was prove to Dee that she had what it took. She would strike out on her own, get her own clients, and solve her own cases. Dee would see how serious she was, and how important it was for Terry to do the job, and Dee would have to take Terry into the business. She would probably make Terry a partner. "Yeah," Terry grinned. Dee would see that Terry could be a damn good investigator.

Terry tapped her pen against the pad. *Where could I start*? Well, she couldn't open her own company; she didn't have a license. She needed a client. "Hmmm…" she dropped the pen and massaged her brow. *Maybe I could learn from the only person I knew.* She could go over to Meyers and poke around, see how they did things, and get a few pointers. She could hang out at the office before Dee got there and observe. She could chat up the employees and maybe sneak a peek at some of their files. At one time, she might have been able to convince Chris, Dee's number one investigator, to help her. He was a flirt and a free spirit, and he used to have a thing for her, before she and David had gotten married. He may have even given her a small lead, if she had asked, back then. But not now; now he was taking himself too seriously. No, he had moved up, and he had a few people working under him. He was all about business.

There was Liz, the researcher. Terry could learn a lot from her. She seemed a little nervous, always pushing her glasses up, even when they appeared to be in place. She didn't talk much. Terry might get some general information from her, but she wouldn't be able to ask too much. Liz was as sharp as she was shy, and she would pick right up on all of Terry's questions and might even discuss it with Dee. The only other investigator that she knew by name was the new guy, Blaine something or other. Terry had seen him a few times, when she visited Dee at the office; she didn't know much about him, but she did know that he was such a tight ass he wouldn't tell her anything at all. Yeah, she could go to the office on Monday morning and hang out for a while. Dee didn't get there until around ten, since she had the twins; Terry could go there as soon as she dropped the boys off at school with the pretense of waiting for Dee. She would fade into the scenery and check things out, stealth like.

"Yeah," She said to herself, that was it.

She would be like a chameleon and skulk around, learn as much as she could.

# Chapter 18

"Ma'am, your bill is now two months past due, and your service is due for disconnection on Monday. Unless you want to make a payment over the phone, there is nothing that we can do. Would you like to make a payment at this time?"

Dropping her face into her hand, Terry quickly jerked her hand away, remembering the facial mask that she'd applied when she crawled out of bed. "No. Look, I sent a check," she lied. Well, she didn't actually lie; she told herself. She did send them a check. Just not in the last two months. "You can't turn off our electric."

"Ma'am, unless you pay the total balance on your bill, there's nothing we can do. They have state organizations that may be able to help you."

"Okay. What if I contact them now?"

"You'd have to wait until Monday, ma'am."

"And by then there's the possibility that my lights will be turned off?"

"Yes, ma'am."

Terry felt what little self-control she had left slip. "Look, stop playing with me. You guys just can't turn off my electric; I will freak the hell out. I'm not playing with... hello... hello?" Terry looked down at the table at the bills spread before her. The telephone bill read, 'Turn off Notice' and had today's date. She felt a scream building in her lungs. "Mother fu..." She gripped the phone, banging it against the table several times, until the front and back halves separated.

She threw her head back taking a deep breath. "Okay. This is going to be okay." The doorbell chimed and Terry groaned. "Now who the hell could that possibly be? Probably the hospital coming to tell me that, after fourteen years, I owe them money, and they want to take DJ back." She snorted. "Could I even be so lucky?" She snatched the door open and was greeted by a tall, dark, and oh-so-sexy man.

"Hey," Wade grinned down at her.

"Hey," Terry said with a squeak. She leaned against the door; instinctively striking what she thought was a sexy pose. Dropping her voice an octave, she said, "What a nice surprise."

"I told you that I would be here early."

"I remember," she lied and smiled coyly.

***

Wade let his eyes travel down her body, his gaze resting momentarily on her full breasts that were barely covered by the white spaghetti-strap tee that she wore. He mentally kicked himself for openly leering, before his eyes met Terry's, and he saw her coy smile turn slightly wicked.

"Um, you've got a little..." he grinned and, using his hand, he made a circular motion around his face.

***

Remembering the facemask and groaning inwardly, Terry pushed herself off the door. "Yeah, I know that, too. Come on in." She left him to close the door as she led the way to the kitchen. "You weren't kidding when you said you would be here early."

"I have a neighbor who wakes me around 6 AM, regardless of if I want him to or not; so, for the last month, I've pretty much been a morning person."

Terry crossed the room to the sink and opened one of the overhead cabinets, grabbing two coffee cups and sitting them on the counter. She looked into another cabinet and removed a jar of instant coffee, sitting it next to the cups. She turned around and crossed the room, heading toward Wade.

"Why don't you make coffee, while I go and change? I take mine with cream and two sugars," she said as she passed him, practically oblivious to the surprised look on his face and the box that he held.

***

Wade watched Terry's white, blue, and pink striped bottom sway down the hallway and disappear around the corner. "Lord, help me," he groaned setting the box on the counter.

Since he'd dropped Terry off last evening, Wade had felt like a walking hard-on. All he could do was think about those gorgeous hazel eyes, luscious breasts, and delicious behind. He heard what sounded like the shower coming on and his body grew even tighter as he pictured her bare breasts swaying with each step she took across the bathroom and stepped under the stream of water from the shower.

"Oh yeah, now I'll have that image in my head for the rest of the day," He muttered to himself.

Wade grabbed one of the coffee cups and searched the nearby drawers for a teaspoon. He filled the cup with water and popped it into the microwave. After three minutes, he put in a spoonful of coffee and leaned against the counter, looking around the small tidy kitchen. The bright white cabinets and high ceiling gave the appearance of a much larger room, while the gold terracotta tile floor and matching marble countertops gave it a warm feeling. There was a pass-through between the kitchen and dining room with a matching marble countertop, and tall white stools. A small round maple table sat next to the window, with two white chairs. In the center of the table sat a broken phone and a vase of yellow and white artificial daisies and mums that looked surprisingly real. Taking another sip of his coffee, Wade stood and left the kitchen, taking the cup with him into the living room.

"Hi," Terry's cousin Keisha said, walking down the steps. "Mr. Nelson, right?"

"Wade. Keisha?"

"Yes."

"Hi, Keisha. You wouldn't happen to know where Terry's car keys are?"

"Yeah, I do, but I'm not supposed to touch them."

"I'm going to need them if I'm going to work on her car."

Bringing her hand to her face, Keisha looked toward the steps and nervously bit her thumbnail. "I don't know…"

"I'm sure she won't mind if you give them to me," Wade assured her.

" 'Keisha, if I catch you touching my keys again, I'm going to break off your fingers, one by one, liquefy them in the blender, and use them as fertilizer for my roses.' Does that sound like someone who wouldn't mind me giving you the keys to her car?"

Wade laughed. "That is graphic."

Keisha nodded. "Isn't it? So I don't think it would be in my best interest to hand over the keys."

A moment later, Terry came bouncing down the stairs wearing the sexiest heather gray sweat pants and tiny pale pink tee Wade had ever seen. The tee allowed a peek of silky smooth skin, and a gold belly ring. Wade watched as she crossed the room toward him and Keisha. Terry's hips swerved with each step and it made him think of a sexy belly dancer.

"Keisha, did you give Wade the keys to the car?" he heard her say, but for the life of him, he could not look up from that belly ring that he imagined himself tugging gently with his teeth.

"You told me not to touch the car keys. You said that if I touched-"

"I said that if you drove my car without my permission again, we were going to have a problem," Terry interrupted. She looked up at Wade and frowned. "What?"

He felt the tip of his tongue tingle as the fantasy of him licking a trail from that sexy-as-hell belly ring down to Terry's…

"What?" Terry's demanding voice brought Wade's attention back to the room.

He finally looked up, met her gaze, and suppressed the urge to wipe away any signs of drool that he was sure was running down his chin. "Um, nothing."

"These are my yard clothes. I'm helping you. I honestly don't know what I'm doing, but I'll be your helper anyway." She headed for the kitchen. "You don't know how much this means to me. Hey, did you make me a cup of coffee?"

"Um, no," Wade said to her, who only gave him a grunt. He then looked back at Keisha.

She hunched her shoulders. "I guess I could have given you the keys, and you should have made the coffee."

## Chapter 18

Wade grinned at her while both he and Keisha followed Terry to the kitchen.

***

Terry walked into the kitchen and crossed to the counter. Spotting the white box, she opened it and peeked inside.

"My neighbor, Hugo, works at Miceli's Ristorante," Wade said. "He brought these pastries over yesterday, and I thought that you, Keisha, and the boys might like them."

"Thank you," Terry said as she examined the pastries.

"I know Hugo," Keisha said.

"Do you?"

"Yeah, I work there part-time." Keisha crossed the room, standing next to Terry and peeking inside the box. "He's a great guy, cute too. And he's a really good cook. Kind of shy, though."

Keisha chose a cherry tart while Terry scooped a spoonful of coffee into one of the cups. She glanced back at him. "Do you want some more?" she held up the jar of instant coffee. He shook his head. She turned back to the counter. "I hope you bought tools, we don't have any around here. Maybe a screwdriver and I think there's a hammer somewhere." She turned to face him, taking a sip from her cup. Grabbing a glass from the cabinet, Keisha moved to the refrigerator and poured a glass of milk.

Wade leaned against the doorframe, watching Terry as she sipped her coffee. "Don't worry, I brought my own." He glanced at Keisha and then at the table. "You don't do well with phones, I take it?"

She met his smiling gaze, and heard Keisha snicker. Terry glanced at the table and then, setting her cup on the counter, she reached under the sink, opened the cabinet door, and grabbed a small garbage can. Crossing to the table, she pushed the parts of the phone inside.

***

Wade reached inside the bed of his truck to remove a two-foot round, ten-inch deep tin pan and a toolbox.

"Do you do this often?" Terry suddenly asked.

"No, I usually take my truck to the shop to have it serviced. I do most of the maintenance on my bike myself, though. 'She's' my baby!"

He turned and passed Terry the pan and then reached inside the truck for a ratty blue blanket.

"No," she said, taking the blanket without looking at it and rolled it into a ball. "I mean, do you just up, and help strangers? Do you just meet people on the street and go home with them to fix their cars?"

"No, I don't," he said, leading the way to her car.

Terry frowned, following Wade to the car. He took the blanket from her arms, folded it in threes, and dropped it. He squatted and slid the pan under the front end of the car. Reaching under the car, he moved his arm, feeling around the undercarriage for a moment; then Terry heard a drip, and then what sounded like liquid draining from the car to the tin pan.

Terry watched as Wade opened his toolbox, took out a couple tools, most of which she couldn't identify, and begin fiddling with things under the hood. After a few minutes, he sat down on the blanket.

"I'll need you to pass me the tools I ask for."

Terry nodded, grinning down at him. "Yep, that's what I'm here for, your trusty helper."

## Chapter 18

"Okay then, let's do it!" Wade said, lay back, and wiggled until the top half of his body was under the car.

"You said yesterday that you would hope someone would help your mother and sister if they needed it. You only have one sister?"

Wade remained silent for a moment. "I also have a brother. And there's my grandmother and my parents, two nieces and a nephew."

Terry leaned against the car, folded her arms, and looked down at his jeans-encased legs. His legs were long; they seemed to go on for miles. His jeans were loose fitting, but not too loose that she couldn't see that his legs were muscular and the apex that met at the junction of his thighs was… *mmm baby. He is so hot. I'm not afraid to say that he's hotter than Patrick. I guess I'll have a new star for my battery-operated, fun-filled evenings*. She grinned, biting her lip.

Wade leaned his head to the side, glancing up at Terry. "Can you pass me the socket…"

Terry suddenly realized that he'd stopped in mid sentence. Her throat tightened and she felt her face flush; oh God, he must have noticed that she was staring at is crotch. His member seemed to have eyes and a mind of its own, because it jerked with the knowledge that it was being watched. Instantly, she turned to look him in the eyes, and Wade gave her a crooked grin. Terry rooted around inside the toolbox, pulling out what she thought he wanted.

"No, that's the monkey wrench," he said. She reached in, pulling out something else, and held it up. "Nope, channel locks."

"Whatever," Terry snapped, passing him both, the channel locks, and the monkey wrench. Still grinning, Wade looked at her and at then at the tools. She held the tools toward him, shaking them in an impatient manner, and he chuckled, taking them from her and moved back under the car.

Looking at the front porch, Terry contemplated going and getting one of the two cedar porch rockers. Changing her mind, she sat on the ground next to Wade's outstretched legs.

"Where is your family from?"

"Chicago," Wade said. He glanced at Terry. "My father's from Chicago and my mother is from Malaysia."

"Do your parents live here in Chicago or Malaysia?"

"Chicago."

"Oh. Do you have any family in Malaysia?"

Wade sighed. "When we moved to the states, my grandparents stayed in Malaysia. My grandfather died when I was nineteen, and my grandmother, Nenek, moved here to be close to my mother."

"Does she ever go back home, your grandmother? Does she go back home to Malaysia to visit?"

***

Wade didn't want to tell Terry that he believed that his grandmother didn't go back to Malaysia because she was afraid to leave his mother alone with his father. He didn't really want to talk about his family at all, but he found himself answering her. "Only once."

"I bet it's beautiful there," Terry said. "I would love to go there. My mother's mom is still living; she lives in Atlanta. My dad's mother passed when I was in my late teens." She picked up a pebble and tossed it in the nearby grass. "Both of my parents died when I was very young; my mother when I was two and my father when I was eight." Wade glanced at her, watching as she picked up another pebble. "I have my cousin Dee and Aunt Jean, that's Dee's mother, and of course Keisha and the boys."

Wade slid away from under the car and stood, and Terry scrambled to her feet. He leaned inside the hood, unscrewing the bolts that held the radiator in and lifted it out. Terry followed him to the side of the house where they had hooked up the water hose.

"So, tell me about your parents," Terry said.

Wade set the radiator down and walked back to the car, removing a few things from the toolbox, and then walked back to the side of the house.

Terry waited for him to return before she said, "You didn't answer my question."

"Question about what?"

"I asked you about your parents."

Wade's jaw tightened. He glanced at Terry, who watched him with her arms folded as she patiently waited for an answer. "My mother is a nurse; she and my father met in Malaysia. They fell in love, got married, had three children, and moved to America."

Terry looked up at him and blinked. "Wow. That was way too much information. You know, you really need to hold some of that back, buddy," she said sarcastically. Wade glanced at her, and she held up her hands. "Hey, if you don't want to talk about your family, that's no problem. I'm just trying to be friendly."

"My father managed one of the pipelines in Malaysia in 1965. While he was working, they had a spill; he fell, broke his collarbone, and he was taken to the nearby hospital. That's where he met my mother. A year later they were married."

"And they're still together?" Wade only nodded. "After forty years, that's wonder-"

"Could you get me an extension cord?" Wade said in a tone that had a little too much bite. "I need it to plug in the soldering gun."

Terry glanced down at the tool that he held and nodded. "Sure."

She turned and walked to the front of the house. Wade took a deep breath. He didn't want to talk to Terry about his past. The past was just that, the past. Why look back? Terry rounded the house with an extension cord, dropping one end next to Wade. She walked to the end of the house and plugged the male end into an exterior receptacle on the side of the house. Walking back to Wade's side, she picked up the female end of the cord. They stood in silence for a moment, Wade looking into her eyes. *She had beautiful eyes*, he thought. They sparkled like amber glistening in sunlight. She leaned forward slightly, so close, that her sweet smell curled through his senses.

Cocking her head to the side, Terry said, "Where do you want to stick this?"

Wade's lips twitched in amusement. "Sorry for snapping at you. I don't like talking about my family."

"No problemo." She passed him the end of the cord.

"It's just that my father and I don't get along."

"I understand. Sometimes two people just don't see eye to eye." She said as she watched Wade fill the radiator with water.

When water started leaking from three spots across the front, he pulled a magic marker from his pocket and marked the spots.

"I'd give anything to have my parents back, she said. "Especially my dad; I was so young when my mother died that I don't remember her, but my dad, he was great." she hesitated. "Sometimes it's hard to get past the things that hurt us. Sometimes it's hard to forgive, but it's easier to forgive then to hold on to the anger."

Wade's jaw clinched again. "It's a little hard to forgive the bastard who broke your mother's ribs because she allowed you to go to the movies with your friends when he initially told her that you couldn't."

Terry flinched at the anger and hurt in his voice. "I'm sorry, I didn't know."

Wade turned away from her. "Of course you didn't. But sometimes you just can't get over things."

# Chapter 19

By 11:30 am, Wade had Terry's radiator soldered, placed back inside the car, and hooked up. When Terry had risen that morning, she was looking forward to a semi-child free day. But, when Keith wandered from the house at 9:45, interrupting Terry in her not-so-handy, mostly ogling, role of helper, and informed her that he was bored, she knew what she had to look forward to for the remainder of the day. She was relieved when Holly called saying that both she and Tyler had to work. Holly asked if it would be possible for them to drop Abby off for a few hours. Holly had arranged for Abby to spend the day with a friend, but the mother said that she had a change of plans and would pick Abby up around noon. Terry assured Holly that it would be no problem for Abby to spend the entire day with them.

DJ was holed up in his room. He had come downstairs for breakfast, and again for lunch, and, after washing the dishes, Terry had not seen him. Keisha was nowhere to be found. Terry assumed that she was at work, so Abby would be a welcome diversion for Keith.

Terry looked at the pile of bills scattered on the table in front of her and grimaced. It was times like this that Terry wished that she was a kid again and could hang out at the mall all day, instead of worrying about the problems that plagued her.

# Chapter 19

"God, sometimes it really sucks being me," Terry muttered, dropping her face in her hands and then running her hands through her hair.

"What's wrong, Aunt Terry?" Abby asked.

Terry looked up, meeting her bright eyes. "I don't even know where to begin; I don't have the money to pay the mortgage again. Shit!" she said, more to herself.

Abby frowned, probably at Terry's choice of expletives. "Mommy and Tyler have stopped cursing. Well, they've almost stopped. We have a takeout jar, and when Mommy and Tyler say curse words, they have to put a quarter in it. They don't want to put money in the jar, so they stop cursing."

Terry removed her hands to blink in confusion at the child. "What? What in the world is the takeout jar?"

Abby leaned on the table. "When mommy and Tyler curse, they put a quarter in the jar. Every month we use the takeout jar to get food, takeout. Usually pizza, but sometimes we get Burger King or McDonald's. Mommy says it helps them stop cursing. Which is good, but sometimes we don't have enough money in the jar for takeout. That's not so good." Abby paused a moment and frowned in contemplation. "Maybe you should have a jar too." Her smile quickly turned mischievous. "Or you can use our jar."

Terry glanced at her, not missing the child's meaning. *Damn, the kid is almost as smart as I am*. "Girl, if I put a quarter in that jar every time I swore, there would be enough money to pay your mamma's mortgage payment for a month."

Abby paused, and frowned. "So, why don't you then?"

"Why don't I what?"

“Why don’t you put a quarter in a jar every time you say a curse word? That way you'd have the money to pay for the house.”

*Because, I’d probably have to borrow the quarters from your mama or Dee.* Terry wanted to say, but instead she said, “You know, in theory that sounds like an excellent idea. I just might have to make you my financial advisor. Look, why don’t you go in the other room and see what Keith is up to? Hey, I forgot to tell you, guess what I borrowed from the library?” Abby watched her expectantly. “The Tinkerbelle DVD.”

Abby squealed. “Thank you!”

Terry grinned at her. “Hey, I have to look out for my sidekick. I’ll be in in a few minutes to watch it with you guys.”

“’Kay,” Abby said racing from the room.

Terry looked at the ring on her right hand; the ring that she’d been wearing for the last eight years. Her grandmother, her mother’s mother, had given it to her for her twenty-fifth birthday. It was the engagement ring that her father had given her mother. She was told that her father had received it from his grandmother and had given it to her mother. Her grandmother had said that Terry’s paternal grandfather had given it to his wife, and then when Terry’s father asked her mother to marry him, he gave the ring to her. Terry didn’t know how her other grandmother had gotten the ring, since it should have gone to someone on her father’s side of the family, but she was just happy to have it. One day, when DJ became engaged, she would give the ring to him.

She didn’t think it was worth much: the diamond was small, tiny really, and it was a simple ring, but it was old, and that should count for something. She spun it around on her finger. She hadn't taken it off since her grandmother gave it to her. Heaving a heavy sigh, she rose from the table. In the living room, Keith and Abby were lying in front of the television set watching the Saturday morning *Disney* cartoon, *Teacher's Pet*.

"Hey, guys, put your shoes on," Terry said, walking to the sofa and stooping to pick up Abby and Keith's shoes and hand them to the kids. "We're going out for a while."

***

"What are you doing here?" Terry asked Dee when she walked into the house toting one baby on each hip. She thrust baby Kyle into Terry's arms and closed the front door.

"I just stopped by to see what you were doing, and to visit for a while. Are you busy?"

"No, just taking care of a few bills. I have a job interview this week, it seems promising."

"What about the daycare?"

"It's going to take some time to get that going; I'm going to find a temporary job until then."

"You know, you can start taking care of Ben and Kyle now, and Holly will have to place Abby somewhere soon; Sandra's only doing child care for the remainder of this year, then she's moving to Tennessee to help her daughter with her children."

"Yeah, I know, but I wanted to wait until I got my license," Terry said, walking through the house to the kitchen.

"You don't have to have a license to take care of family children."

"I know, but I just want to wait. Have everything legit."

"Okay, just let us know when you're ready," Dee said, sitting at the table and allowing baby Ben to slip from her lap, while his brother slipped from Terry's. "Where are the kids?"

"DJ went to the mall with friends, and Keith is in the back yard with Abby. Can I get you something to drink?" Terry rose from the table. "I have water, Kool-Aid, water, hot tea, and water. I was going to make a cup of tea."

"Sure, I'll have a cup of tea," Dee said, watching Terry move around the kitchen.

Terry winced as she realized that Dee could see the bills scattered across the table. Could she see the balance on the electric bill, which read $674.25? Terry hoped not.

"Terry, how is everything?"

"Everything is good," She said, trying to sound convincing – but sure she was failing.

"If you need help, you know you can always come to us."

Terry walked to the table carrying two mugs. "Yeah, I know."

When Terry passed one of the mugs to Dee, she looked down at Terry's hand and saw the light circle on her middle finger where Terry's mother's ring used to be. Dee knew that Terry never took that ring off; she knew what it meant to her cousin. If she did not have it on, that meant that Terry had either sold it or pawned it. Either way, it was an indication that things were worse than even Dee realized. She felt tears burning her eyes as she looked away, taking a sip of her tea. She glanced up at Terry, who was gathering up the bills from the table. She carried them across the room and put them in one of the drawers next to the sink.

## Chapter 19

Three days later, Terry sat at her usual spot at the kitchen table going through the monthly bills. She'd just received $300.00 from Keisha, and she hoped that the mortgage company would take that, and work with her for the balance of the money due. She knew she had a better chance of turning into a six-foot, blond Amazon, but it was worth a try.

"Mrs. Meyers?" The billing rep said.

"Yes," Terry replied, practically holding her breath.

"You don't have a payment due at this time."

"Are you sure you're checking the right account? Terry Meyers, um, I mean, Wilkerson."

"Yes, ma'am, I'm checking the correct account, and there isn't a payment due at this time. Your next payment is not due for another three months."

"Oookay..." Terry said slowly, before she hung up the phone.

She didn't know what was going on, but she sure as hell wasn't going to argue with their record keeping. She only hoped that when they found their error that it wouldn't cost her more in fees. She heaved a sigh and opened the utility bill. Scanning the bill, she saw the past due amount: $625.76, the payment due this month: $261.78, and the balance due being: $0.00!

"What the hell...? Dee," Terry said, even as tears sprang to her eyes before she'd realized it.

No one would have done this for her except Dee, Dee and Ben. She rested her face in her hands as she let the tears flow. She couldn't believe how lucky she was to have family that cared for her, to help her when she was in need, and she cried for the father that her sons didn't have any longer, the father who had a new life and didn't want her boys in it.

She wiped her eyes with the back of her hand as she picked up the phone and dialed Dee's number.

# Chapter 20

Slipping her left foot inside the black Cole Haan loafers she had borrowed from Dee, Terry turned to check herself in the mirror. She laughed; most of her wardrobe came from Dee, with a few things from Holly. Whenever she needed something new to wear, she could always count on Dee to help her out. Holly, on the other hand, knew to only lend Terry things that she had no desire to have returned. Dee pretended that she was upset when Terry asked for something to wear, but when Dee would bring the asked for item, she always brought something extra. If Terry asked to borrow a blouse, Dee would bring the blouse and a skirt or slacks. She would always say that it was a loan and never asked for it to be returned, and Terry usually forgot.

She smiled, turning from side to side, admiring her outfit. She wore form-fitting black slacks and a black button down top, and the shoes were the finishing touch. "Yes, the perfect outfit for the successful PI."

Terry picked up a black leather jacket from the bed and left the room. She trotted done the steps. "DJ, I want you to keep an eye on your brother for me for a while."

DJ switched off the television and walked around and halfway up the steps. "I don't want to."

Terry froze and spun around, walking to the bottom of the steps, and looked up at her son. "What?"

"I don't want to watch Keith. Can't Keisha watch him?"

"No, Keisha isn't home yet, and I don't want her to keep an eye on him, I told you to."

"But, why do I have to do it?"

"Because I told you to! And, because I'm your mother, and you will do as you're told. Don't think you're grown up because you're taller than me, Mister Man. You know better."

DJ looked at his mother, clearly prepared to argue. He looked around and then back down at Terry, and then reluctantly said, "All right."

Terry grabbed her purse and looked inside. Digging around, she found an envelope that Keisha had given her earlier during the day. She peeked inside and quickly counted it. One hundred and fifty dollars was left after she'd gone grocery shopping. She took out thirty dollars, her driver's license, and turned to DJ. "When I get home, I expect to find your brother in one piece. Understand?"

DJ just nodded. She shoved the money into the back pocket of her slacks and rushed out of the front door.

Terry parked her car on the opposite side of the parking lot, approximately four hundred feet from Imagine Photo studios. She had driven around the lot until she spotted Chadwick Henderson's Silver Lexus, and then she parked what she thought was a reasonable distance away from his car and place of work, and waited. She looked around the parking lot, watching the comings and goings of the business complex. Terry picked up the pen and pad that she had brought from home, making a circular mark on the pad to be sure that the pen worked. She couldn't believe how easy it was to obtain the information for this case. It practically fell into her lap, which only went to show that this is what she was meant to do.

When she went to Meyers Investigation to learn what she could about being a PI, the new receptionist, Pam/Patty/Paula, or whatever her name was, had greeted Terry with a friendly smile, and a tale of how she had risen two hours earlier than usual, rode the bus for an hour, and skipped breakfast to get to work on time. Terry looked at the woman's hollow cheeks and extremely thin upper body, and thought that she of all people didn't need to be skipping any meals.

Terry had told the woman who she was and headed down the hall to Dee's office, and to her surprise the woman let her go with no ID or confirmation of who she really was. Terry looked around Dee's office for any books on PI training. Ten minutes after she had entered Dee's office, Paula rushed in, asking Terry if she could keep an eye on the front desk. Paula said that she had to run across the street for something that was crucial.

"Sure," Terry had said.

She knew that the only thing on the other side of the street open this early in the morning was the Starbucks. It would give Terry time to get a peek into some of the files in the front office. When Paula left, Terry laughed to herself as she walked down the hall to the reception area. Terry knew Paula wouldn't be keeping her job for long. If Dee walked in and found her missing, and figured out that she had made a coffee run when she was supposed to be working, Dee would shit a thirty-pound brick, right before she pitched her out on her skinny butt.

While at the front desk, Terry searched a few files, trying to memorize the format of the reports that Meyers used. She checked the dates on a few files, and when she found one that was over a year old, she took a couple of sheets from the report, folded them and slipped them into her purse. Ten minutes after she sat down at the receptionist desk, a call came in from a prospective client. Excitement welled inside her as she wrote down the new client's information and put the message in her purse next to the notes from the report. Shortly after that Liz, Dee's research specialist, entered the office. When she saw Terry sitting behind the front desk, she asked where the new receptionist was. She said that Dee had an early appointment and was coming in a little earlier than her usual time. Checking the clock, Terry saw that it was 8:40 AM. Liz said that Dee was due to come in at 9 AM, which meant that Dee's prompt ass would come walking through the doors at 8:50. Terry had hoped that she would be out of the office long before Dee's arrival. She watched Liz walk down the hall to her own office while thinking that if Ms-ten-hot-minutes-away-from-being-unemployed didn't bring her bony ass back soon, that's what she was going to be, unemployed. When Paula returned, Terry quickly escaped from the office and headed in the opposite direction from where she knew Dee always parked. When she reached her car, she called her new client to set up an appointment to meet with her.

Terry had arranged to meet with Mrs. Henderson at the Starbucks a mile from her home. Before she arrived, Terry went over the notes that she'd taken from Dee's office and wrote down some questions to ask during her initial meeting. When Pauline Bleeker-Henderson walked into the Starbucks, Terry knew her immediately. She was a tall woman, close to six feet with copper hair and expressive brown eyes. She had a majestic look about her, but also looked like she wasn't afraid of hard work.

## Chapter 20

After questioning Mrs. Henderson, Terry learned that the Henderson's had been married for twelve years and that they didn't have any children. Pauline said that when she'd married Chadwick, at age thirty-two, her family wasn't happy. She said that her family was not against her getting married, but were against whom she was marrying. Hers was a family of means, but she assured Terry that that wasn't the reason for everyone trying to convince her that the marriage was a bad idea. Everyone, her parents, her grandparents, and even her three sisters, just didn't care for Chadwick. For months, her sisters tried to convince her not to marry him; her eldest sister, who was what she called the proverbial prude, even suggested that she and Chadwick live together. But she was in love and so they were married.

"Chadwick has always seemed a little secretive," she had told Terry.

At the beginning of their relationship, she had chalked it up to him being shy and introverted; but as time went by she realized that her husband wasn't as shy as she thought he was, and she attributed his secrets to just being the way he was. In the last few months, he had grown more secretive. He would sometimes go into the back yard to use his cellphone. He wouldn't let her use his car, and once she asked for his car keys to retrieve a bag that she'd left in there from a shopping trip that they'd taken earlier that day, and he blew up at her.

"He just started screaming at me," she said.

At the end of their meeting, Terry had casually mentioned how reputable Meyers Investigation was, and how everyone including herself had a backlog of cases. Pauline had said that she could understand, and that Meyers had come highly recommended. By the end of their meeting, Terry had Pauline agreeing to hiring Meyers Investigation, and gladly saying that she didn't have any problems with the timetable. Terry was relieved, she figured it would take her at least that long to figure things out, and come up with something to give Pauline. At the end of their meeting, Pauline offered to write a check for the down payment. Terry was so tempted to take it, but she told her that they would send her a bill once the case was settled.

After ten minutes, Terry realized that she was doodling. She focused on the bubble lettering that she had doodled and noticed that the words she'd written said Terry and Wade. She scratched them out, tore out the sheet of paper, and balled it up to throw over her shoulder and into the back seat. Out of the corner of her eye, she saw a man exit Imagine studio. He was a big man, a couple inches over six feet, and probably about two hundred and fifty pounds, but Terry thought he looked a lot bigger than the description, and a lot meaner than the photo she'd received from Pauline.

Henderson turned and locked the front door of the studio, and walked to his parking space directly in front of the store. He got into his car, and from what Terry could tell, he placed a phone call before starting his car and pulled from the parking lot.

"Yeah!" Terry nearly screamed, both excited and nervous. This was her time to shine.

Terry pulled her car to the end of the block and watched as Henderson got out of his car, locked it with the remote, and trotted across the street to an apartment building. She looked around, trying to figure out her next move.

"He would have to go to an apartment instead of a house. Shit," she mumbled.

## Chapter 20

Terry watched him as he opened the door leading into the lobby and disappeared. She watched for a moment, trying to decide what to do, and then let her head drop against the headrest.

"Man. Shit, shit, shit," She grumbled, and then looked across the street at the apartment again. She watched as a rail thin woman walked from the apartment building. She looked about thirty, but it was hard to tell because her hair was scraggly and her complexion haggard. "She looks awful," Terry whispered.

If that woman stood in the dark and was silhouetted with a backlight, she'd look like a skeleton. Terry watched as she sat on the steps of the apartment building, looking up and down the street, as if she was waiting for someone. Terry slid out of the car, locking the door, and slipped her keys in the pocket of her slacks. She walked across the street, stopping a few feet away from the woman.

"Miss," Terry said. The woman looked up at her. "Um..." Terry started and paused, pretending that she was unsure of what she wanted to ask. "I'm looking for the man who was driving this car; would you happen to know what apartment he went into?"

"What's it to you?" the skeleton asked. "Are you a cop or something?"

"No, I'm not a cop," Terry answered hesitantly as she watched the woman size her up.

Terry noticed that the skeleton was paying particular attention to her jacket. Eventually her eyes moved from the jacket back up to Terry's face.

"If you ain't no cop, what you asking about the owner of that car for?"

Terry looked away, she didn't know if this woman knew Henderson or not, odds were she didn't, but she did look like the sort of person who knew and saw what went on in the neighborhood.

"Um, look, I'm his girlfriend, and I want to see what apartment he went into, make sure he's not cheating; you won't tell him you saw me, will you?" Terry added knowing that this woman probably didn't give a damn who she was or what she did.

"I don't give a shit. I don't even know him," The skeleton said, confirming Terry's belief. "But I do know the chick he's laid up with, and I don't want to cause her no trouble."

"I won't cause any trouble; I don't even care about her." Terry forced out a fake sob and tried to produce faker tears. "She probably doesn't even know that he has a girlfriend. We just had a baby." She sobbed again. "God, he's such a jerk."

The skeleton snorted phlegm from somewhere deep inside, and it took everything in Terry not to grimace in disgust. The skeleton leaned over the edge of the steps, spitting a huge wad of phlegm in the grass, and Terry shuddered.

"Well," Skeleton said, "I could tell you which apartment he went into, but you have to promise that it ain't gonna be no mess."

Terry crossed her heart, and raised her hand as if to take an oath. "Swear."

The skeleton paused, eyeing Terry's jacket once more, "All right, but it's gonna cost you," she said, standing and walking toward Terry.

Terry glanced up and down the street and then at the apartment complex. Sighing, she reached into her back pocket, pulling out the thirty bucks that she'd stuck in there before leaving the house.

"Okay. Well, I can give you ten bucks, that's all I have…" Terry said, moments before the money was snatched from her hands, and the skeleton darted in the opposite direction of the apartment complex. “Shit,” Terry muttered, taking off after the other woman.

The way the skeleton ran reminded Terry of a gazelle, all arms and legs. She dodged between two moving cars and sprinted in front of a moving UPS truck like an Olympic champion, before cutting a path toward a nearby park. Terry was in hot pursuit. She’d be damned if she was going to let someone that was all of sixty pounds outrun her and get away with her money.

When Terry almost reached the curb, a car pulled up, stopping in front of her. She threw her leg up and over the car, rolling across the hood. She’d seen it several times on television and in the movies, and they had made it seem so easy. She hit the hood with a loud thud, slid down, and over the grill. The edge of the grill scraped her from thigh to hip, before she ended up on her knees in front of the car. Scrambling to recover, she tripped and banged her knee on the sidewalk.

“Look what you did to my car, you crazy bitch,” the owner of the car yelled.

“Son of a bitch!” Terry cursed, scrambling to her feet and hobbling as fast as possible, which wasn’t very fast, after her prey. “Wait ‘til I get my hands on that skinny bitch,” she said through gritted teeth.

The Skeleton dodged through the park and seemed to slow down, until she looked over her shoulder to see Terry in pursuit. Terry’s chest was burning, and her heart was pounding so loud that it was the only thing she could hear; but she wasn’t going to let that bitch get away with her thirty bucks. Gritting her teeth, she pushed passed the pain and cut through a cluster of bushes. When she rounded a patch of trees, Terry saw the skeleton duck behind tall shrubbery and, to her amazement, slide down a drainage pipe. Terry looked around, then cursed her stupidity. She took a deep breath, threw caution to the wind, and slid down the pipe behind the skeleton. Terry expected to go down like she was an athlete sliding down a luge, but she slid down slowly about eight feet, and then stopped. She moved her arms and found that she was wedged in tight. Not tight enough not to have movement, but tight enough to know that she wasn't going down any further.

"This can't be happening. This can't be freaking happening!" Terry wiggled a little, trying to push herself up, only to slide down a few more inches, becoming wedged in tighter. "Shit, shit, shit."

"Hello," a female voice called from above.

Terry froze, closing her eyes. Great, all she needed was for Dee and Holly to find out about this. She'd never live it down. And, this would prove to Dee that she didn't have what it took to be a partner at Meyers Investigation.

"Is someone down there?" Terry remained silent. "Hello?" Terry heard another voice, but couldn't make out what they said. "I know I heard a voice, I'm positive I did. They might be hurt, I'm calling the police."

"No!" Terry said quickly.

"Hello, do you need help?"

"No, I'm okay. Just…um, taking care of some things… I've got this, don't worry about it. Why don't you just run along? I'll be fine."

"I really think we should call for-"

"No! Don't do that."

"Are you in the drain?"

Terry hesitated, and then in a sarcastic tone said, "Uh, yeees."

"That seems awful small. Are you stuck?

*Uh, it is a small opening, what do you think?* "Um, no, I'm… peachy." Terry couldn't hear everything that was being said, but she heard the words fire department and police. "No! I'm coming up," Terry said in aspiration. She wiggled her hips and braced her feet, one in front of her and one behind, trying to push herself up when the shoe slipped from her right foot. She froze. "No!"

"What's going on?" The voice from above called.

"Nothing. I'm coming up. Shit." Terry wiggled her foot and pressed the front against the pipe, trying to get her shoe back on. That's when she felt it. It felt as if the breath rushed from her lungs, traveled down her leg, through her right foot and whooshed from her body, along with Dee's four hundred dollar Cole Haan loafer.

"Mother fuc…" the rest of her statement was drowned out by the sound of her shoe clanking and scraping as it slid down the pipe.

"Are you all right? That settles it, I'm calling for help."

*No bitch*. "No, I'm coming, I'm coming," Terry called out.

She struggled, pulling her arms up. Even with her jacket on, it felt like she was scraping the skin from her arms. Using her right foot, she prepared to push the shoe from her left foot.

She paused, shivered. Whispered, "Shit," and pushed the other shoe off.

Using her toes to push herself up, she inched her way to freedom. In what seemed to be hours, but was actually ten minutes, Terry saw that she was less than two feet away from the end of the drainpipe. Suddenly, a pair of strong hands gripped her arms and pulled her up.

*Damn, but this bitch is strong*, Terry thought as she was heaved out of her short-term hell.

She came face to face with an extremely gorgeous blonde-haired woman.

"Are you all right?" the blond asked, stepping close and examining Terry's face.

Terry took a quick step back and staggered, slightly off balance. She tripped and tumbled backwards to fall into the arms of her savior.

"Easy," a rich voice said from her left and above her, and then he immediately laughed. "Amazing."

She glanced up and into the gray eyes of Wade Nelson!

# Chapter 21

Terry recovered quickly, pushed at his chest, and stepped away from him.

She muttered, "Great, just great. This night keeps getting better and better." She tugged indignantly at the hem of her jacket and looked up at him. "I always seem to be running into you. Good lord, don't you ever stay home?"

"No, I don't. And evidently you don't either." He tilted his head slightly and grinned. "I'm a little afraid to ask." He paused and then grinned. "Do I even want to know why you'd be hanging out inside of a drainage pipe?"

Terry glared at him and snapped, "I'm sure you do, but don't ask."

"Um, I'd like to know," the blond spoke up, a hint of humor replacing the concern in her voice.

Terry cut her eyes in the other woman's direction. "I bet you would," she murmured under her breath, and then turned back to Wade. "Well. Thanks for the hand. It was nice seeing you again. Have a good evening," She said with such fake cheerfulness, that it even made her cringe.

She looked around quickly to get her bearings and then, after deciding which direction, she had parked, she turned and headed in the direction of her car.

Wade laughed. "Hey," he called as Terry walked away. "Do you need a ride?"

"Nope," she said waving, but not bothering to look back.

She squared her shoulders, held her head high, and marched with the confidence of someone who had been stuck in drainage pipes all the time and thought it was no big deal. She only hoped that Wade and his companion didn't notice that she wasn't wearing any shoes.

***

Wade watched Terry's shapely hips swaying from side to side as she walked to where he assumed she had parked her car. *Man, she was something*, he thought, grinning. He took her in from head to heel and realized that she wasn't wearing shoes. He laughed again, shaking his head.

"Do you know that crazy woman?" Jennifer said.

"Yeah, she's the mother of one of my students. Her name is Terry, Terry Meyers."

"She seems a bit… odd."

"No, not odd… different. I don't know what it is, but I like it."

"Wow." Jennifer peeked at him and smiled. "You like her?"

"Yeah, I think I do."

"Maybe you should ask her out."

Wade slid his hands in his pockets, watching Terry cross the park. "Mmm, maybe I will," he said, right before he saw Terry look down at something that she'd obviously stepped in. He wasn't positive, but he could swear that he heard a string of curses coming from her. He couldn't keep from laughing again. He glanced in the direction that he and Jennifer had just come from. Jennifer had a photo shoot, and she had asked Wade to meet her there. They'd planned to go out to dinner afterwards. The photographer was examining the lens on his camera while he talked to his assistant. He turned back to Jennifer. "Are you finished here?"

"Yeah, we're done."

Wade took her hand and he led her in Terry's direction. "Let's make sure she gets to her car safely."

***

*How humiliating*, Terry thought as she marched barefooted across the park.

She held her head high, trying very hard to hold the revulsion and nausea of knowing that she still had the residue of dog poop on her foot and look composed at the same time. She didn't know what was worse, being stuck in that stupid drain, having Wade rescue her, his gorgeous girlfriend witnessing it, or stepping in dog poop. Terry glanced over her shoulder seeing Wade and the beautiful blond following her. She picked up her pace.

Without a doubt, having Wade rescue her was definitely the worse part. There was no telling what he thought about her, not that she cared, she told herself. She didn't care if he thought that she was some freaky-assed drain dweller that went running barefooted in the park and stepping in dog poop whenever she got the chance. When she reached the edge of the park, she saw Henderson slipping behind the steering wheel of his Lexus.

"Great," she murmured and sprinted in the direction of her car. By the time she reached the car, opened the door, and got in, Henderson's car was around the corner and out of sight. "Just great."

When Terry walked into the house, the sound of voices coming from the kitchen drew her attention from the wad of paper towels that she gingerly held. When she'd gotten in her car, she had quickly put napkins on the floor to keep from getting doggie poop on it, and then driven a block away before using the roll of paper towels she kept in her trunk, and the bottle of water in her cup holder, to clean her foot.

She paused as she identified each voice, Dee, Holly, and Keisha. Dee must have ridden with Holly, since Holly's car was the only one in front of the house. She looked down, debating on whether she should go upstairs and take a shower first. Then she decided against it. Dee and Holly would definitely become suspicious and ask questions, if she didn't come into the kitchen and say something to them before going upstairs. She looked down at her bare feet and then glanced at the stairs, wanting to go and at least put shoes on first. After abandoning that idea, she took off her coat, hung it in the closet, fluffed her hair, and took her blouse out of her slacks, making herself look a little more rumpled, before she walked into the kitchen.

"Hey, guys," she said as she entered the kitchen. She briskly crossed the room and dropped the paper towels in the trash. "How long have you been here?"

"Not long," Holly said. "We just stopped by to see you."

"What's that smell?" Keisha asked, her nose turned up.

Terry cut her eyes in Keisha's direction before saying, "Thanks." She walked to the sink, washed her hands, then turned, leaning against the counter to cross her arms across her breasts as a beautiful and extremely statuesque girl entered the kitchen.

# Chapter 21

"Keisha, where are the glasses?" she asked, not giving Terry, Dee, or Holly a glance.

The three watched in complete silence, all of them wearing surprised looks.

"Oh, hold on a sec." Keisha rose from the table, crossed the room, and took two glasses from the cabinet.

She gave them to the girl, who walked to the refrigerator, poured two glasses of Kool-Aid, smiled at Terry and headed toward the living room.

Terry was the first to snap out of her momentary stupor. "Um, who the hell are you?"

"Oh, that's Lindsey," Keisha said before the girl had time to respond.

Lindsey looked at Terry for only a moment, smiled, said, "Hi," and walked from the kitchen.

"And who the hell would that be?" Terry said, giving Keisha a murderous glare, ignoring the shocked looks on Dee and Holly's faces.

"I told you, that's Lindsey."

Terry's jaw clinched. "Care to elaborate?"

"She's a friend of DJ's," Keisha said. "I think she's his girlfriend. Isn't that cute? DJ having a girlfriend, I mean. She's a real nice girl."

"David Jerome Meyers!" Terry bellowed, her eyes never leaving Keisha. A moment later DJ entered the kitchen and Terry turned to him. "DJ, who is that girl walking around my house like she owns the place?"

"Oh, that's my friend, Lindsey. Keisha said it was okay that she came over."

Terry glared at her cousin. "Keisha can't be extending invitations; she's here on borrowed time her dammed self."

"Mom, we're studying together."

"DJ, its almost 8:00 pm, study time is over. She needs to go home, now!"

"She's waiting for her mother's boyfriend to come and pick her up. She talked to him a little while ago, and he said he would be here soon," DJ said, before he turned, leaving the kitchen.

Terry stood staring at the spot where her son had just been standing a moment before. *What the*? She turned her glare on Keisha, who only hunched her shoulders, utterly clueless as to why Terry might not want her fourteen-year-old son alone in his bedroom with a girl who looked like a younger version of a Playboy centerfold.

"If it's okay with you guys, I'd really like to kill Keisha now."

Holly laughed. "No, Terry, you can't kill her. Not now, not ever."

"Please."

"No."

"I'll do your laundry."

Holly paused, bit her lip as if she had to think about that for a moment, and then shook her head. "No, Terry."

"Anyway," Dee said, drawing Terry's heated gaze from Keisha.

Terry watched Keisha for a few moments more. *Note to self, when Dee and Holly leave, kill Keisha.* She got a moment's satisfaction when Keisha squirmed under her scrutiny, before she turned back to Holly and Dee.

"You guys, I'm losing control of my household. DJ has a Hooters babe in his room; I have an unwanted houseguest. The next thing I know, Keith will be shooting craps on the front porch."

"Terry Ann, I don't think…" Keisha started to say, when Terry gave her an evil look. Keisha quickly crossed the kitchen, sitting at the table between Dee and Holly.

"And I don't know about this Lindsey. Something seems off." Terry paused to collect her thought. "She seems a little older than a fourteen or fifteen-year-old girl, don't you think? And, it's weird but, she sort of reminds me of someone."

"Really?" Holly asked.

"Yeah, I don't know who…" Terry paused again, seeing the look that passed between Holly and Dee. "What?"

"She should remind you of someone," Dee said quietly.

"Who?" Terry said.

Holly hesitated before speaking. "You. I mean, not now, but when you were… I don't know, I guess around fourteen or fifteen. You remember how you were just a bit… How should I put this? Frisky."

Keisha looked between Holly and Dee and then she glanced at Terry. "I think I'll just… Um…" She slipped out of the chair and eased out of the kitchen.

Terry frowned at Dee and Holly. Tilting her head, she thought back to when she was fifteen. "Yeah, I guess I was a bit of a handful." Terry gasped. "No!"

Holly nodded. "Yep. I sort of picked up on it right away."

Dee nodded as well.

"You guys are joking with me, right?"

Dee frowned and shook her head. "Nope, honey, 'fraid not."

Terry felt mortified. She quickly pushed herself from the counter, marching across the kitchen. "Oh, hell no!"

When Terry stormed from the kitchen, the only thing she saw was red. No way in hell was her fourteen-year-old son going to be behind closed doors with a girl like that. When Terry was fifteen, she was a little boy crazy; she would admit it. No, she was *totally* boy crazy, and the boys were crazy about her. There wasn't a time all through high school that she didn't have a boyfriend. She didn't have sex with any of them; she had waited until she turned seventeen for that. But that didn't keep her from having a reputation; most of the guys spread rumors about her being easy and putting out, but she didn't care. At the time, it made her popular, and that was the most important thing, to be popular and cool. That didn't mean she didn't know about sex though. Hell, she knew enough to teach the sex education teacher a thing or two, or twenty.

If she knew anything, it was that kids today were a lot freer with sex than they were back when she was in high school, and she'd be damned if this girl was going to be teaching DJ about the birds and bees, or the fish, or mice, or whatever the hell they taught these sex fiend kids these days. It took everything in Terry not to kick the door in when she rushed into DJ's room. DJ and Lindsey were lying on his bed, shoulder to shoulder, looking at a book that lay before them.

DJ jumped, when the door banged opened, his eyes as large as saucers. "What? What happened?"

"Why is this door closed?" Terry demanded.

"I don't know," DJ answered, seeming confused. "You never said anything about me closing the door before when I had company."

"Well, I am now. I want this door to stay open."

"I… I…What's wrong, Mom?"

"Nothing. Don't close this door." Terry looked at DJ and Lindsey, who were now sitting up on the bed. "Go get a chair," she told DJ and then pointed to Lindsey.

"And you, sit on the chair next to the desk. I don't want either of you sitting on that bed."

"But…" DJ said, still clearly confused.

"Do it!" Terry said, pointing to DJ and turned to leave the room. She turned back to see Lindsey looking at her, more angelic then Mother Teresa, and DJ looking just as confused as he had when she entered the room. "How old are you, little girl?"

Lindsey's angelic look turned to one of unease. "Um…" she hesitated. "I'm fifteen; I… I'll be sixteen in January."

"What classes do you have with DJ?"

"We're in the same algebra class, mom."

"I struggle with math," Lindsey said. "And DJ's really a whiz, and he offered to help me."

Terry watched as Lindsey squirmed under her scrutiny. She looked suspiciously at DJ, whose chest was so puffed up it looked as if he had been pumped full of helium, to Lindsey, and then back to DJ.

Turning, she pushed the door open as far as it would go, and then pointed two fingers at her eyes and then at both teens, using the gesture to mean that she was watching them, before leaving the room.

# Chapter 22

Walking Jennifer to the entrance of her apartment building, Wade watched her wave to the door attendant before she crossed the corridor and stepped onto the elevator. He got back into his truck, started it up, and pulled out from the parking lot. Wade drove down Washington, made a right on Clark and another right on Madison, heading west.

After leaving the park, he and Jennifer had gone to Filene's Basement, a department store on State Street. She had said that she had met a woman at the airport, and they struck up a conversation and the woman told Jennifer that she could get great buys there. They walked around the store for almost an hour and a half; Jennifer picking up this and that, showing it to Wade, who only nodded and said, 'That's nice'. After showing Wade some hideous item of purple and red, Jennifer finally realized that Wade's mind was a million miles away and suggested that he take her home. When they arrived at her apartment, Wade had apologized, saying that he had things on his mind and telling her that it was work related. Jennifer assured him that she understood and told him that she would call him in a few days.

Drumming his fingers on the steering wheel while he waited for the light to change, Wade thought about the real reason that he was distracted: Terry Meyers. He thought about the flustered looked on her face when he eased her out of the drainage pipe; the way she stumbled and he caught her, and the brief time that he was able to hold her. The look on her face when she realized that he was the one to aid her, the way her chin jutted out and the way she held her head high when she turned and walked away.

He grinned and felt a sudden rush of heat, as he remembered the way her sharply hips swayed when she tried to trudge as gracefully as she could through the park, while barefooted. Well, she was graceful until she stepped in those animal feces. He laughed. What in the hell was she doing? Was she hiding from someone, was she in trouble? He hadn't seen anyone around when they were there, but if she were hiding from someone, they could have looked for her, not found her and left. Who would think that someone would actually hide in a drainage pipe? When Jennifer insisted that she had heard someone in the pipe, and he realized that she was right, it had surprised the hell out of him, and he had seen some strange things in his life.

Maybe he needed to do a little investigating on Terry Meyers. He only knew the basics. She was thirty-four, and divorced with two sons. She had an AA in general studies from City College of Chicago, and one year of Early Childhood Education at Columbia. She had had different jobs over the last fifteen years, the longest lasting two years, and she didn't have a criminal record.

Wade pulled the truck to the curb in front of his parents' house and leaned forward. He looked up at the window on the top floor. His parents' bedroom light was on, and he could see movement behind the blinds. The height and size of the figure suggested that it was his father. Good, he didn't want to deal with his father this evening.

Wade sat back, watching the house. He looked at the window at the far side of the brown and beige bungalow. That was the room he and Adam had shared; now it was a guest room. Wade thought back to the days when he and his father had still had a relationship. To the day when he had lost what little respect he had left for the man who was once his hero.

When Wade's father started drinking, Wade was confused. He didn't understand what was going on, so he went to his mother and asked her. She said that his father was sad and that was why he was drinking. Wade still didn't understand, and he wanted to know why their father seemed so sad.

"Wade, your father has a lot of thing on his mind," his mother had told him.

"Is dad sad because we moved here to Chicago?"

His mother hesitated. "In a way, yes."

"Then we should go back home, back to Malaysia."

His mother smiled at him sadly. "Wade, it's not that easy. Come, sit down and have a snack."

He sat at the table, and she cut him a slice of cherry pie, poured him a glass of milk, and sat with him, asking him about school and his friends. Soon he had his mind where she wanted it, off the subject of his father and his father's drinking.

Eventually, his father's drinking became worse, and Wade grew surer that it was best for them to move from Chicago. Being there had changed his father. He and his father had once shared a bond; his mother always held a special place in his heart, but he was his father's oldest son. When they were in Malaysia, they used to spend a lot of time together. Chicago had changed that. Not only did he and the family have to live in a situation where things were getting progressively worse from his father's drinking; now they had to deal with other people knowing about Wade Sr.'s drinking problem. It was terribly embarrassing because, as a child, Wade felt like everyone knew that his father was a drunk; so he decided that he would do something about it.

One evening, his father was sitting in front of the television after work. Wade waited until his mother had left the room to go check on dinner, before he broached the subject of Malaysia.

He walked to the sofa, perching on the arm of the couch."Dad?" his father remained silent. "Dad?"

"Don't you see me watching the damned TV?" His father bellowed.

Wade flinched, his heart lodging in his throat. His hands trembled, and his body tingled from fear. He was afraid, and he didn't know why. Their father had never hit them. He yelled. In the last year in a half that was all he ever did, but he'd never hurt his family. Wade didn't understand his fear and something deep down inside told him to get up and leave the living room, but he had to do this, he had to get his father away from Chicago, and what was making him drink.

"Dad, do you ever miss home?"

"What the hell are you talking about, boy?"

"Do you miss being back home? Back home in Malaysia?"

His father gave him a nasty glare. "Boy, I am home." He turned back to the television.

"But you're not happy here; if we went back to Malaysia, you could be happy again. Then you can stop drinking."

His father moved so fast, Wade hardly saw him. He slapped Wade, knocking him off the arm of the sofa and to the floor. "Boy, don't you talk to me about my drinking! You don't have a right to talk to me about anything, do you hear me?"

His mother rushed into the room, and seeing what had happened, she rushed to Wade to check his face. She turned to her husband. "Wade, what is wrong with you?"

He stepped closer to her, leaned down, and spoke to her through gritted teeth. "You know what the hell is wrong. It's you. It's all of you. You killed my relationship with my family. You killed my mother."

Wade's mother stared at her husband stunned. "But…" she started before he shoved her, knocked her off balance so she stumbled, tripping over the coffee table and landed on the opposite side.

"It's your fault! My mother, she didn't want me to marry you. She died broken-hearted and angry, and my family blames me."

She shook her head. "Wade… I-"

"Shut up!" Wade Sr. bellowed and took an angry step toward his wife. "Shut up, I don't want to hear anything from you. If I hadn't married you, things would be different. My family would accept me, and my mother might still be alive."

His father turned and stormed from the house. He was gone for two days, and when he returned no one spoke of that day. The day when Wade Sr. first hit his child and pushed his wife; the day that he decided that Wade was the enemy, and Wade's mother was that bitch who protected his enemy, that was the day Wade Jr. lost his hero.

Wade had gotten his first job the summer that he turned fifteen. He worked at the grocery store as a bagger and helped customers load their cars. Wade had gotten his first paycheck. He hopped on his bike and headed home. It was a Friday and, if he remembered correctly, the banks stayed open late. If he got home in time, maybe his mother could take him to cash his check. He was so excited, thinking about all of the things that he would buy. He'd get some Snickers for Shalan, they were her favorites, and he could send them to her at school. He'd buy Adam the He-Man action figure that they saw last week when they went to K-mart with their mom, and he would give his mother some pretty-smelling soap. He'd even get his dad a gift; maybe a pair of socks or a tie. No, his dad didn't wear ties, but he'd think of something.

When Wade turned the corner, he saw his father's car. He slowed his bike. Wade, Sr. was usually out late on Friday and part of Wade wondered if something was wrong. He rode around the block and parked his bike in the back yard. He walked onto the porch and entered the house, going in search of his mother. When he walked from the kitchen to the living room, Wade spotted his father sitting on the sofa clutching a beer can, all of his attention focused on the television. Wade hesitated and then quietly passed through the living room to the stairs leading to the upper level.

"Boy, don't you see me sitting here?"

His father's voice made him jump."Hi, dad."

"Where the hell have you been?"

"Um," Wade looked back toward the kitchen, cursing himself for venturing into the living room. "I was at work."

His father grunted. "You come sneaking in here and don't even open your mouth. I guess you're a big man now that you have a job. Since you're a man, you don't need to respect your father. That right?"

Wade didn't know how to answer that question. If he disagreed with his father, it would get him in trouble, and of course agreeing with such a statement was almost certainly a death sentence. Wade's eyes shifted from side to side.

"Is mom home?" He asked instead. "I got my check today, and I wanted to see if she could take me to the bank."

"She ain't taking you no dammed where. Jahan, get your ass down here!" Wade, Sr. bellowed. Wade looked up, meeting his mother's gaze as she descended the steps. "Jahan, you ain't taking that boy nowhere, you hear me? He's a man, let him figure out how to cash that check himself, damn him!"

His mother looked at Wade and then nodded slightly. "Wade, go up stairs and get washed up for dinner."

"No," Wade, Sr. said. "He's going to sit his ass down here with me." His father looked at Wade. "Boy, sit your ass down." Wade hesitated; evidently, to his father, it was a moment too long. "I said sit your ass down!"

His father hurled the beer can at Wade. The can barely grazed his arm, but beer splattered the wall. When the can hit the floor, beer puddled on the carpet. Wade's mother descended the steps the rest of the way, and crossed the living room to Wade at the same time that his father rose from his chair.

"Didn't I tell you to do something, you little asshole?" Wade, Sr. said shoving Wade in the chest.

Wade stumbled backwards and instinctively reached out to grab something to keep from falling. Wade Sr. obviously thought that Wade was trying to defend himself as he went into attack mode. He pushed Wade from him, and Wade tumbled backwards and slipped in the puddle of beer.

## Chapter 22

"You think you're going to hit me, you little bastard?" Wade Sr. bellowed as he reached down and grasped Wade's hair, pulling him up.

Nurjahan immediately rushed to Wade's defense, trying to place herself between her husband and her son. Wade Sr. slapped her and she screamed, falling to the floor. To Wade, everything seemed to go too fast. He remembered his father pushing him, and reaching out for something to break his fall. The next thing he remembered was his father's fist striking the side of his head, and then his mother crawling to him and covering his body with her much smaller one as his father kicked angrily at him.

Later that evening, his mother came to his room. She walked slowly, and Wade could tell that she was in pain, but she never groaned or winced. She told him that she was sorry; sorry for what his father had done, sorry for not being strong enough to protect him, and sorry for moving to America. She held Wade while he cried, and when she left, Wade promised that he would never treat someone like that. He would never hurt a woman or a child. He would never get married.

The next day, when his father came home from work, he walked into the house as if everything was as it had always been. But, Wade knew he would never look at his father the same way again. When he looked at his mother, so small and delicate, with nasty yellow and green bruises from the beating she took to protect him, he knew that he would hate his father forever.

Pushing his memories away, Wade took the keys out of the ignition, got out of the truck, and headed up the walkway toward his parents' house.

# Chapter 23

Terry held baby Kyle in her arms as she tried to keep him from biting his brother. She was four and half weeks into her new career as a childcare provider, and she knew she'd made a terrible mistake. She had three other children besides the twins and Abby, two brothers and a sister; eleven-year-old Roland Briggs, his nine-year-old sister Ronisha, and their six-year-old brother Rodney. They were good kids. Their mother would drop them off at Terry's house at 7 am, she would feed them breakfast, and at 7:45, she would walk them, along with Abby and Keith, to the bus stop.

The way it worked out now, she only had baby Ben and Kyle during the day, and at 3:10, she would put the twins in their double stroller and walk down to the bus stop to pick up the other kids. Even though she liked getting the much-needed money for the Briggs children, she knew that this just wasn't for her. The first few days were great, she even had fun, but by the sixth day, she wanted to kill all of the children, and by the twelfth day, she wanted to kill everybody within a five-mile radius. There was running and jumping and screaming in the house all of the time, not to mention the constant crying. At the beginning, Terry would try to be calm when she talked to the children.

# Chapter 23

"Please do not run in the house", or, "Screaming is not necessary", or, "Please don't jump from the top step of the back porch, you could get hurt." She soon moved to, "I've asked you guys to please not run in the house, I've asked you not to scream, and haven't I asked you a million times not to jump down the steps?" Now she was to the point where she was resorting to threats. "If you don't stop that damn running, I'm going to tie you to a chair," and, "Good heavens, if I hear you scream again, I'm going to gag you," and, "If you do that one more time, I swear, I'm gonna beat your asses."

She just couldn't take it, the constant arguing, bickering, and crying just was not cutting it. And, every now and again, Rodney would do something that was so overly annoying that it just made Terry want to smack him. It was driving her insane.

The upside was that with Abby, the twins, and the Briggs children, she was finally able to sleep at night without worrying about her finances. Things were looking up. The lights were not in jeopardy of being turned off, they had food in the fridge, and DJ had pants that actually fit him. She was even able to send small amounts of money to her creditors.

Baby Ben made a growl. The one that babies sometimes made right before they struck, and Terry jerked his brother back before teeth met skin.

"Aunt Terry," Abby said.

Terry was so busy trying to keep the twins from chomping each other to death that Abby had to call her several times before Terry could even think about answering.

"What, Abby?" she finally said.

"Roland ate a crayon."

"What?"

"He did. A crayon," Abby said, looking up at Terry. "He ate it. Just broke it and ate it. Just like this." Abby simulated Roland's actions, pretending that she'd put a crayon in her mouth.

"Roland, why would you do that?"

"'Cause Abby dared me," Roland said.

Terry glared down at Abby, who smiled at her sheepishly and hunched her narrow shoulders. Terry looked down at the broken crayon.

"Great, you had to eat the black crayon, see all the blues and greens, why not eat one of those. No, it had to be the black one."

"But, Aunt Terry, he ate a crayon."

"Don't worry about it, it's nontoxic. He'll be okay."

After the last child was picked up, Terry raced upstairs to change her clothes. Going to her closet, she selected a dark blue, long-sleeved silk tee and her better pair of jeans. Laying them out on the bed, she went into the bathroom to take a quick shower. When she walked back into the bedroom, she looked at the clothes on the bed and shook her head. Putting them back in the closet, she chose a plain white pullover top and worn jeans. She slipped on blue tennis shoes and a hat, and grabbed her Sony digital camera before trotting downstairs.

"Keisha!" she called, heading toward the kitchen.

Keisha was exiting the kitchen and nearly ran into Terry. "Yeah?"

"Are you going out?"

"I'm meeting Deion. Where are you going?"

"Out. Can you fix dinner for DJ and Keith?"

Keisha waited a beat before she asked, "Can Deion come for dinner?"

"Yeah, I guess so. But, I don't want any funny business going on. No messing around."

## Chapter 23

"Terry Ann, I know that."

Terry glared at Keisha and opened her hand, reaching for the girl as if she were going to grab her, but instead closed her hand into a fist, making her knuckles crack. She turned grabbing her purse from the sofa and rushed out the front door.

Terry drove back to the neighborhood where she had followed Henderson, and parked on the corner where she had parked four evenings a week for the last three weeks. After sitting in the car for almost two hours, she started nodding off, when the blaring of a horn snapped her awake. She looked around, momentarily confused, and then focused on the movement on the street, when she saw the silver Lexus sitting at the curb. She looked across the street, seeing Henderson walking inside the apartment building.

"Shit," She said, under her breath.

Terry jumped out of the car, locking the door. She skipped across the street, and tried to peek inside the apartment building vestibule to see what apartment Henderson had entered. She saw a door on the lower level closing, but was not able to see if it was in fact her subject.

"All right, what would Dee do?" She looked up and down the street. "Okay, no one else went inside. So that had to be the right apartment."

She scratched her head for a moment, and shoved her hands in her pockets while she walked back to her car. Sitting in the car, she contemplated what her next move should be.

"It has to be the right apartment," she told herself.

She reached inside her purse, pulling out the digital camera, and got out of the car, taking her purse with her. She walked to the back of the car, putting her purse in the trunk, and then walked across the street to the apartments and around back. She walked the length of the building, looking at the lower windows. The apartment to the far end had its bedroom light on. Terry walked by the window, peeking inside. When she did, she saw a woman about thirty going through one of the drawers of a dresser. Terry stepped to the side of the window, peeking inside. The woman removed a black pair of thongs and a black teddy, laying them on the bed.

"Ma'am, what are you doing?" Terry heard a strong man's voice say, and she spun around, only to have a bright light shined in her eyes.

She raised her hands, blocking the light. "Hey, I can't see."

"Ma'am, what are you doing?" came the same question, followed by the squawk of a police radio.

*Great*. "Officer, I know what you must be thinking. This can be so easily explained."

"I'm sure it can. I'm going to need you to come with me."

***

"Detective Lawson, we have someone here who says she knows you. We caught her peeking in someone's window."

Holly sighed, muttering. "Damn it, Dee," as she rose from her desk and walked to the intake area. She slowed when she saw not Dee but Terry slouched in one of the gray chairs, staring up at the ceiling. "Terry, what the hell are you doing here?"

"She says she's a PI working on a case," the desk sergeant said.

Holly frowned, glancing at Terry, who beamed at her like a fool. "This is so not cool," Holly groaned.

## Chapter 23

***

When Terry was seated in the chair next to Holly's desk, Holly leaned back in her seat and folded her arms. "Okay, let's hear it. What happened?"

Terry shifted in her seat, biting her lower lip. "Well, I really want to be a PI, but Dee won't let me. So, I figured I could solve a case and prove that I can learn to do it."

"So, you advertised as a PI? Terry, you could get in a lot of trouble doing that."

"No… I sort of… borrowed one of Dee's cases."

"You what?"

"It was either that, or find one on my own, and I didn't know how to go about doing that. But don't worry; I'm not going to mess this up."

"Oh my lord, girl, Dee is going to kill you."

"No, no she won't. 'Cause I'm going to solve this case and she'll get paid for it. Everything will work out, just you wait and see."

"And you were peeking in someone's window because?"

"I saw what apartment that this guy, Henderson, that's the perp's name…" Holly opened her mouth to say something, but shook her head and let it go. "...Went into, and I wanted to take pictures of him with his girlfriend. I didn't see him in the room; I had just walked back there. And why were the cops hanging out behind an apartment complex anyway? Don't you guys have anything better to do?"

***

Holly closed her eyes. "Good lord, why can't I have normal friends? Why can't I have friends that take their kids to the park and go to work doing normal nine to five jobs? But no — not me; I have to choose friends who, if they were in an asylum, would be the ward leaders." Holly opened her eyes, looking at Terry.

"I'm sorry," Terry said, her brows rose in question.

"Yeah, sure you are. You're sorry your ass got caught."

"Yeah, I'm sorry about that too." Terry frowned and scratched her nose.

Holly shook her head. "You are aware that my boss hates me, right? And, I can tell you, he's going to hate you even more if you start doing the off-the-wall stuff that your cousin does. I'm sure I can get you off this time, but you need to give up this crazy idea."

"I can't. I have to do this. I do."

"Dee's not going to like this, when I tell her."

"You can't tell her."

"Terry, I can't keep this from her."

"You can't tell her. Please. Promise you won't tell her. I'm begging you."

"Terry…"

"Please, I have to do this. I swear, this is not a fad, this is so important to me. I know this is what I'm meant to do. I just need a chance to prove myself. Please, please, please!"

"Okay, okay. But promise me that you'll stay out of trouble."

"I will, I swear."

Holly grunted. "Now, where the hell have I heard that before?"

## Chapter 24

Terry couldn't believe her luck. When she pulled around the corner, all set to spend a fun-filled evening sitting and staring at the door of the apartment building, waiting for her subject and not having him show up; she was elated to see Henderson and his girlfriend getting into his car. She pulled to the curb at the end of the block and waited until his car pulled from its parking spot, and then followed. She stayed close behind, not wanting to lose him, and hoped that he wouldn't spot her following them.

Walking into the restaurant, she passed the hostess without breaking her stride and waved saying, "I'm meeting someone."

She glanced around, seeing her quarry sitting at a table with a stunning redhead. Terry took a quick step backwards and slid to the side next to a five-foot wall lined with plants, and peered over it.

"Damn it," she whispered standing on her toes to get a better peek.

One of the pots tilted forwards. She grabbed it in time to keep it from falling, only to have the one directly next to it slip and fall over with a crash, which was followed by a shriek.

Terry closed her eyes and cursed. Standing on her toes, she peered over the wall. Henderson and his companion looked in her direction for a brief moment, and then turned away. She peered down at the couple whose dinner she was sure she had ruined and sucked in a deep breath.

"Oh, mother fu…"

***

Wade looked at Jennifer's pink sweater that now looked like a hand grenade filled with marinara sauce had exploded all over it and then up, only to meet a pair of hazel orbs staring back at him. Wade let out a snort, shook his head slightly, and dropped his head into his hands.

"Why am I not surprised?"

"I—am—so—sorry!" Terry said, rushing around the wall, all the while keeping her face averted from Henderson.

Wade looked up, glowering suspiciously at Terry. "Terry! What are you doing here? What did you do?"

"Nothing! I didn't do anything. I was looking for the people I'm meeting and touched the wall. I guess I must have hit one of the plants. I'm sorry. I swear I'll clean it. If anyone can get the stain out, I ca…" Terry touched the sweater, and seeing that it was cashmere, she stuttered, "Oh… um… oh lord, I'm sorry."

"Don't worry about it," Jennifer said, grabbing the hand that dabbed at the stain, which was only making it worse. "Really, it's just a sweater."

***

## Chapter 24

In her peripheral vision, Terry saw Henderson laugh at something his date said, and then he leaned close and kissed her. *Great, that would have been the perfect photo.* She met Jennifer's gaze and then frowned. "Don't I know you?"

Jennifer laughed. "No, I just have one of those faces. Everyone that meets me thinks they know me."

Terry studied her closely. *Yeah, one of those faces. Not.*

"So," Wade suddenly asked. "Who are you meeting?"

Terry stared across the table at his intense gray eyes, and for a moment, her mind went blank. "Uh… my cousin." She looked around the restaurant, seeing every table full except one. The Middle Eastern family that she spotted sat at one of the largest tables, one with eight seats. "There they are," she said, smiling at Wade. "Nice seeing you." she turned to Jennifer. "And again, I'm sorry about your sweater. Wade can give you my number, and we can work something out."

"Don't worry about it," Terry heard Jennifer say, as she turned and walked away from the table.

She approached the table of eight, sliding into the only empty chair. "Hi, I'm doing a survey for the restaurant."

Everyone looked at her and nodded blankly. Terry cut her eyes to the right, seeing Wade watching her. She sat her purse on the floor next to her, reached to the woman on her left, and touched her arm, laughing as if the woman had said something funny. She looked around the table at all the stunned faces that stared back at her.

"So," she said, reaching for a roll, breaking it apart, and picked up the butter knife from the place setting in front of her and spreading a generous amount of butter on the roll. “How is everyone’s evening going?” she heard a round of murmurs as everyone glanced at each other nervously. “I know you’re not going to believe this, but I'm not crazy, really.” She dropped her voice a little. “I'm just sort of hiding in plain sight.”

“Who are you?” A teenaged boy finally asked.

“Not important.” Terry waved his question away with a hand, before turning to the woman on her right. “What’s your name?” The woman looked so startled Terry had to bite her lip to keep from laughing.

“Um…Um… Janna.”

“Well, Janna, the important thing here is that I get out of here without blowing my cover.”

“Are you a spy?” A boy about ten-years-old asked in awe.

“That’s my husband’s seat and he's coming,” Janna said to Terry, a look of sheer relief on her face.

Terry looked over her shoulder in the direction that Janna had indicated with a nod of her head, and saw a man walking toward the table.

“Of course, why wouldn’t he be coming at this exact moment?” she whispered.

Terry glanced in Wade’s direction, seeing him still watching her, and then grabbing her purse. She stood quickly and walked toward the approaching man. Stopping in front of him, she spoke in a low voice. When he gave her a huge smile, she touched his arm and squeezed it in what she hoped looked like a show of affection, and then walked passed him toward the restrooms.

Terry hid in the hallway leading to the restrooms for a few minutes and then crept around the corner. She looked out, seeing that Wade and his date were preparing to leave, and decided that she had to get out before he saw her. She slipped passed the hostesses and out the door, hoping that they wouldn’t be too pissed when Janna's husband tried to get the twenty percent discount for being the 1,000$^{th}$ customer that she had told him he would be receiving.

When she reached the parking lot, she sprinted to her car, opened it, and slipped inside just as Wade emerged from the restaurant. She slid down in her seat and watched Wade and his date exit the building, and silently prayed that he didn't still have her phone number. Not because she didn't want him to call her, but because she sure as hell didn't have the money to pay for a freaking cashmere sweater.

***

"You don't think she's involved with your case, do you?" Jennifer asked Wade when they got inside the truck.

"I don't know." Wade watched the front of the restaurant for a moment. "I don't think she has anything to do with it, but she's into something, and I don't know what. She always seems to be in some sort of dilemma."

Wade had done more checking into Terry's background. As far as he could tell, nothing indicated that she was involved in anything illegal or unethical. She had no friends that fit that description either. Her nearest family and friends were pillars of the community.

"Maybe it's just bad luck," Jennifer said. Wade gave her a look of disbelief. "Well, it could be."

"I don't believe in luck. I don't know what's going on with her, but I need to find out. You know my rules."

Jennifer laughed. "Yes. Don't go in unprepared. Make sure you're always armed."

"And...?"

"And," Jennifer sighed, "Don't shit where you eat. Has anyone ever told you that you're very cynical?"

Wade stuck his key in the ignition, started the truck, and put it in drive. “I’d rather be a live cynic than a dead optimist.”

# Chapter 25

Wade stared at his computer monitor, not really seeing the words that were before him. He looked at the phone and back at the monitor. Picking up the phone, he held it for a moment, and then hung it back up. Sitting back, he crossed his arms, watching the phone for a moment, before he sat up straight and picked up the phone again. He dialed the phone number that was scrawled on a piece of paper laid out on the keyboard.

"This is dumb," he chastised himself. "This is so damned dumb." The phone rang three times before it was picked up. "May I speak to Terry please?"

There was a short pause, and then, "That depends."

Leaning back in his chair, Wade hesitated. "On?"

"On… who this is?"

He laughed. "Wade Nelson."

"Oh," Terry said, and laughed too. She asked him to hold on a second, and then he heard her yell. "Do your homework this instant, mister. Don't you look at me like that." A moment later, she was speaking into the receiver in a normal and pleasant voice. "Hey, how have you been?"

"I see you're screening your calls, are you in the witness protection program?" Wade couldn't help but ask.

Terry snorted. “I wish it was that easy. So,” she said, before he could delve deeper into the topic, “to what can I owe the pleasure?”

“I was wondering if you were free later? If so, maybe we could grab a cup of coffee.”

***

Parking at the far end of the parking lot, Terry got out of her car, not bothering to lock the door, and headed across the lot to *Our Neighborhood Grill*. She walked inside and scanned the small crowd for Wade. He smiled when she spotted him, and rose when she approached the table.

“Hey,” She said.

“Hi,” He replied, rounded the small table, and pulled out the chair for her.

Terry quickly slipped her coat off and laid it across the back of the chair, before sitting. She picked the menu up and scanned it. After placing an order and adding cream and sugar to her coffee, she turned her attention on Wade. “How have you been?”

He nodded. “Great. And yourself?”

After making small talk about the weather and both their jobs, Terry sipped her coffee and eyed him over the rim of her cup. *Man*, she thought, *he is truly gorgeous*.

Wade set his cup down. “Okay, are you going to tell what that thing in the restaurant was all about?”

“What do you mean?” she asked, hoping her features only showed the innocence that she wanted to portray.

Wade rested his arms on the table, leaning toward her. “Those beautiful eyes and succulent lips…” His eyes traveled to her lips, and then snapped back to her eyes. “Might fool other men, but not me, sweetheart.”

## Chapter 25

Terry's tongue darted out, and she moistened her bottom lip. Wade's eye immediately slid back to her lips, and a seductive smile spread across his face. "Well…?"

Terry gazed into his grey eyes, shining with excitement and mischief. "Um, you see. This is what happened…" *Damn*. "Well, it has a lot to do with..."

Wade smiled, his eyes going to her lips again. "A lot to do with what?"

She shifted nervously in her seat; God, she felt like a naughty student being scolded by her teacher. "Um, well you see…"

"See what?" Wade leaned closer still.

"You're confusing me."

Wade grinned. "Am I? I wouldn't think that a woman as beautiful as you are could become confused so easily."

Terry watched him for a moment, her breathing speeding up, and then she batted her eyes. "Are you hitting on me?"

"No, if I were, I would saying something like, 'You have the most beautiful eyes I've ever seen. I think I love you.' "

She laughed at that. "Wow, that was witty. I don't think I've ever heard that one before. Does it work for you?"

Wade laughed. "Not as much as you would think."

"Thanks for coming." Wade tugged on her jacket and she took a step closer to him.

"Thanks for the invitation. I needed to get out."

Reaching up, he ran his finger along her jaw, tracing her lips, then let the back of his hand stroke her cheek. Her eyes fluttered, and he brushed his thumb across her lips.

"Do you think we could go out again?" he said. "I could call you next week."

Terry looked up at him. Her libido was yelling, *hell yeah*, but her conscience told her, *go slow. Take your time*. It reminded her of her decision to not date for a year. *Damn conscience*. "I had a good time. Maybe we can hang out some time. Give me a call." she turned and headed to her car.

# Chapter 26

When Holly entered the house to pick Abby up, Terry ambushed her, pulling her into the kitchen. Abby followed the women.

"What's going on?" Holly asked.

"Nothing, I just needed to talk to you," Terry answered, and looked down at Abby.

"Mommy, today we made Thanksgiving cards. Aunt Terry said that she's going to help us make Christmas presents." Abby looked up from her mother to Terry and back. "I like coming here after school; we have a lot of fun."

"I'm sure you do, honey," Holly said, seeing the anxious look on Terry's face as she looked from Abby to the door leading to the other part of the house. Holly laughed. "But, if Aunt Terry's not careful, she's going to have a few new playmates, courtesy of the Illinois Board of Corrections."

"No, I won't, 'cause I'm not doing anything that I could get in trouble for, and if I were, I won't get caught."

"Ah - huh," Holly said, her tone making it clear that she did not believe her. "If Dee finds out what you're up to, you'll wish you had gotten locked up."

"Find out what, Mommy?" Abby asked.

“Abby, why don’t you go and peek inside the play-pen? Make sure Kyle and Ben are still asleep,” Terry said still watching Holly.

Abby looked at her mother and Terry; she bit her lip and fidgeted from foot to foot as if she were trying to find a reason to stay in the kitchen, but knew that it could possibly result in her getting into trouble. "’Kay." She finally said, and walked slowly across the kitchen, glancing back as she crossed the room.

“Move it, little girl,” Holly said and Abby rushed from the kitchen.

Terry laughed, shaking her head. “I only hope the babies don't have a little ‘help’ waking up.” She turned to Holly. “By the time Dee finds out that I’m working this case, I’ll have finished it.”

“No, she’ll find out long before that.”

Terry gave her a look of utter fear. “You wouldn’t!”

Holly laughed. “I should, but no, I made a promise and I won’t tell.” A look of relief crossed Terry’s face and Holly sighed. “What did you want to talk to me about?”

Terry bit her lip, her eyes taking on a hopeful gleam as she stepped from one foot to the other. “Well, I was sort of wondering if you could get me a fake ID.”

Holly chuckled. “Um, let me think. Hell no!”

Terry dropped down in one of the table chairs. “Man. Why not?”

Raising her hand, Holly said, “Police officer, against the law. Need I say more? So, why do you need a fake ID?”

Terry grinned sheepishly and then turned away. That was when Holly realized what Terry actually meant by fake ID. “Good lord, I don’t even want to know what you have in mind.”

“I was just going to…”

## Chapter 26

Holly raised her hand, stopping Terry. "Please, do not say it. I don't even want to know what strange thoughts are bouncing around inside that head of yours."

"But-"

"Noo!"

"Fine, whatever," Terry huffed and folded her arms. When Holly batted her lashes at Terry, she laughed and rose from the table. "I knew you wouldn't help me get a fake ID, I just thought I would try."

She crossed the room to the stove, taking the lid off one of two pots that was boiling.

"What are you making?" Holly said, walking to the stove, and peeking inside the pot as well.

"Chicken and dumplings."

"Do you think it's time to add the dumplings?"

"I did already," Terry said, staring inside the pot. "I think I might have added them too soon."

Picking up the spoon that was perched on a spoon rest, she stirred the stew. Holly grimaced and turned away from the stove.

"Hey," Dee said entering the kitchen with the twins in tow. "Ooh, what's that smell?"

"Chicken and dumplings; it's almost finished," Terry said happily, and reached in the cabinet for a bowl. "Want some?"

Dee's eyes quickly shifted in Holly's direction. Holly nibbled her lip, suppressing a smile and dropped her gaze to the floor. "I promised Ben that the boys and I would meet him for dinner. Why don't you put some in a bowl for me to go?"

Terry turned back to the stove and dished up a large serving of chicken and dumplings. She reached in the cabinet for a second bowl and filled that one as well. Reaching in a lower cabinet, she grabbed the plastic wrap and covered both bowls, handing one to Dee and the other to Holly.

Holly looked at the bowl and then at Terry. "Oh. Okay, thanks." She sat the bowl on the table and sat down. "Terry, Abby tells me that you've been going out a lot."

Terry quickly glanced in Dee's direction and then back at Holly. "No, not really."

"Yes, you have," Dee added. "Abby told Keith that you've been going out with Wade."

An obvious wave of relief washed over Terry. Holly felt the same way – thank God Dee didn't suspect anything other than that Terry was dating again.

"We've been out a few times, but it's nothing," Terry said quickly.

Dee shook her head. "For you, a few times *is* something."

"Well, normally yeah. But we're just friends hanging out."

Holly picked at the plastic on the bowl and then stopped when one of the twins reached for the bowl. She pushed it closer to the center of the table. "So, you're not interested in him?"

"I didn't say that."

Dee grinned and then frowned when her chair was bumped by baby Kyle trying to crawl under it. "So, you are seeing him?"

"No, I didn't say that either."

Holly leaned toward Terry. "I thought you said that he was hot?"

The twins marched around the table.

"He is," Terry admitted.

Holly looked at the twins, who were now running around the table laughing. They giggled and squealed.

"Then, what's wrong with him?" she said.

# Chapter 26

Terry didn't seem to notice the squealing toddlers as she kept talking. "Nothing. I'm sticking with my decision to not date for a year."

Dee looked surprised. "Are you serious?"

"Yep."

Holly laughed. "Wow. Who would have thought?"

Terry glared at her. "Don't be a smart ass."

"I'm not trying to be. I know how hard things have been for you. Really, I'm impressed."

"Thank you." Terry nodded. "But you know. If I were going to date someone, it would have to be Wade. He seems like a great guy. And he has the best buns I've ever seen."

"Now that's the Terry we know and love." Holly laughed. She rose for the table. "Let me get out of here."

"Yeah I need to meet Ben."

"Hey don't forget your stew," Terry called to Holly before she left the kitchen.

"Damn. Um, yeah… I almost forgot." Holly crossed the room, picking up the bowl while Dee laughed.

# Chapter 27

Terry walked inside of the house, dropping her purse on the sofa. “Hold on there buddy,” she called to DJ, who had grabbed his basketball from the laundry basket that Terry kept next to the front door. “Don’t go anywhere, I’m calling Dee and Ben and see if they can swing by and pick us up.”

DJ sighed, dropping the ball back into the basket. “All right, mom,” he said, going to the kitchen instead, probably to forage for food.

While Terry spoke to Dee, she watched Keith pick up the remote and turn on the television set. He turned the channel to the Cartoon Network, settling back to watch one of his favorite shows.

“Okay, see you guys soon,” Terry said, before she clicked the phone off and then turned to Keith. “Don’t get too comfortable there, Mr. Man, Aunt Dee and Uncle Ben will be here soon; I don’t want you whining when I tell you to turn the television off.”

“Okay, mommy.”

Terry walked back out the front door and down the driveway to her car. She opened the backdoor, taking out the box that she had placed on the seat. The box held a large bowl of tossed salad, a fruit salad, a store-bought cake, and a few snacks for the kids. Lifting the box, she backed out of the car, closing the door with her hip. She turned to see someone standing behind her, and she let out a loud shriek, nearly dropping the box.

"David! What the hell? You scared the shit out of me!"

"Terry, what the hell is your problem?"

"What are you talking about?"

"You know what I'm talking about. Why did you file a claim with Child Support? Now I have to take time off from work to go down there and straighten out this mess you caused."

"Uh, maybe if you gave me money to help with the boys I wouldn't have to do that, but you didn't give me any choice, did you?" Terry sidestepped David trying to walk around him.

He moved with her, not allowing her to pass. "That's bullshit, Terry. I've explained things to you."

"It doesn't matter now, it's already done. Like your mother said, let the courts take care of it."

"Why are you doing this?" David yelled. "You're just jealous, Shareese said that you were jealous of our relationship, but I tried to give you the benefit of the doubt."

Shifting the box in her arms Terry cursed as the bowl that held the fruit salad slid, nearly falling from the top of the box.

"David, go home. I don't have time for your crap," Terry said, pushing passed him.

"I bet you have time for your cousin's husband," David said with venom.

She froze, turning back to him. "What?"

"Yeah, I bet that's what you're doing, uh? Probably trying to get him or some other sugar daddy to take care of you and your kids, since you weren't woman enough to hold on to me. But I guess you're hard pressed to find someone else desperate enough to want a whore!"

“Hey!” Ben said, walking up the driveway. He stepped between Terry and David and in a furious tone asked David. “What the hell is your problem?”

“Are you all right, honey?” Dee asked Terry, while she glared heatedly at David.

“David, why would you speak to Terry like that?” Ben asked angrily. “Why would you speak to the mother of your sons that way?”

“You of all people shouldn’t have to ask me that question,” David said, never taking his eyes from Terry.

“You asshole!” Dee said, taking a step toward David.

Ben grabbed her arm, pulling her back, and stepping in front of her. During the entire exchange, Terry remained silent. She felt her cheeks grow warm, and hoped they weren’t getting too red.

“You know what,” Terry almost whispered. “I did some things that I’m ashamed of and I’ll have to live with them for the rest of my life. But, I’m not going to do this with you. I am not going to let you tear me down. I’ve tried to make up for the things that I’ve done.”

David snorted.

“I think you need to leave,” Ben said, looking ready to go for the other man’s throat.

David shook his head, glaring at Terry, and walked down the driveway toward his vehicle.

Dee slipped an arm around Terry’s waist. “Are you all right?”

“Sure,” Terry said her tone casual. “I’m not letting what he says get to me. I’m so beyond that.” She started to walk passed Ben, but stopped to look up at him. She shifted the box that she held and leaned close, giving him a half hug. “Thanks, cuz.”

## Chapter 27

Ben returned the hug, all while they all continued to watch David get into his car and drive away from the curb. Terry pulled away, never giving David a second glance as she carried the box toward Dee and Ben's SUV.

After looking at Terry's car, Ben determined that it was probably her battery, though he wasn't sure. He only knew that the engine wasn't getting any power. He told her that if she wanted, he'd have the garage pick it up and look at it, but it would not be until Monday.

"Terry, how are you going to get to Holly's house if you don't ride with us?" Dee asked.

"Don't worry about it, I'll get a ride."

"Why don't you stay with Terry, sweetheart?" Ben suggested. "I'll drive the kids over to Holly's, stay there for a while, and then come back to pick you two up. It'll give you some time to talk."

"No, I'm going to be fine," Terry said. "You guys go ahead and take the kids over. I'll be there in no time."

Dee hesitated. "Are you sure?"

"Yes," Terry said in aspiration. "I'm sure."

After Ben drove away with DJ, Keith, and a reluctant Dee, Terry locked up the house and walked four blocks south to the nearby park. The wind whipped around her and she pulled her coat tight, buttoned it, and pulled her gloves from her pockets. After slipping them on, she shoved her hands into the pockets.

# Chapter 28

Opening the dishwasher, Wade's mother removed two coffee cups, and dessert plates. She placed the cups and dishes on the counter, opening the box of confectionary delights that Hugo had given Wade the day before. "Wow, these look delicious."

"They are. My neighbor Hugo makes them," Wade said.

He watched his mother, dressed in a plain flowered dress and neon-yellow socks. She wore her glowing mane piled on top of her head, and when she looked at Wade, her eyes nearly sparkled. Wade smiled, remembering the times that he and his mother spent at this very table having dessert and milk.

"How is everything going at work?"

"Good."

Wade heard movement coming from the living room and he immediately hoped that it was his grandmother. The past week, Wade had been avoiding his father. The last time Wade had visited while his father was at home, his father was rude and belligerent, and Wade thought it best if he avoided the man for a while, to steer clear of an argument. He'd made it a point to ask his mother if she and his grandmother were okay, and she assured him that they were.

A moment later, his father limped into the kitchen.

## Chapter 28

Nurjahan turned at her husband's approach. "Wade, we have dessert." She glanced inside the box as she spoke to her husband. "There are all sorts of goodies here, pecan and strawberry tarts, and I believe that's a slice of German chocolate cake."

Wade Sr. walked to his wife's side, peeking inside the box. He scowled and grunted.

"How you feeling, Dad?" Wade asked his father.

Wade Sr. did not reply. He crossed the kitchen and opened the refrigerator, grabbing a bottle of beer and opening it. Leaning against the refrigerator, he sipped his beer and watched Wade.

Nurjahan chose a strawberry tart from the box and walked to her husband. "Try it; I'm sure it's delicious."

She held the tart for Wade Sr., who scowled again before opening his mouth and allowing his wife to feed him the dessert.

He quickly turned and spit the tart into the sink. "Woman, are you trying to kill me? That tastes like shit!"

Nurjahan glared up at her husband. "That was not called for."

Wade immediately rose from the table. "Mama, I think I should leave. I'll come by and see you in a couple days."

After leaving his parents' house, Wade drove a few blocks and pulled into a 7-11 parking lot. After going inside and buying a cup of coffee, he sat in his truck, sipping from his cup as he watched various vehicles enter and leave the lot. He spotted a man opening the back door of his car and helping a boy out. The man took the child's hand and walked inside the 7-11 while Wade's mind swam with memories.

Wade never understood why his father hated him. Sometimes he would go to his mother, nearly in tears after one of his father's rants, and ask her, "Mama, why does Dad hate me?"

She would say, "Your father doesn't hate you, he loves you. He's just going through a hard time right now."

Wade so wanted it to be true. He would persuade himself that his mother was right and that things would get better.

One night, Wade lay staring at the ceiling. He was tired, but too eager to sleep. Tomorrow he was going to the movies with Sammy Atkins. It was his first real date and Sammy was pretty, funny, smart, and best of all she really liked him. He had been in bed since 10:30 and now it was after midnight. He eased the blanket back and headed down the hall to the bathroom for a drink of water. As he was passing his parents' door, her heard his father's raised voice.

"Nurjahan, I don't want your damned mother here. She'll be spying on me, judging me."

Wade could hear his mother's gentle voice, but could not make out what she was saying.

"Yes she will, and you know it. They're always judging me." He paused. "Don't you look at me like you don't have a clue as to what I'm talking about! They'll probably run back and tell him. I can just hear it, 'Johnny, Wade isn't good enough for Nurjahan, she should have married you.' "

When Wade's mother spoke, her voice was still calm.

"You know damned well what I'm talking about," his father snapped. "They always wanted you to be with Johnny. That's why your mother wants to come here, isn't it? So she can tell Johnny about his son! Wade, that bastard that the two of you conceived!"

Wade's heart lodged in his throat. He backed away from the door and dashed down the hall to his room. Dropping down on his bed, he shook his head. This couldn't be. This had to be a mistake. He knew who his father was; he knew who he was. No, he had to have misunderstood what his father had said. Wade slid under the blanket and pulled it over his head, going over what he had just heard again. This wasn't possible. But, that might explain why his father hated him, why his father treated him so badly. That had to be it.

After a few moments, Wade realized that his father was also mean to Adam. No, this definitely was a mistake. If someone else was his father that would mean his mother was with another man, and his mother wouldn't do that. She would never do that.

He lay in bed until nearly 4 AM before finally drifting off to sleep.

Wade avoided his mother for nearly three days, before she approached him. He was in his room, sitting on a chair, his school books spread out before him on the bed. His mother entered, closing the door behind her.

"Are almost finished with your homework?" She asked. Wade only shook his head. Nurjahan sighed. "Wade, what's going on?"

"Nothing."

His mother watched him for a few moments. Not one to push, she turned, prepared to leave him alone.

Wade blurted out, "Who's my father?"

His mother sucked in a sharp intake of breath before speaking. "You know who your father is. Why would you ask me such a thing?"

"I… I heard you and dad talking."

His mother sighed and took his hand, leading him to the dresser across the room. "Wade look," she gestured toward the mirror. He studied his reflection, seeing his father's grey eyes looking back at him. "How can you doubt who your father is?"

"Mama, I heard what dad said. I heard him say that he wasn't my father."

Nurjahan closed her eyes for a moment and then led Wade back to the bed. "Sit down, we need to talk." She sat next to Wade, taking his hand. "When your father and I met, it was wonderful. We fell in love almost instantly, and within a month, your father proposed. He called his mother to tell her the news, and she was not too happy, but the following month she arrived in Malaysia to meet me and attend our wedding. Upon arriving, she set out to do everything she could to stop the wedding. We did not let her succeed, and we were married anyway. She was so angry with your father that she told him that she disowned him; that she no longer had a son named Wade."

"Why? Why would she do that?"

His mother hesitated. "Because I was… different."

"Because you weren't white!" She didn't answer, and Wade's heart broke for his mother. "But I still don't understand why Dad says that I'm not his son."

"Your father and I had a friend, Jonathon, Johnny. Johnny was your father's best friend; they were like brothers. Somehow your father got the idea that Johnny and I were having an affair." She sighed. "One evening, Johnny came to see your father. Wade hadn't come home from work yet. I knew he would be arriving home soon, so I told Johnny that he could wait. When your father returned home and found Johnny there, he was so angry that he and Johnny argued. That was the last time the two of them ever spoke." Her fingers brushed

Wade's cheek. "Almost a year later, you came along. Your father was so proud, so happy that I had given him a son. Wade called his mother to tell her the good news about his son. She didn't say a word; she just hung up on him. It hurt him so much, and he promised that he would never turn his back on his children; would never hurt them, like he was being hurt." Wade felt tears sliding down his cheeks, his mother brushed them away as she continued. "When we moved to Chicago and your grandmother died, something changed in your father, and he convinced himself that I secretly longed to be with Johnny, and that you were his child and that's why you and I are so close."

"But you told him the truth. He knows that I'm his son."

"Yes, Wade, I have, and he does. Sometimes people don't see the truth when they're in pain. He's just confused. Losing his mother shattered something in him, and he's still hurting." She rose from the bed kissing his cheek. "Just give him time."

That was a month prior to Wade laying in the fetal position on their living room floor, his mother's small body covering his while his father kicked the both of them. Using the back of his hands Wade massaged his weary eyes and dug in his pocket for his cellphone.

***

Terry sat on a bench looking out at the small pond when her cellphone rang for the fifth time in the last half hour. She sucked her teeth, pulling it from her pocket, and checking it. Seeing that it was neither Dee nor Holly, she flipped the phone open saying "Hey," when she pressed it to her ear.

"Hey. How are you?" she heard Wade say.

Terry paused and then said, "Good."

"Is everything okay?"

"Just having a bad day."

"Anything I can do?" Terry looked around the park. When she didn't answer, Wade asked. "Where are you?"

"At the park a few blocks from my house."

"Tell me where it is," Wade said. Terry gave him directions and they hung up.

Within fifteen minutes, Wade's truck was pulling into the small parking lot about forty yards from where Terry sat on the bench. He got out of the truck, walked to the bench, and sat next to Terry.

"Hey."

"Hey," Terry said, hunching her shoulders against a cold breeze that instantly blew.

"So, what's going on?" Wade asked.

Terry looked around the nearly empty park. "Just having a bad day."

"Because?"

"My ex stopped by today."

"And?"

"And he said some pretty mean things, and they sort of bummed me out." Terry continued to look around, not wanting to meet Wade's gaze. "The sad part is that some of what he said was true."

Wade watched her as she became instantly interested in two birds fluttering around the lower branches of a tree. She sighed. "You know, I've done some really horrible things. About ten years ago, I decided that I wanted to marry a wealthy man. He had everything I thought I wanted, a fancy penthouse and millions in the bank." She paused before going on. "The problem is that he was seeing Dee." She looked at Wade, trying to read his reaction to her statement. "Of course, nothing happened between us, not that I didn't want it to. I was at a place in my life that I didn't care about anything but getting what I thought I deserved."

"Terry, we've all done things that were a bit crazy in our lives, things that we regret."

"Yeah, but we all didn't go to the extremes that I did."

"I don't care what you did in the past. I don't care what happened between you and some other man." he paused. "As long as you've come to terms with what's happened and you've learned from it, that's all that matters. I'm interested in who you are now." He watched her for a moment and then said, "Terry, I just care about who and how you are when you're with me."

Terry turned, resting her leg on the bench and faced him. "Um, a few months ago, I made the decision that I wasn't going to get into any relationships. Not for a whole year."

Wade smiled at her and nodded slightly saying, "Okay."

"I really like you though. And, I was just wondering…."

Wade leaned forward, pressing his lips against hers. As cold as it was, his lips were so warm and soft that Terry instantly moaned and melted into him. When she drew back, they looked into each other's eyes for a moment.

"I'd really like for us to get to know each other better" She said, barely above a whisper.

"I would too."

"Nothing serious; we can go slow and see what happens." Terry grinned at him and then leaned forward for another kiss.

Wade was the one who drew back this time. He stroked her cheek with the back of his fingers. Her cheek was as cold as ice. He frowned. "How long have you been sitting out here? You're freezing."

"Not really," Terry said, feeling the cold once he mentioned it.

"Come on," he said, rising from the bench and taking Terry's hand, pulling her to her feet. "Let me take you home."

"I'm supposed to go to Holly's house. She and Dee have called me about fifty times; I should really be heading over there. Do you think you can drop me off?"

By the time Terry reached Holly's house, Ben and Tyler were absolutely elated to see her.

"I'm so glad you're here," Tyler said. "It took everything Ben and I could do to keep these two from sending out a search party."

"Where were you?" Holly and Dee both demanded as they crossed the room to Terry's side.

"Are you all right?" Dee asked, massaging Terry's back.

"I'm fine, Dee." Terry looked at the concern on all of their faces. "I am, really."

"Dee said that you told them you were coming right over," Holly said, her tone accusing.

"I had to make a stop."

"You look upset," Dee said, examining Terry closely as she continued to rub her back.

"Why do you keep rubbing my back?" Terry said, pushing at Dee's hand. "What, do you think a genie is gonna pop out my ass? Geez."

Tyler and Ben both laughed, Tyler saying, "She's definitely all right."

"We're just concerned. Are you sure you're all right?" Dee said.

"Yes, I'm fine, give it a rest," Terry said, pushing

past Dee and Holly, and marching in to the kitchen.

Looking inside the refrigerator, Terry pulled out two bowls, one with potato salad and the other with the tossed salad. She carried the bowls to the counter and looked inside of the top drawer, retrieving two serving spoons. After removing the plastic wrap, she put a spoon in each bowl.

Holly walked into the kitchen from the dining room and crossed to the sink, rummaging in the utensil drawer. After a few minutes, she closed the drawer and turned on the water, rinsing her hands. She gave Terry a sideways glance and then leaned toward her, bumping Terry's shoulder. "You're good?"

Terry nodded and smiled. "I'm good."

After dinner, Holly suggested that they take a walk, saying that Dee needed to walk off those two extra helpings of potato salad. Ben and Tyler volunteered to stay with the children in order to give the women some alone time.

"Are you going to tell us where you went before you came to Holly's?" Dee asked, as soon as they left the house.

"Nope," Terry said, and Dee gave her an evil glare. "Okay. I just went for a walk, then a friend called, we met up, talked for a while, and I asked him if he could drop me off."

"Friend, huh?" Holly asked. "Anybody we know?"

Terry hesitated. "Yeah, Wade."

Dee grinned. "Ah, hot teacher Wade."

"Sexy motorcycle Wade?" Holly teased.

"Please, he ain't all that," Terry lied.

She didn't want to tell Dee and Holly that she was considering seeing Wade. She didn't want them to know that she was thinking of abandoning her pledge to not date for a year, at least, not yet.

"That's not what you said last week," Dee teased.

"I never said he was hot or sexy."

"Yeah, you did, you said if you were ever going to forget your oath to not be with a man for a year, you'd do it for him."

"Yep," Holly added. "I heard it myself."

"I didn't mean that I would actually give up my celibacy for him. I mean I might, but who wouldn't? Come on, the guy's a god. He's gorgeous, and he's smart and funny. Any woman would be lucky to have him." Terry scrunched up her nose and then quickly added, "But that doesn't mean I want him."

"Sounds like she's protesting a little too much. I think she likes him," Dee teased.

"I think she more than just likes him. I think she loves him," Holly said, using what they all knew was one of Abby's teasing voices.

"No, I don't," Terry snapped.

Dee jumped right on that. "Oohh she denied that way too quickly. She *is* falling for this guy."

Terry rolled her eyes. "Uh, no."

"Oh my goodness," Dee let out a fake sob fanning her face. "Holly, our baby is falling in love."

Terry laughed and lightly swatted at Dee's arm before walking ahead of them. Throwing her head high and putting a little extra swing in her hips she said, "Aw, both of you, bite me!"

# Chapter 29

"I can take Terry and the kids home," Tyler was saying, as Dee and Ben packed up the twins, preparing to leave. "If you guys take her and the kids home, you'll be going in the opposite direction."

"Thanks, Tyler," Terry said, taking their coats out of the closet.

"Okay. You know what," Dee said resting her hands on her hips. "This is so ridiculous, Terry you need a new car."

"Yeah, well, that's not going to happen right now, is it?"

"We could lend you…" Dee started to say.

"No," Terry cut her off.

"But…"

"No, I've borrowed enough from you, all of you. I have to do this on my own."

Ben slipped his coat on and turned to Terry. "Terry, look at it this way. What if something happened and you had to pick up Abby and Keith? How are you going to drive the two kids, the twins and any other kids you have in that small car? It's not logical. If you're going to be watching the kids, I'd like for them to be safe. So, a new vehicle would be just that, a safer means of transportation. When you get on your feet, you can pay us back, if you feel as though you have to."

Terry looked at the faces staring at her. Dee looked as if she was preparing for a fight; Ben looked as if what he'd just proposed was the most logical thing in the world, and Tyler's look was almost identical to Ben's, while Holly looked as if she was trying to come up with another argument as to why Terry needed a new vehicle.

Terry sighed. "Okay, but it has to be an older car. And it has to be something that I can afford."

"Absolutely," Ben said.

Five days later, Terry was standing on her front porch across from a red-cheeked man of about fifty, who was handing her a clipboard and a set of keys to a silver 2008 Dodge Caravan.

"Ma'am, I just need you to sign here," he pointed to a space on the clipboard. "And she's all yours."

After signing the necessary documentation, and handing the keys and title to her old car over, she walked down to inspect her new vehicle. Since baby Ben and Kyle were napping, she only spent a few minutes quickly looking around the interior of the van, before she rushed back inside the house.

She went into the kitchen, searching the list of telephone numbers that she kept next to the phone and dialed Ben's office. Once she was connected to Ben's office, she immediately said, "Hi, Ben, thanks for having the van delivered."

"No problem. Did they tow the old one away for you?"

"Yeah. Thanks for that too."

"Good."

"Um, I don't mean to sound ungrateful or anything like that, but, I thought we decided that I was going to get an older vehicle. Something I can afford."

"It is older, it's a 2008."

"But it only has 175 miles on it. That's not an older car."

"It's older than the 2009."

"Ben, you know what I mean!"

"Yeah, Terry, I know what you mean. Listen. You're family, and what good does it do for me to work and make a ridiculous amount of money if I can't help my family?"

"Yeah, but..."

"No buts, hear me out. I know you want to do things on your own, and I agree with you a hundred percent, but sometimes we all need a little help. I won't make it a habit of meddling in your affairs, but if I see that you're really trying and that you need help, I won't hesitate to interfere."

Terry paused and then said, "Thanks, cuz. I really appreciate it."

"I know you do."

"I'll pay you back."

"No, I don't want you to pay anything back. It's a gift for you and the kids." Ben hesitated. "But, there is something you could do for me."

"Sure, anything."

"It would be great if you would not let my sons eat anything like crayons or paste and justifying it by reminding us that such items are non-toxic."

Terry laughed. "But, they *are* non-toxic."

"Yeah, I know, but I'd rather the twins not eat any of those things, all the same."

Terry laughed again. "Right, no crayons, no paste; got it."

# Chapter 30

"Chicken nuggets and succotash?" Terry scrunched up her nose and shook her head. "Na, green beans."

She sat at the kitchen table, Dee and Holly next to her, and wrote on the weekly menu that she kept on the refrigerator.

Keisha walked in, crossing to the sink. She retrieved a glass from the dish rack and filled it with water. Leaning against the sink, she turned to watch Terry at the table.

"What's up, Keisha?"

"Nothing," she answered, taking a sip of water. "What'cha doing?"

"Writing the menu for this week."

"The daycare thing is going really well for you, huh?"

"It's going okay." Terry paused. "No, it's going better than okay. I can't believe I'm saying this, but I really like it. The kids and I have a good time together. I help them with their homework; sometimes we do crafts and play games. They make me laugh."

"Oh, I can tell, you seem much happier. And look at you, you're really good at it. I could just see you having people practically knocking down the door to bring their kids here."

## Chapter 30

Suspicion immediately sparked Terry's senses, and she looked up from what she was doing to eye Keisha. "There isn't something that you need to tell me, is there?"

"No, of course not; I'm just saying that I see you being really successful in your new business."

"Um hm." Terry placed the pen on top of the schedule and clasped her hands as she watched Keisha fidget under her gaze.

Keisha suddenly blurted out, "Terry Ann, I was wondering if Deion could spend the night."

"Nope." Unclasping her hands, Terry picked up her pen and scanned the menu again.

"Why? It will only be for tonight, and I did ask you. I could have done it without saying anything."

Terry continued to scan the menu as she spoke. "You asked me because you knew that if you let him spend the night without my permission, and I found out, which I would, I'd kick your ass. And the answer is still, no."

"But I pay rent. And Deion says that if I pay rent, I should be able to let whomever I want stay the night."

She looked up at Keisha. "Why can't you stay the night at Deion's place… oh sorry, he doesn't have one."

"He lives with…"

Setting the pen back on the table, Terry held up her finger, silencing Keisha, and ticking off her comments as she spoke. "For one, this is my house. When Deion contributes to the mortgage payment, I'll gladly allow him to have an opinion as to what goes on around here. But if he did contribute, his opinion still wouldn't mean shit, because I rule all of this." She twirled her finger indicating the space around her before ticking off another digit. "And two, you eat more then you contribute, so don't be telling me how you pay rent, little girl. You only pay a portion of your food cost, and I mean a portion; a very small portion." Terry picked up her pen tapping it against the menu.

"Terry An… um… Terry, I really like Deion, and we want to spend time together. His mom won't let us stay there."

"Hmm. Wonder why?" Terry looked up at Keisha, faking thoughtfulness. "Okay, this is how it's going to be. The only person who's going to be doing the nasty in this house is me. Got it? Good." Terry went back to writing her menu.

"But…" Keisha pleaded.

"No."

"But-"

Terry held her hand up, saying, "Uh," every time Keisha opened her mouth to speak.

Keisha left the room in a huff, mumbling about things not being fair, and a few other things that Terry didn't give a damn about.

A few hours later Terry barged into Holly's kitchen. "I'm going to have to do something about Keisha," she said, flopping down in the kitchen chair.

"Come on, Terry," Dee said, "she's not that bad."

"I don't know if I can last much longer without killing her."

"I'll admit, she can be a bit much at times, but she has a lot of good points," Dee said.

"You know, Dee's right," Holly said. "Maybe if you focus on the positive things, she won't get under your skin so easily."

"Well, she's a great cook; I'll give her that," Terry said.

"Good." Holly nodded. "What else?"

"Um… and she gets along wonderfully with the kids."

"See," Dee said. "Those are very good attributes. Now, what's the problem?"

"A lot of things. For starters, the guy that she's seeing, Deion, I told you guys about him. I know he's a loser, and that she's spending her money on him. She actually had the nerve to ask me if they could have a sleep over. Like I'm running some sort of kiddy camp, or worse, a whorehouse," Terry said with a snort. "And this dickhead told her that since she pays rent, she has a right to have whomever she wants to stay over. What kind of shit is that?"

"You know how it is when you're young and in love, Terry," Dee said.

"She's in heat," Terry stated flatly.

"Terry, you don't know that. She might be in love with this guy," Holly said.

"Well, Reds, I have an idea. Why don't you let them come to your place and bump nasties?"

Holly scrunched up her nose. "Uh, no thanks."

"I didn't think so," Terry replied. "It's not one specific thing that she does. It's sort of like having a hangnail, and you don't have a pair of nail clippers handy. You try biting it off, and then you find yourself biting and nipping at it. The next thing you know, it's driven you so crazy, that you've damned near gnawed your arm off trying to stop the torture."

Holly laughed as Dee shook her head at Terry's description.

"Okay, listen to this," Terry added. "The other day, we drove across an overpass, and Keisha asks me where all of the cars were going? I'm looking around, not seeing what she meant; I mean, we're on the road; of course there are a lot of cars. She points to the cars driving under us and says, 'Right there, where are they going?' I was like, 'Um under the bridge.' She sat there blinking for a moment and then said, 'The traffic flows under the bridge? Hmm, I never thought about it, but that makes sense.' When I looked at her, I realized that she was serious. I was so dumbfounded, I swear I had to have been staring at her for a full minute, because I almost rear ended an SUV."

Both Dee and Holly laughed. "You're kidding."

"No. I'm not, really." Terry laughed with Holly and Dee thinking about the serious look on Keisha's face. "Oh yeah, and guess what the hell she did the other day. She used my Fendi without my permission," Terry practically yelled.

Dee and Holly looked at each other.

"The suede one?" Dee asked.

"Yep." Terry huffed.

"The one you borrowed from Dee last fall and never returned?" Holly said in a singsong voice.

Terry ignored her. "The other day, when it was raining, 'Einstein' decided that she needed a larger bag to carry her books in." Both Dee and Holly groaned. "One that was waterproof. And, of course, we all know that suede is waterproof." Terry shook her head as she spoke.

"She didn't?" Holly gasped.

"Oooh…" Dee groaned.

"Ruined-com-plete-ly."

"Not good," Holly said biting into a carrot stick. "You know what? I love Keisha too, she's really sweet, but sometimes she tends to get on my nerves, and I don't have to live with her."

"See!" Terry said waving her hand at Holly. "It's like everything with her turns into a job, and not a small job, but an enormous project. And if she calls me Terry Ann one more time, I swear to goodness, I'll kill her."

## Chapter 30

"Terry Ann?" Keisha called as she walked into the kitchen.

Both Dee and Holly looked at Terry and their gaze followed hers to the cake plate in the center of the table. Next to it sat a cake knife. The three of them dived for the cake knife; Holly grabbed it first and rushed to the sink, laughing.

"What's going on?" Keisha asked, seeing the three women nearly rolling across the kitchen table.

"Nothing," Dee said, laughing as well.

Terry glared at both Dee and Holly, folding her arms across her chest.

Bang. Bang. Bang.

Terry walked into the kitchen when she heard the cabinets doors slam for the third time. She eyed Keisha, who stomped around the kitchen. Bang. She slammed the cabinet under the sink.

"Whatever's wrong, the cabinets didn't do it," Terry teased.

Keisha looked at her and rolled her eyes. "This doesn't makes any sense. I can't believe that we don't have any more teabags. Not a damned teabag in the house!" She snapped.

"Okay," Terry said, stretching out the word. "I think someone needs a time out." Keisha glowered at her. Terry sighed. "All right, what's going on?"

"Nothing."

Terry waited a moment, debating on if she wanted to convince Keisha to talk to her. Deciding to give her cousin some space, Terry turned to leave the kitchen.

"Deion is such a jerk."

Terry turned back to her. "Uh, he has a penis; of course he's a jerk."

Keisha dropped down in one of the chairs, tears glistening in her eyes. Terry sighed and sat down across from her.

"All right, what happened?"

"Deion and I had a fight." The tears that glistened in her eyes a few seconds ago spilled over the rims. "He's always openly checking out other girls."

Terry took her hand. "Honey, sometimes guys do that. I really don't think they mean anything by it. We look too. When you see someone who's attractive, it's natural to look."

"He doesn't just look. He leers. If a pretty girl walks by, he watches her for a long time. He even turns around and watches them when we're walking down the street, and he doesn't care that I'm there with him."

"Maybe you guys need to spend some time apart." Terry paused, hesitating before she spoke again. "Maybe Deion's not the guy for you." Terry watched as Keisha swiped angrily at the tears flowing down her cheeks. "I have an idea." She rose from the table, going to the living room and returning with her purse. She dug inside and produced the envelope that Keisha had given her with $300 for rent. She pulled off $160.00, removed a $20 from the $160, and then added it again. "I want you to go to the mall and pick out some outfits, try to get things that are on sale," Terry quickly added. "I want you to get something conservative. I have a few errands to run, and then I'll meet you at Holly's. I'll see if Wade's busy and if he's not, maybe Holly, Tyler and the three of us can go out. You never know, you might meet someone, and if you don't, at least you can go out and have a good time."

Terry wasn't able to reach Wade, and Holly and Tyler didn't feel like going out. Terry told Holly about

Keisha being down in the dumps, so they made plans to go to dinner and dancing the coming Saturday. Terry also told Holly that Keisha would be at her house in a few hours and she asked that Keisha wait there for her.

When Keisha walked into the kitchen, Holly nearly dropped the glass that she was holding. "Keisha, Terry said she sent you to the mall to get some new clothes."

"She did. I just got back."

Holly, Dee, and Tyler looked at one another and then at Keisha's outfit. She wore a jersey blouse with a leopard print bodice and black midriff, black jeans that had gold specks in the material and that were so tight that they looked like she had to oil herself up in order to slide them passed her hips. Her breasts were squeezed together so tightly that it honestly looked painful.

Holly slowly asked, "Um, honey, has Terry seen you yet?"

"No, she told me that she'd meet me here."

Holly looked at Dee and then Tyler again.

Tyler cut his eyes in Keisha's direction and then hesitantly said, "Baby, maybe you guys should take Keisha to the mall before Terry gets here. You know, give her a hand."

"Why, what's wrong?" Keisha asked confused.

"Nothing," Dee said rising from the table. "Not really, it's just…"

"Just what? I like it, and Deion said he loved it."

"Deion?" Holly asked, remembering what Terry said about him.

"I bet he did," Tyler said under his breath. Holly elbowed him. "What?" He asked innocently.

"Tell you what, why don't you keep that outfit, and we can go and get something a little more conservative too." Dee grabbed her purse. Holly nodded, moving away from the counter and toward the door.

"Hello!" Terry yelled from the living room.

"Oops, too late," Tyler said.

Terry walked into the kitchen. "Hey guys," She said laying a shopping bag on the table. She glanced at Keisha, did a double take, and then frowned. "What in heaven's name are you wearing?"

"The girls at the store helped me pick it out." she held out her arms and did a pirouette, showing off her outfit.

"Where the hell did you go shopping, Whores-r-us?"

Tyler snickered and Holly elbowed him in the ribs again. "What?"

"Keisha, when I sent you shopping, I wanted you to get something less flashy. Something that wasn't so…"

"Something more conservative," Dee added quickly.

"Yeah, okay," Terry sniffed. "What she said."

"But this is conservative," Keisha said.

Terry snorted. "Honey, that's only conservative if you're working somewhere where they sell cheap twats and ta-tas."

Tyler suppressed a laugh and Holly elbowed him yet again. "Ow!" he rubbed his belly in an exaggerated fashion.

Dee dropped her purse on the table. "Terry, come and help me bundle up the twins, and I'll go to the mall with you and Keisha."

"No. You don't want to take the twins to the mall; it'll be like a mad house," Holly said. "If you can take Abby and Keith home with you, Tyler and I'll go to the mall to help Terry with Keisha."

"We will?" Tyler asked, surprised.

"Yes, we will. Keisha needs a male perspective ."
"Oh yeah, a male's perspective like Deion's."

Almost two hours later, Terry, Keisha, Holly and Tyler, walked from the mall, each carrying a shopping bag. Tyler opened the door of the SUV, and Holly took Terry's bag, going around to the back to store them, while Terry walked to the back passenger door to get inside. When she got into the vehicle and closed the door, she looked around. A few yards away, she saw a tall familiar figure leaving the door of Macy's department store. He walked at a leisurely pace next to a tall blond. Terry was too far away to get a good look at her, but she thought it was the woman that Wade had been with before. Jennifer, that was her name. Wade had mentioned her before, saying that they had known each other for years. Terry couldn't make out her features, but she could see that the woman wore an expensive cream wool coat and 4-inch cream boots, her blond hair glistened in the sunlight and her cheeks seemed rosy from the cold wind.

They approached a blue BMW Mini Cooper and stopped as the woman used a key and opened the door. Wade stood talking to the woman for a moment, and then he leaned forwards, his lips quickly brushing hers, before she got into her car. Wade watched, waiting for her car to leave the parking lot before he crossed the lot, getting into his truck.

"Jerk," Terry groaned through clinched teeth.

"What's wrong, Terry Ann?" Keisha said, fastening her seatbelt.

Terry met Keisha's gaze and then bit her lip. "Nothing." She turned away to look out the window and watch Wade's truck pull from the lot. She swiped at an unchecked tear that ran down her cheek "Freaking asshole," she muttered.

She should have known better. She should have known not to trust a man like Wade. One who was so sweet and caring, it was probably all bullshit. She knew he was too good to be true. He probably was just hanging around her until he got tired of her or until she put out.  He would use her and discard her. The vehicle was eerily silent. She glanced around: Tyler, Holly, and Keisha were all watching her.

"Are you all right?" Holly asked, concern shining in her eyes.

"Yeah, I'm all right," Terry said, forcing a smile. "Do you think Dee and Ben will mind keeping the kids a little longer? I feel like a margarita." She turned glancing out the window again as they pulled from their parking space. *You are not going to get away with this, Wade Nelson. I am not the one.*

# Chapter 31

The following Friday, Terry merged into the flowing traffic on the L street. It was 7:10 pm and she had told Wade that she would not be at his house until eight. She figured that she would be there in another ten minutes and was hoping that he would not be ready when she arrived. If things went as she had hoped, she would have time to look around his apartment for any signs of him having a serious relationship, before he had finished his shower. When she arrived, Terry parked her van across from the apartment building and sat watching Wade's window. He was sitting at his computer desk, studying the monitor. He opened the drawer, pulled out some papers, and flipped through them before he reached for the telephone. As he, dialed the phone, he kept looking up at the computer monitor. He talked for a few moments, laughed, talked for a few more moments, and then clicked the phone off to set it on the desk next to the keyboard.

Terry immediately wondered whom he had called. *Probably his girlfriend, the bastard.*

***

Wade pulled his truck into the parking space. He glanced over at Terry, who had been uncharacteristically quiet the entire evening. He and Terry had gone out several times in the last few weeks and the one thing that he had learned about Terry was that she was *always* late. This evening, she had arrived at his apartment twenty minutes before the agreed upon time, which was odd. She rushed him along when she entered his apartment, saying that she didn't want to be late for the movie, and hadn't really spoken to him since they left the apartment, except answering any questions he might ask.

He turned on the ignition as he watched her. She looked in the direction of the theater, but her mind seemed to be miles away. Reaching for her hand, he gently tugged, drawing her attention to him. "Hey, babe, is something wrong?"

Terry looked up at him, and blinked. Wade wasn't sure, but it looked to him like she could cry at any moment. "No, everything's all right. Let's get inside. I want to get some popcorn, and get a good seat before the theater fills up."

Before Wade could get out of the truck and walk to Terry's side, she had already opened her door, got out and was headed across the parking lot.

***

They walked down the steps and slipped past several people, making their way to the center of the row to sit down. Terry scooted forward in her seat, slipped her coat off, and put it on the seat to her right. Wade waited until Terry's hands were free, and then gave her the popcorn and drinks to hold while he removed his coat. He leaned across Terry, placing his coat on top of hers.

He looked into her eyes and smiled. "We were in such a hurry when we left my apartment, I didn't have the chance to greet you properly. Good evening, beautiful."

***

Leaning toward her, his lips gently brushed hers, and then he drew back only a fraction, his eyes meeting hers. She could see the heat there that was meant for only for her, before his mouth covered hers. Terry's eyes fluttered closed, and a soft sigh escaped when his tongue brushed hers, sending a surge of electricity through her. She could swear to anybody who asked that her toes literally curled. Wade nipped her lower lip lightly before ending the kiss, and Terry opened her eyes just as the lights went down.

"Woooow," Terry heard one of the women sitting in the row of seats behind them say.

"Damn, makes me want to go home to my husband," another said in a husky voice. "I wonder if she'll consider changing seats with me."

Terry closed her eyes again, and tried to ignore what she knew was the sound of her heart shattering. She thought about the key hidden in the side pocket of her purse, the one that she had swiped from Wade's apartment no more than thirty minutes ago. Tomorrow, Terry would know what was going on. She would know if Wade was the sweet loving man he appeared to be, or if he was someone who used women and tossed them aside. Damn, she was glad she had talked Wade into coming to see *My Sister's Keeper*. That way, when she cried for the family in the movie, she could also cry for herself.

# Chapter 32

Terry got out of the SUV and reached into the back seat for her tote bag. She hefted the bag onto her shoulder and froze, hoping that Dee didn't hear the three spray-paint cans clink together. Dee got out of the vehicle and walked around to stand in front of it.

"Tell me again why you wanted me to come with you, if you're just picking up Wade's laundry."

"Because, I have a surprise for him," Terry said, patting her tote.

"What sort of surprise?" Dee said, reaching for the corner of the tote to peer inside.

Terry pulled the bag out of Dee's reach. "Nothing much; I'm going to fix dinner for him, and I was hoping you'd help."

Dee grinned at her, nodding. "Sure, I'll help." She followed Terry across the lot and into the apartment building. "Did you bring candles?" Terry glanced over her shoulder as Dee went on, "I'm thinking that we can set the table really nice. Once we get the meal started, I can run down to the store for a bunch of flowers and candles, if you forgot them."

"Ah… sure."

"Terry, this is so romantic."

"Yeah, romantic."

## Chapter 32

Terry walked up the steps with Dee close behind, talking a mile a minute. They stopped at the apartment door, while Terry dug the key out of her pocket. Before putting the key into the lock, Terry knocked on the door.

She glanced at Dee and grinned. "Just in case."

Dee grinned at her and nodded while Terry unlocked and opened the door. They entered the apartment and Dee casually looked around as Terry turned and headed down the hallway towards the bedroom.

"Be right back. Don't do anything yet," She told Dee.

"You don't want me to get started on the meal?"

"No, let me go and make sure Wade's not in the bedroom, napping, or something."

Dee nodded and stood next to the door, her hands in her pockets, waiting for Terry to return.

Terry walked down the hall, and when she reached the bedroom, she rushed across the room, dropping her bag on the bed and opened the dresser drawers, looking for any sign of a woman's personal belongings. Not seeing anything, she went into the bathroom and checked in the medicine cabinets and the cabinet under the vanity.

Nothing!

She went back into the bedroom and checked the closet – nothing again. Walking to the bed, she opened the drawers of the nightstand and her stomach dropped. In it was a photo of Wade sitting on a bench; his arms wrapped around Jennifer, and she was leaning back against him. Wade smiled broadly for the camera, while Jennifer had a look of someone who was happy and at peace with life. Terry felt tears burn her eyes and she clinched her teeth to fight the desire to sob.

She dropped the photo back inside the drawer. "Hump, figures, bastard!" She slammed the drawer, glancing up and out the window. Across the parking lot, she saw Wade backing his motorcycle into his usual parking spot. "Aw shit! Kiss my ass!"

She turned, headed for the bedroom door, froze, spun, and grabbed her tote bag before she bolted down the hall. Running toward the living room, arms flailing, Terry bellowed, "Abort mission! Mayday! Mayday! May—Daaay!"

Dee's eyes grew large as she looked around, a panic-stricken expression on her face. She immediately stepped from one foot to the other as if she was preparing to run. "What, what the hell are you talking about?"

When Terry reached Dee's side, she grabbed her arm and tugged her in the direction of the bedroom. "He's coming, we need to hide."

Dee pushed Terry's hand away, still looking around. "What, what's going on? Who's coming… Hide? What do you mean, hide?"

"You know! Hide! That thing you do when you don't want someone to see you!"

Dee's eyes grew even larger, if possible, and then she gasped, "You said that Wade knew that you were doing his laundry, you said that you were going to-"

"I lied!" Terry cut off the rant that she knew was coming. "So, we need to hide, right now!"

Terry hurriedly pulled Dee down the hall in the direction of the bedroom.

"Oh shit! Shit, shit, shit. Girl, what the hell did you do?"

"This is not the time! We're about to have a major problem!"

"God, I swear I'm going to kill you!" Dee was saying as she frantically looked around the bedroom for somewhere to hide.

"Where are we going to hide?" Terry anxiously jerked on Dee's arm.

## Chapter 32

Dee stepped from foot to foot again, looking as if she might wet her pants at any moment, while she glanced around the room. A part of Terry thought that if this situation were not so dire, she would have laughed. "Uh…Under the bed." Dee darted toward the bed.

Terry frowned, propping her hands on her hips. "What? What sort of idiot hides under a bed?"

"The same sort of idiot who gets her cousin to commit breaking and entering. Now move your ass!"

"Under the bed, right!" Terry pulled the comforter up preparing to crawl under the bed when she noticed that the bed was a platform storage bed. "What in the hell is that?"

Dee spun around, pulling the closet door open, and they both saw that it was crammed full of boxes. She spun grabbing Terry's arm. "Living room closet!"

They ran down the hall and reached the coat closet just as the front door swung open and Wade stepped inside.

Wade jumped, startled, and dropped the stack of papers that he held. They went fluttering to the floor. "What the hell?"

Terry froze when they reached the door, and Dee ran into her back, knocking her slightly off balance. She looked up and into Wade's surprised face. "Um… Hi, I, um, we can explain."

Wade eyes narrowed. "Terry, what the hell are you doing in my apartment?"

Dee stepped from behind Terry and plastered a huge smile on her face. "Hey, Wade, how are you? I'm Dee, Terry's cousin." She reached out her hand and turned up her smile a notch. He glared at the extended hand and then back up at her. She withdrew it slipping it behind her back. "Well, um, we… There's a perfectly good explanation for us being here. Right, Terry?"

Terry’s emotions went from startled, to surprised, to angry in a matter of seconds. She glared at Wade and immediately folded her arms under her breasts; her right foot was making a muffled but steady patting sound on the carpeted floor.

Dee nudged her forward. “Terry, tell Wade that we were just passing by and...”

“You said that you and your little buddy Jennifer were only friends.”

“Uh?” Both Dee and Wade asked simultaneously.

“You heard me.” Terry’s head moved from side to side as she poked a finger in Wade’s chest.

Dee stared at her cousin for a moment, her mouth agape, when realization suddenly hit her. “Oh-my-god.” She groaned, covering her eyes. “I’m going to be an inmate's bride.”

“What the hell are you talking about?” Wade gritted out.

“Why would you tell me that you and Jennifer were only friends, when there is clearly more to your relationship?” Terry demanded.

“Oh lord, just kill me now, why don’t you?” Dee muttered.

Glancing down, Terry eyed the scattered papers. She squinted, seeing photos. Most of the photos were of females. Not just any females, but females that looked young enough to be high school girls. Terry’s mouth hung open for a moment. “What are you doing with those?”

“A project I’m working on,” Wade said and quickly leaned over, gathering the papers.

His jacket shifted slightly and Terry saw the dull black handle of a… "Oh my god! Gun! Gun!" Terry screamed.

“What?” Dee asked, confused.

## Chapter 32

"Gun! Dee, he has a gun!" Terry took a step back, grabbing Dee's arm and jerking it.

Clearly moving on instinct, Dee took a quick step forward, and with her free arm gave Wade a sharp jab to his right eye. As Dee struck, Terry took that opportunity to run forward. She tried to push past both Dee and Wade and out of the apartment.

"Freeze!" Wade yelled, his right hand automatically going for his weapon after the assault. He must have felt more than seen Terry rushing toward him, as he quickly pushed her back with a sweep of his left arm.

Terry stumbled back a few feet, only seconds before Terry and Dee both screamed and tried to scatter, running into each other.

"I said freeze! Shut the hell up!" Bending at the waist, Wade grabbed his right eye with his left hand, while his right hand rested on his weapon, all the while he kept his good eye on the two lunatics standing in his living room. "Are you fucking crazy?" He yelled through gritted teeth.

"Oh lord! Please don't kill us!" Terry begged.

"My husband knows where we are!" Dee was saying at the same time.

"I said, shut up!" Wade pulled his badge from his back pocket, holding it toward the two cowering women.

They froze and Dee reluctantly moved closer, she sucked in a deep breath. "Oooh, ho–ly–shit." she glanced over at Terry and through clinched teeth said. "God, I hate you."

"I can't believe this; I hit a law enforcement officer; not just any law enforcement officer, but a freaking FBI agent. Oh God, I am in so much trouble."

"Just stop it," Terry said. "Just calm down. This is not as bad as it seems. It was a mistake, and besides, you didn't even hit him that hard. Geez."

Dee gave Terry a heated glare. "Did I mention that I hate you?" Terry rolled her eyes toward the ceiling. "Ben is going to be pissed. I promised him just last week that I wouldn't be getting into any more trouble. Oh lord, I can't go to jail—what about my babies—they're not even two yet. And what about the new baby?" She placed her hand on her round belly, "I can't give birth in jail. They may not have the right drugs," Dee babbled. "No, I'm sorry I can't do it. I can't do the time; I just can't do the time."

Folding her arms Terry looked toward the kitchen where Wade mumbled and cursed as he banged the cabinet doors shut. His long-sleeved light blue tee shirt hugged his wide shoulders and back and tapered to his waist where it was tucked inside of his jeans. Terry's eyes traveled down his body to his tight butt, and his muscular thighs. She grinned when he shook out a blue plastic bag, stepped in front of the refrigerator, and pushed the button for the ice dispenser. Ice flowed from the dispenser, falling into the bag and out a hole in the bottom. Cursing, he threw the bag inside of the sink. He looked inside the cabinet, grabbed another bag, and picked up the ice cubes from the floor shoving them inside.

*Damn, he's even hotter when he's mad.* Terry looked to her left, seeing Dee glowering at her. "What?"

"Why are you smiling?" Dee growled. "There is nothing funny about this situation."

"My man is really hot, isn't he?" Terry said looking at Wade and then turning back to Dee. "Tell the truth, he's hot."

## Chapter 32

Dee narrowed her eyes, giving Terry a furious glare. Terry had seen that look before; she had seen it on one of the old Twilight Zone episodes. It was the same look that this six-year-old monster kid gave some poor sap who'd pissed him off. A look of heated rage that made the kid turn this guy into a giant jack-in-the-box and whisk him into the cornfield. Terry shuddered and looked away.

Wade walked in from the kitchen, carrying a blue grocery bag with ice cubes in it that he had placed on his eye. He sat on the coffee table in front of Dee and Terry.

Dee groaned. "Oh lord, what am I going to do?"

"You? What about me? What am I going to do? What about the boys? Who's going to take care of them? And, what am I going to wear? I can't wear olive drab," Terry said, shaking her head.

"Um, I'd take care of the boys for you. Ben and I will take really good care of them. We'd make sure they had everything that they needed and got a good education. We'd even bring them to see you every visiting day and make sure that they never forgot you." she paused. "And besides, you'd make a much better jail house wife than I would."

"Ah—yeah, right. I barely made an adequate heterosexual wife; I'd make a horrible prison homosexual wife. Hey! What the hell do you mean, bring the boys to see me?"

"No, you'd be okay," Dee said, skipping the question about the kids.

Wade looked at the two women, clearly – from the expression on his face – not believing what he was hearing. They had to be nuts, they had to be, here they thought that there was a chance of them going to jail and all they could think about is who'd make a better prison wife.

"You were a great wife," Dee went on.

Terry shook her head. "But, you cook better than I can."

"Yeah, true." Terry looked at her with huge eyes, and Dee quickly said. "But cooking isn't everything; your cell would be spotless."

"You think so?"

***

Wade had had enough. After running his free hand through his hair, he decided that it was time to put an end to the foolishness. "All right."

"Sure, your house is always in order, it's always so tidy," Dee said as she kept talking.

"Cut it out," Wade raised his voice a little more.

Dee went on. "And you're great with the laundry. Your whites are always so bright."

Wade whistled. Both Terry and Dee looked at him as if they had just remembered he was in the room. "Enough!"

Bringing his free hand to his face, Wade groaned and winched at the pain in his eye. He was helplessly in love with the most beautiful, craziest woman he'd ever met. Dropping his left hand, he looked back up at Terry with his good eye.

"Lemon juice," Terry whispered to Dee.

Wade glared at her. Terry made a motion of locking her lips with a key and throwing it away.

"Okay. This is your last chance. I want the truth, and I want it now!"

"Um…" Terry began. "See… this is what happened…"

"Oh-my-freaking-god," Dee knew – from experience – that when Terry began a story with, "See, this is what happened," it was bound to be a lie. She brought her hand to her forehead. "I can't believe this. I can't freaking believe this. We're going to jail."

# Chapter 33

Terry bit her lip and glanced at Dee from the corner of her eye. She paused, and must have quickly decided to go on the offensive, as she suddenly glared at Wade. "And you, I can't believe that you didn't tell me who you really are. You're an FBI agent. What are you doing impersonating a teacher? Why didn't you tell me what you really did for a living?"

Wade opened his mouth and closed it again. He couldn't believe what he was hearing, was she crazy? She had to be crazy, she had broken into his apartment with the intention of doing lord knows what, and she had the audacity to question him? Unbelievable.

"You don't get to ask questions," he said firmly, and watched as Terry raised her chin in defiance. He shook his head slightly. "The first thing I want to know is what the hell you are doing in my apartment?"

***

If she thought it would work, Terry would try to bullshit her way out of this mess, but, she could tell by Wade's demeanor and the set of his jaw that he was having none of it. Terry looked down and scratched her brow before looking back up at Wade. "Okay, I'm going to tell you the truth." She looked at Wade and then Dee, and then back at Wade. “Well, we came to see you.” Dee snorted and Terry cut her eyes in Dee’s direction. “You see, I just wanted to stop by and say hi. The door was ajar, so I thought; why not just wait for you inside?”

Dee huffed. “Hah! Oh, now you come up with a convincing lie.”

Terry glared at her. “Shut up!”

“Terry,” Wade cut in, “if you’re not going to tell me the truth…”

“Okay-okay,” Terry said, when she saw Wade rising from the chair; she exhaled dramatically and then sighed. “Okaaay… last Tuesday Holly, Tyler, and I took Keisha to the mall. When we were leaving, I saw you with that… blond.”

Wade frowned; cursed under his breath and used his left hand to wipe the water away that had dripped from the plastic bag onto his jeans. “Blond? What blond are you talking about?”

“You know what blond!” Of course Terry knew her name. She knew it was childish, but she did not want to say Jennifer’s name when she had to tell Wade that she’d been so jealous that she’d resorted to breaking into his home. “You know, your… ‘friend.’ ” Terry said, making quotation marks in the air.

“Jennifer?”

“Yeeess, Jennifer,” Terry said in a mocking but goofy voice. Wade frowned at her again, and Terry bit her lip going for a contrite look. “…Um, at the mall you two seemed really chummy. When she was getting ready to leave, you kissed her, and I wanted to see if you were playing me.”

Wade blinked at her. “And breaking into my home was the best way for you to find out if I was seeing her?”

"Breaking in is such an ugly term," Dee supplied quickly. Wade glared at her. "Well, it is. I prefer, sneaking. Yeah, sneaking; Ben would understand sneaking much more than breaking in."

Wade shook his head and then turned back to Terry. "And, how did you get in here?"

"I found the… key?" Terry made it a question more than a statement.

He tried to give her a menacing look but didn't think he pulled it off with one eye. "Found the key where, Terry?"

"All right, damn it!" She yelled, and then mumbling, she folded her arms. "I found it on your desk."

Wade sighed. "Terry, why couldn't you just come right out and ask me what you wanted to know? Why would you go behind my back like this?"

"What?" Dee blinked at him. "Have you even met my cousin?" she asked, obviously totally shocked at his question.

Terry elbowed Dee, rolling her eyes. "Because," Terry said, her eyes shifting from Wade's. "You're a man, and men lie."

"So, just because you've had bad experiences in the past, you think that every man you meet from now on is going to do you wrong? You don't think that I could be different?"

"Well, maybe. I mean, I wanted to think you were different, but… okay, I'll admit, I handled the situation wrong. I didn't mean for you to come home and catch us. No, I mean, I was just going to look around…Wait! That sounded just as bad, didn't it? Look, the truth is…"

"Okay, I have an idea," Dee interrupted. She scooted to the edge of the sofa and whispered in a conspiratorially tone to Wade. "How about if Terry comes and cleans your apartment a few days a week? For… let's say, a month?"

"What?" Terry's head snapped in Dee's direction.

Dee looked around the living room. "This place can use some sprucing up, and she can do a couple loads of laundry while she's at it."

"I can't believe you! Are you pimping me out?"

"Hush," Dee said waving a hand in Terry's direction, her eyes still on Wade.

Wade grinned at the look of incredulity on Terry's face. "Can she cook?"

Dee glanced at Terry, frowned, and then said, "Oh…" Before sitting back.

"Look, babe," Wade slid to the edge of the table, taking Terry's left hand in his; he tugged her hand, clearly trying to get her attention. "If we're going to have a relationship, you're going to have to learn to trust me."

"I can cook!" Terry said abruptly, still looking at Dee. Dee bit her lip and turned away. "I can, damn it!" Terry demanded.

"Yes, you can, honey," Dee said, reaching over and patting the back of Terry's hand that Wade held, and then she slid to the edge of the sofa again. "Okay, check this out," Dee suddenly said to Wade. "How about if my housekeeper comes over here a couple days a week; let's say… for the next month? She can fix you three meals each time and put them in your freezer. How about Tuesdays and Fridays? Ben won't notice a few days for a month. I can cover for her."

Wade laughed, and Terry snatched her hand from his. With indignation, she said, "Oh, Ben will know all right. He'll know just as soon as I tell him."

"Oh, be quiet, you. You can't tell him anything, it's your fault we're in this mess to begin with."

"You were the one who said I should check out any guy that I'm interested in. So, technically, this is your fault. I remember when you told me, 'Terry, you need to be careful about the sort of man you date. Check them out and see what they're about.' Now, all of a sudden, you're changing your mind?"

"Yeah, I did say that you should check them out, but I didn't mean that you should break into his home. And, I surely didn't mean for you to make me an accomplice. For crying out loud, we could go to jail!"

"Oh please. Don't be melodramatic," Terry huffed.

Wade dropped the plastic bag that held the ice onto the coffee table next to him and let off a loud whistle, bringing both Terry and Dee's attention back to him. Both women got a chance to get a good look at his eye. It was turning a rather ugly shade of red. They both winced, and Wade scowled at them.

Terry shook her head. "You know, it's not as bad as you might think." She tried to reassure him and prayed that her face didn't give her away. "Um… right, Dee?"

Dee, on the other hand, had a pained look on her face. "Ho–ly shit."

# Chapter 34

Terry got out of Dee's car. Well, more like jumped out. Dee was so pissed off that she barely stopped to give Terry a chance to place her foot on the sidewalk before she sped away. After keeping them at his apartment for almost an additional hour, Wade finally let Dee and Terry leave. He warned them that if they told anyone he was FBI, they'd both be charged with obstruction of justice. Dee was only too glad to agree to anything he said.

By the time Terry and Dee left Wade's apartment, Terry was sure that Dee was ready to offer up all of her worldly goods, including her unborn child, if only Wade promised not to tell Ben that they had broken into his apartment. Terry wasn't worried. Well, not too worried. Wade was royally pissed. Terry didn't know what he would do. So, she solemnly told Wade her entire plan from beginning to end. She even made a point of using the word 'snuck', instead of 'broke in.' She figured that if she admitted to breaking into Wade's apartment Dee would probably have had a massive stroke.

She even confessed that she was going to spray-paint 'Cheater' on his bed and bedroom walls with black paint if she found any proof that he was cheating on her, or Jennifer. She thought being completely honest with him would win her a few brownie points, but instead, both Wade and Dee just sat there staring at her as if she had lost her mind.

At that moment, Terry remembered what her grandmother always said to her about always being honest and how honesty would set you free. *Well, hell*, Terry thought now as she walked up the sidewalk and onto the porch. *That's a bunch of crock.*

Terry walked into the living room, seeing Keisha, Deion, and two other men wrestling with what looked to be a bed headboard as they tried to push it up the steps. "What the hell is going on?"

"Hey, Terry Ann, we're taking my new bed upstairs," Keisha said, pointing to what had to be the largest king-size headboard that Terry had ever seen.

Made of what looked like some dark exotic wood, each post had to stand six and a half feet with intricate carvings in it. The headboard alone probably weighed close to a hundred and fifty pounds.

"New bed? What the hell do you need a new bed for?"

"The other one was too small, so I got a bigger one."

"You can't afford that." Terry waved a hand at the massive piece of furniture. "That thing has to cost in the neighborhood of a thousand bucks."

"No, I rented it. I got the bed, box spring, and mattress for $65.00 a week."

Terry turned to the two men that stood on the step with the massive headboard. "Freeze!" She turned back to Keisha. "Keisha, there isn't enough space in that bedroom for a king size bed. The way the room is shaped, they probably couldn't get the mattress and box spring through the door. And if they could, there would barely be enough room for anything else in there."

## Chapter 34

Deion walked over to the armchair and plopped down. "Maybe you could cut the mattress and box spring in half. That way it would be easier to get it into the room."

Terry looked at him and blinked. "And how do you propose we put it back together?" she folded her arms, waiting for him to answer. He looked at her and she could tell that he was trying to give it some serious thought. One of the rental center employees was laughing uncontrollably and the other just grinned, obviously sharing the same thought that Terry was having. *This kid is an idiot.*

She glanced at Keisha, who looked at Deion as if he was absolutely brilliant. Or, it could have been lustful hunger. With Keisha, Terry was never sure. Shaking her head, Terry turned from Keisha and Deion.

"You!" Terry pointed at the moving men, "do not move. That shit is going back. You!" she pointed at Keisha, "come with me." Deion stood to follow Terry and Keisha to the kitchen. Terry turned to him. "And you, you just sit there and look pretty." He blinked at Terry a few times as if he couldn't comprehend what she'd meant. "Sit!" She demanded, and then, turning toward the kitchen, she marched away with a reluctant Keisha following behind.

"Okay, missy, just what the hell do you think you're doing?"

"I was thinking that I could use a bigger bed."

"You were thinking, or was all of this Deion's idea?"

"Well, we both…"

Terry put her hand up stopping Keisha. "No, there is a full-sized bed in that room and that's big enough for your rotund ass. Don't be making any permanent plans to stay here, because you've worn out your damn welcome, and don't be entertaining the idea of your little boy toy lying up in my house. Got it, sister?"

Keisha nodded.

Terry spun on her heel and walked back into the living room. She was almost past Deion before she slapped the back of his head and knocked his cap off. "Look shit-head," she stopped in front of him poking a finger in his chest. "You need to stop giving Keisha these stupid-assed ideas. There is no way in hell that you're going to be sleeping, napping, or screwing in my damned house, so you'd better forget it. If I catch you doing any of the things that I just mentioned, I'm going to take my baseball bat and break your kneecaps. Got it?" She poked her finger in his chest extra hard for emphasis. He had the decency to look like a chastised child before he nodded and leaned forward to pick up his hat. "And don't put that damned hat on in my house again." She barked turning away from him. She pointed the index finger of both hands at the movers and then pointed toward the door. "Move it out, boys."

The younger of the two, who was clearly the boss, smiled at Terry. "Yes, ma'am."

# Chapter 35

Terry stood in the mirror looking at her profile. She held her head tilted to the side, and saw every imperfection. Maybe she should have forgone those shortbread cookies and hot chocolate last night. When all was said and done, she didn't look too bad. Her breasts were still high, and her hips and thighs were still shapely. But, it was that little bit of a pouch that her eyes kept zooming in on. She held her shoulders back.

"Before, after, before, after," She chanted a mantra, sucking in her tummy and letting it back out several times, before her shoulders sagged. "Damn. Maybe I should go for something low cut. Something *really* low cut, that'll take the focus off my gut. Yeah," she said crossing the room to her closet and selected a plum-colored lightweight sweater with a plunging neckline and cream slacks.

Searching through her lingerie drawer, she selected a purple pushup bra and matching panties. Grinning, she went into the bathroom to get ready.

Wade reached for the blue plastic bottle of liquid soap and squeezed a large dollop in the towel.

"Yeah," he called in answer to the tap on the bathroom door.

"Can we talk for a minute?" Jennifer asked.

“Sure, I'll be out in a minute.”

“No, take your time,” she said, her voice becoming louder as Wade immediately realized that she had entered the bathroom. “We can talk in here.”

Wade heard the clicking of her heels on the tile floor. Even though the shower door was frosted, he could make out Jennifer’s silhouette sitting on the toilet with her legs crossed and one elbow resting on her knee with her chin propped on her fist.

“Jenn, um… If Terry were here, she would have a bit of a problem with you coming in here while I’m in the shower.”

Wade saw her head turn in the direction of the shower. He was sure she hadn’t realized what she’d done. She felt so comfortable with him that she didn’t think anything of his being in the shower.

“I’m sorry,” she said, standing and heading toward the bathroom door. “I didn’t mean...”

“I know you didn’t.”

“I’m just so used to…”

“I know…

“I know you like Terry, and I don’t want her to get the wrong impression. I really don’t want to cause a problem.” She quickly left the bathroom.

Ten minutes later, Wade walked into the living room wearing a black long-sleeved shirt and black jeans. He walked to Jennifer to wrap her in an embrace. “Care to tell me what’s going on?”

She sighed, resting her head on his shoulder. “I don’t want to lose you, you’re my best friend.”

“I’m not going anywhere.”

“Yes, you are.” She sighed again. “Do you remember me telling you about Seth’s girlfriend, Hanna?”

“Yeah.”

# Chapter 35

"And, I told you how sweet she was, and how much Seth seemed to love her?"

"Um hm."

"Well, I didn't tell you how, when Hanna and I met, things seemed to change with Seth and my relationship. Whenever I called to invite him and Hanna out to dinner, Seth made arrangements for us to meet, and then within hours of our meeting, he'd call and cancel, saying that he and Hanna had something planned and he'd forgotten or hadn't checked with her first."

"Jenn, you know Seth, he's always been a self-absorbed asshole. He didn't check with his girlfriend before making a dinner date with you…"

"Seven times, Wade. It's happened seven times. And, this is not the only time something like this has happened. Whenever I have friends, and they meet someone, their women don't want me around. That's why I don't have any female friends. It's like they don't trust their men around me, and so they don't even want to be my friend."

"That's their insecurities; it has nothing to do with you."

"But it does. My friends are the only family I have; when you guys are gone, who'll I have? I understand the insecurity of these women, I really do. Lord knows, I feel insecure at times, but I can't help the way I look or who I am." She heaved a heavy sigh, backing out of Wade's embrace. "You're my best friend, and I just think of you like one of the girls."

"What?"

She laughed at the look on his face. "Not one of the girls, but you know what I mean. I don't think of you in a sexual way."

"I know that."

"But, will Terry know that?"

“Sure she will,” Wade assured her, pulling her into another embrace. He sure hoped that Terry would know that; if not, he didn’t know what he was going to do.

Terry looked at the woman sitting across from her closely. She could tell that Jennifer’s hair was naturally blond with brilliant gold highlights. She had perfect teeth, a perfect nose, and perfect full lips that no way came from a surgeon’s scalpel. Her long gracious fingers were tipped with smooth manicured nails and her outfit was impeccable. As she talked about her last job and her upcoming assignment, in Hawaii, she occasionally reached across the table and affectionately touched Terry’s hand.

*Of course she’s a model*, Terry thought. *What else would she possibly be*?

Terry watched the sincerity shine in Jennifer’s eyes when she had asked Terry what she did, and Terry told her that she was a childcare provider.

“Oh good lord,” Jennifer had said. “It takes a special kind of person to take care of children. I could never do that. I love children, don’t get me wrong, but I don’t know the first thing about taking care of them, least of all be a childcare provider.”

Terry tried to dislike her, she really did, but Jennifer’s personality was so pleasing and open that it would turn a spinster’s cold cruel heart into sweet fluffy cotton candy.

*God,* Terry groaned, *she’s so perfect, she could make Barbie want to slit her own wrist.*

“I’ll be in Hawaii for the photo shoot of next summer’s issue of National Sports magazine. After that, I think we’ll be off to Australia,” Jennifer was telling Wade and Terry. “I’ll be gone for Christmas, but I’ll be back before New Year’s. I know someone who’s having a party, and I'd really love for you guys to come with me," She said, before reaching out and touching Terry's hand again.

"So," Terry said, gently removing her hand, picking up her glass, and taking a sip of water. "How did you two meet?"

"We met when I lived in California." Jennifer looked at Wade, and he nodded slightly. "Well. I had just moved to LA and I met this guy. He told me that he was a movie producer and that he wanted me to come down and audition for a part. I was young and naïve, so I went. It turned out this jerk wasn't a producer, but a drug dealer, and it was just my luck that not more than three minutes after I arrived, the cops and FBI raided the place. Wade was one of the agents. After they figured out that I didn't have a clue as to what was going on, they told me I could leave. I went outside, sat on the curb, and bawled my eyes out."

"Really?"

"Yep. You see, I had left home almost a month before that, bad family situation. When I thought that this was going to be my big break, I had splurged on an expensive outfit and new shoes, spending what little money I had left. Wade found me sitting on the curb crying like a baby. He drove me to the dump that was my apartment, and later he helped me get a job as a waitress in this upscale bistro. He even drove me to auditions when he wasn't busy. One afternoon, I met Tito, a scout for the agency that I model through now. He liked my look and they signed me on. Wade and I have been best friends ever since. He's like the brother I never had, even though I have two brothers. My family is just… well never mind about that. Wade is just a wonderful guy." Jennifer reached across the table, taking Wade's hand.

Terry watched the exchange between Wade and Jennifer for a moment. "Excuse me."

She rose, dropping her napkin on the table, and reached for her purse, heading in the direction of the restrooms. A few minutes later, she walked out of the stall to the sink and washed her hands. She pulled several paper towels from the dispenser, when the bathroom door opened and she looked up to see Jennifer enter the restroom. *Great.*

"Terry, can we talk?" Jennifer asked.

"Sure, what's on your mind?" Terry said as she dropped the paper towels into the garbage bin and opened her purse, searching for her lipstick.

"I could be wrong, but I get the feeling you don't like me."

Terry paused during her search, looked up in the mirror to meet Jennifer's sincere blue gaze and sighed. She turned to the other woman. "Unfortunately, I do." Seeing the confused look on Jennifer's face Terry added, "I mean, I like you."

"And why would that be unfortunate?"

"Look at you, you're perfect, you're sweet, and you're successful."

"You're a beautiful woman, Terry." Jennifer snorted. "You know you are, and, I'm not the least bit interested in Wade."

Now it was Terry's turn to snort – in disbelief. "You'll forgive me, but I don't quite believe you."

"I'm not. Wade is a wonderful man, and I love him, but he's not the sort of person that I'm attracted to."

Terry folded her arms leaning against the counter. "Wade is an extremely handsome man, so I find it hard to believe that you don't find him attractive."

"Wrong gender," Jennifer said quickly.

"Uh?"

## Chapter 35

Jennifer sighed. "Terry, I would be more interested in you than I would be in Wade." Terry stared speechless, her mouth open. She let it snap shut. "I've never told anyone, I don't want anyone to know. Wade knows, and a select few friends, but I don't want anyone else…"

"I wouldn't, I mean, I won't." Terry would have never guessed. This woman, this beautiful woman that more than half the men in the world would want, was a lesbian. She realized she was staring again. "I'm sorry. Look, Jennifer, I don't mean to be rude. It's just."

"You don't see how I could be a lesbian?"

"No, that's not what I was thinking." Terry paused and then said, "Yeah, I guess I was thinking that too; but, I was also thinking, how can you hide something like that?"

"Easy, the women I date don't want anyone to know that they're lesbians."

"But why?"

"A lot of people are still narrow-minded, and I like being a model. I'm afraid of what will happen when I finally come out. I just hope…" Jennifer shook her head.

Terry took her hand and squeezed it. "I'm sure everything will be fine, and I won't breathe a word to anyone."

Jennifer smiled. "Thanks. I want you to know that I was being honest when I said that Wade was like a brother to me. He's always been there, looking out for me, like a big brother would do. Neither one of us has now, or in the past, had the idea that we were anything more." She took Terry's hand adding, "So don't worry."

Terry looked at this stunning woman standing before her with such sincerity and warmth shining in her eyes. She couldn't help but smile. "Thanks."

"For what?"

"Coming in here to talk to me; most women wouldn't bother."

Jennifer waved the comment away. "He really likes you, you know."

"I like him a lot too."

"Good. All I ask is that you treat him right."

When they returned to the table, Terry was more relaxed. By the end of lunch, she had even invited Jennifer to Thanksgiving dinner at Dee and Ben's.

# Chapter 36

Rolling onto her back, Terry groaned, reaching for the phone. "What?" she murmured into the phone.

"What are you doing?" David said not trying to hide his distain. "It's almost noon, are you asleep?"

"What do you want, David?"

"Why are you in bed? What the hell are you doing?"

"David, what do you want?"

He paused. "I want to spend some time with Keith. It's his birthday."

"Not today, David. I'm not feeling well. I'm waiting for Dee to come and pick Keith up and do something with him. I'll do something special with him tomorrow."

"Terry, I want to spend time with him."

"David, no, not today. It's not a good time."

"It's the perfect time." He hesitated as he waited for Terry to answer and then said, "Look, Terry, I'm serious this time."

"I don't want him disappointed on his birthday"

"I don't either. I know I haven't kept my word before, but this time I will. It's just going to be me and Keith this evening; just the two of us. I want to spend his birthday with him, make it special. Shareese is going to her mother's house. They're having some kind of party, Mary Kay, Avon or some woman thing. She's taking the boys with her and they're spending the night. I swear, it'll be just me and Keith. If you can just bring him to my job around 4:30, I'll be waiting. Please."

Terry followed the car, the car she knew only too well, from the parking lot. It was 4:30, she was there, Keith was there – and David was not! This was until she saw him and 'that woman' pulling out the back way. So, she'd followed. Now, finally, they were stopped. So, she pulled up behind them and jumped out of the driver's seat.

"David, what the hell? You asked me to bring Keith, you begged me to bring him."

David gave a little jump of surprise as Terry came up alongside his car. The prick was so timid; he actually left the window up as he spoke to Terry. "I'm sorry, Terry; I'll make it up to him. Shareese met me at work and reminded me of something we had to do. I'm sorry, really I am this time."

Terry glared at the woman who smiled smugly at her from the passenger seat. Terry walked to the front of the car and leaned on the hood. "No, you're not going anywhere, damn it. You're not going to hurt my baby. Not any dammed more!" Clasping both hands together, she used her fists and banged on the hood of the car.

"Terry, get the hell away from my car." David said, throwing the driver's door open and getting out.

"No!" Terry kept yelling, as she banged the top of the car. "You're not going to hurt my babies again."

Shareese opened her door, stepping out of the car as well. "Get away from the car, bitch."

She looked at Terry with disdain. Terry's hair was disheveled and her eyes were so red from fever that one might have thought she was possessed.

## Chapter 36

Terry glared at Shareese, and through clinched teeth, she uttered. “Don't do it, little girl. I've had a shitty month and an even shittier year, and I'd like nothing more than to kick someone's ass. And the opportunity to kick your ass, well, that would just make me, oh so, happy.”

Shareese looked at David and then back at Terry before getting back into the car.

***

Wade massaged his brow, trying to ease the headache he’d had for the last two hours. He tried to focus on what Jennifer was telling him about her last photo shoot, but he had too many things on his mind.

It was Saturday afternoon, and Jennifer had popped in for a surprise visit. When she found out that Wade was home alone, she had dragged him out of the apartment for a day of fun. He had hoped that he and Terry could do something, maybe take the boys to the movies. He called her that morning, but only got her answering machine. Now he was trying to figure out what was going on. He and Terry seemed to be getting close; he could tell that she cared for him, and he was hopelessly in love with her. The problem was, whenever they seemed to take two steps forwards, she seemed to take one step back.

“So, I only have today and tomorrow before I have to hop on a plane and head down to…” She paused and glanced over at Wade. “Hey.”

“Hmm?”

“Are you okay?”

“Sure.”

“You seem awful quiet. What’s going on with you?”

"Nothing. Same old, same old."

"How're things going with Terry?" Wade remained silent. "Right. What happened?"

"Nothing. Other than her son dislikes me, and our relationship seems to be at a standstill." They sat behind a line of cars waiting for the traffic to move. "Before Terry and I met, she decided that she wasn't going to date or get into a relationship for a while. Whenever I think things might be progressing, she seems to put on the breaks, and reminds me of her choice not to start any relationship."

"Wade, she's just being cautious. You can understand that, she's divorced and doesn't want to make the same mistake."

"Yeah, I know."

"I can tell she cares for you a lot. Just give her some time." She looked over at Wade.

He turned away, watching two children run down the sidewalk, and caught his own reflection in the car's window. Oh God, did he really look that forlorn?

She smiled. "You love her, don't you?"

"Yeah," Wade said without hesitation still watching the happy children.

"Don't worry," she said, and reached for his hand, squeezing it. "Everything will be fine. Geez." Jennifer groaned, "What's going on?" she inched her car slightly over the line to see the traffic at the front of the line. She leaned forward, peering out of the windshield. "Uh, Wade. Is that your girlfriend standing in the street yelling and waving her arms frantically?"

Wade looked at Jennifer for a moment before fully comprehending what she'd just said. He opened the car door getting out quickly and saw Terry ranting and raving, her arms flying all around. Jennifer opened her door stepping from the car.

## Chapter 36

"Stay," Wade commanded, using the voice he would use on his students and the people that worked under him.

"I will not!" Jennifer said indignantly as she walked around the car, following Wade in the direction of the commotion.

The traffic in all four directions was at a standstill as Terry stood in the intersection between two police cars, her arms flailing, her coat billowing around like a cape.

As they got closer, Jennifer laughed. "I just knew when I first met Terry that I was going to love her."

***

"You said that you were going to take Keith for the day, damn it, and you're not going to disappoint him!" Terry yelled at David as he stood on the other side of the car.

"Terry, I told you that I can't."

"He's here, and you're here. Why the hell can't you?"

"Damn it, Terry, I told you, Shareese and I have things that we need to do, and he's just going to have to grow up and deal with it."

Terry felt like she was about to explode. She let out a savage growl and darted to her left running around one of the police officers and one of the cars. She made three circles around the car, hot on David's heels as the little coward ran from her, before strong arms grasped her around the waist and lifted her off her feet.

"Get your damned hands off of me!" she screamed.

"You need to lock her up! That bitch is crazy!" David heaved, bending over as he tried to catch his breath.

"I've got your bitch right here!" Terry yelled, struggling within the arms that held her. "Get off of me! Get off!"

"Calm down, babe," Wade said in a soothing tone, while Terry kept struggling and fighting against the arms that held her.

"I'm gonna kick your ass," Terry yelled, her arms and legs floundering about. "Then I'm gonna kick your skank slut's ass, and then I'm gonna kick your bitch of a mother's ass for giving birth to you, you-lowlife-bottom-feeding-shit-bag-son of a-"

Wade quickly placed his hand over Terry's mouth. "Officer, she didn't mean that." Terry promptly bit his hand. "Ouch!" Wade snatched his hand away from Terry's mouth.

"Fuck you!" she threw over her shoulder at him.

"Terry's a friend of mine," Wade told the police officers as he backed away. "Just give me a minute to talk to her, and she'll be fine. I promise."

Wade walked away from the fray, toting a struggling Terry with him.

"Okay, what happened?" Wade said, after setting Terry's struggling body on her feet.

She spun around, her fist balled and her eyes narrowed, prepared to take a punch at him. For the first time, she realized who he was, and her eyes immediately filled with tears.

"Hey, it'll be okay," Wade said calmly, stepping closer, and taking her in his arms. "It's okay, babe, I'm here." He breathed into her hair. "Tell me what happened."

Terry was silent for a few minutes, sobbing into Wade's chest. When she had quieted down, she said, "Today is Keith's birthday, and I was going to take him to the movies and to dinner, but when I woke up this morning I didn't feel well..."

***

Wade leaned back and took a good look at her. She was in pink and white flannel pajamas; one leg was tucked inside of her brown snow boots, and a red fleece robe that hung more than a foot below her gray wool coat. Her hair was in a lopsided ponytail, with messy wisps sticking in different directions. There was perspiration across her brow and upper lip, her eyes were bloodshot, and her nose was as red as a beet. Reaching up, he pressed the back of his hand against her forehead.

"God, you're burning up."

Terry rambled on. "…and David kept calling me, asking me to bring Keith to his job, he said that he wanted to do something with Keith for his birthday. I didn't feel well, but I didn't want Keith not to have a happy birthday. He begged me to bring Keith, so I said yeah, and when I got here, I saw him pulling out of the parking lot. I followed him, and when he got to a light, I got out of the car and went to ask him why he left and to tell him that I had Keith in the car waiting for him." her voice broke and a small sob escaped. "…And he tells me something came up and he can't take Keith. Keith is sitting right in the car, and I know he knows what's going on. I got so mad that I started beating the car, and I was going to beat David but he ran and then the police came, and they stopped me before I was able to get to David. David said that Keith needed to grow up and deal with it. I was so mad, I wanted to *really* beat him, and, and then he ran some more…" her lip trembled.

Wade pulled her close, holding her and rocking her again. "It's okay, babe. It'll be all right."

"No, it won't. Its Keith's birthday, and he heard what David said. He knows David didn't want to spend time with him, and it's his birthday." Terry rambled on, sobbing against Wade's chest.

Wade looked down the street at Terry's ex. He stood with his arms folded, leaning against his car with a young woman standing next to him. It took everything in Wade not to cross the distance and knock him on his sorry ass. He pulled back a little, tilting Terry's face up to meet his gaze. "I'll tell you what, why don't I take Keith overnight?"

"No, I couldn't…"

"Sure, it'll be great. We'll go out for pizza and then to the movies. I can probably pick up my nephew, Jack, and make it a guys' night out. He'll have a great time. He and I can get to know each other better, and it'll give you time to take care of yourself."

"You'll do that for us, for me?"

"I'd do anything for you, babe." He kissed her forehead, and tears welled in Terry's eyes again. Wade tugged up his shirt and, using the edge, he wiped Terry's eyes. After holding her for a few more minutes, he asked, "Are you okay to go back over there?"

She nodded.

When they walked back to the car, Wade could see Jennifer sitting in the back of Terry's van, chatting with Keith, while the gathering police officers looked on. When she looked up as Terry and Wade approached, she slid from the backseat.

"Everything okay?" she asked Terry.

Terry nodded and smiled up at her. "Thanks."

Terry sat in the van next to Keith, "Hey, I have a surprise for you." he looked up at her with sad eyes. "It's a really good surprise; I promise you'll like it."

## Chapter 36

"Mommy," Keith whispered, his lip trembling. "I don't want to go with Daddy anymore."

"You don't have to, honey." She reached for his overnight bag and took his hand, helping him from the van.

"Hey, buddy, how are you doing?" Wade squatted in front of the child. Keith kept his eyes trained on the ground in front of him. "Happy birthday."

"Thank you," Keith said in a barely audible whisper.

"How would you like to hang out with me this evening? We could go out for pizza, and maybe go to the movies to see Iron Man. I was going to get you a birthday gift, but I didn't know what you wanted. Maybe we could go pick out something together."

Keith finally looked up, giving Wade a sad smile and a nod. "My daddy didn't want to take me." He said in a small voice.

Wade stroked the child's cheek with a finger. "No, you're a great kid, who wouldn't want to spend time with you, especially on your birthday? I had to beg your mom to let you come with me. She nearly cried."

"Really?" Keith looked up at his mother, and she gave him a tearful smile. "Don't cry, Mommy. I won't go, if you don't want me to."

Terry squatted next to Keith as well. "I feel bad that we can't hang out for your birthday, but I'm a little sick today. I'm sure I'll feel better tomorrow, and we can do something special. I don't want you to miss having a great day because of me, so why don't you go with Wade and have a good time?"

Keith looked across the street at his father and then dropped his eyes again.

"I'm sure your dad just got tied up with work," Wade lied, getting Keith's attention back to him. "That's the only thing that would make him break his date with you." Wade rose to his full height. Terry rose with him, and he reached for Keith's overnight bag, taking it from Terry. "We'll be fine," he assured her. "We're going to have a great time, aren't we, buddy?"

# Chapter 37

The following afternoon, Wade got out of his truck and pulled out Keith's overnight bag, and a shopping bag they had gotten from their trip to the grocery store. Wade's nephew, Jack, and Keith climbed out the passenger door, and met Wade when he rounded the truck to the driveway. Walking toward the front door, Wade laughed and shook his head as he listened to the boys debate about which one of them belched the loudest during their ride from the Burger King to Terry's house.

Walking onto the front porch, Wade rang the doorbell. Hearing music coming from inside the house, he looked down at Keith, who only hunched his small shoulders and shrugged. After ringing the bell again, they waited a few more minutes before Wade tried the doorknob. It was unlocked; they stepped inside, and Wade looked around the living room. There were empty bowls and cups on the coffee table, the throw pillows from the sofa and chairs were strewn around the room, and there were several coats and jackets piled on the coffee table.

Wade turned to Keith to give him his overnight bag and said, "Hey, buddy, why don't you and Jack take your things to your room? I'm going to go say hi to DJ and then go check on your mom. And then we can get dinner started."

Wade raised the bag slightly and nodded toward the steps. Keith grabbed his bag, and he and Jack both turned and bolted up the steps while Wade headed toward the kitchen. Setting the grocery bag on the table, Wade crossed the room and opened the door that led to the basement. When he made his way down the steps, Wade saw DJ and his friend Roderick sitting on an old sofa. There were three other boys, beside DJ and Roderick. Wade recognized them, but didn't know their names. They looked a little older than DJ, and they were sprawled on another sofa, opposite the one DJ occupied. Standing between the facing sofas were two girls. One wore a tight turtleneck and a barely-there skirt, the other girl, Lindsey, wore a green button-down blouse, on which the button at her breast was the only one in use, and low-riding jeans. Both girls held cigarettes, and all of the boys watched, mesmerized as girls danced and gyrated to music coming from a music video that was playing on the television.

The small cots that Terry had for the daycare stood stacked in the corner, the pillows the children used during their naps were tossed haphazardly on the floor, along with the throw pillows from the couches. Wade crossed the room, stepping over the pillows, and unplugged the television set.

The room fell quiet, and in a low and calm voice, Wade said. "Out. Now."

All eyes immediately went to him and then there was an immediate sound of rustling as the teens gathered whatever belongings they had dropped, and rushed upstairs. DJ headed toward the stairs, along with the group of teens.

"DJ!" Wade called, stopping the boy in his tracks. DJ turned to him. "I'm going to assume that your mother doesn't know that you're having this little…" Wade looked around the room at the mess, and then back at DJ. "…Get together." DJ didn't say anything, which was answer enough. "I'm going to check on your mother. When I return, I expect to see this mess," he thrust his chin in the direction of the sofas, where the bulk of the mess lay. "And the mess in the living room, cleaned up. And then I'd like you to meet me in the kitchen."

Without a word, Wade walked past DJ and up the second floor to Terry's bedroom. He found her under a mountain of blankets, sound asleep. Crossing the room, he squatted next to the bed, running his fingers across her brow. Her eyes fluttered open and he smiled at her.

"Hey," He said.

"Hey."

"How are you feeling?"

"Much better. How did things go with Keith? Did you guys have a good time?"

"We had a great time. The movie was good, and Keith and Jack got along like old friends. I promised to take them out together in a few weeks." He felt her forehead. "When was the last time you've had something to eat?"

"Day before yesterday, I think. I haven't been hungry."

"How about a little soup and a cup of hot tea?"

"I don't know about the soup, but the tea sounds good."

He brushed her hair from her forehead and kissed her brow. "I'll be back in a few minutes."

Wade looked up as DJ entered the kitchen. "Are you finished in the living room?"

DJ glared at him but answered, "Yeah."

"Have a seat." DJ looked as if he wanted to argue, but Wade didn't give him the chance. "Now."

Pulling out a chair, DJ dropped down in it.

"DJ, you're a smart young man. I can't believe that you would invite people into your mother's house, and let them nearly run amok while your mother is sick in bed. You know that's not acceptable."

DJ kept his eyes on the table, his tennis shoe clad foot tapping a rhythm on the floor. Wade watched the hostile clinch of DJ's jaw. He knew that hostility. It was caused by the hurt and betrayal of someone you loved and idolized.

"DJ, when's the last time you spoke to your father?"

DJ's eyes flashed on him, and then narrowed. "Why?"

"Maybe you need to talk to him, tell him how you feel. Tell him how angry you are."

"That's none of your business. I don't want to talk about my father."

"I don't want to talk about your father either. I'm just suggesting that you speak to him. I understand how you feel."

DJ hastily rose from the table. "You don't know anything." He turned abruptly leaving the kitchen.

When Wade entered the bedroom, he found Terry under the blankets, sound asleep. He set the bowl of soup and cup of tea on the nightstand and pulled the cover over Terry's shoulders. He allowed his fingers to brush her brow, and then let the back of his knuckles gently brush her cheek. It felt as if her temperature was close to normal. She was still a little warm, but not as hot as she was the day before. He leaned down and kissed her brow, and she moaned, smiling in her sleep. He stood watching her for a moment. Even being as sick as she had been, she was beautiful.

## Chapter 37

While her soup and tea were cooking, he had come to check on her, and she was in the shower. He stripped the sheets from the bed and put on fresh linen, and then left to return to the kitchen.

Now it was time to let her rest. He stepped out of her bedroom and headed for the stairs, and heard movement behind him. Turning, he looked over his shoulder, and saw Keith and Jack standing in the doorway of Keith's room.

"Is Mommy still sick?"

Wade placed his finger to his lips, and then crossed to the room and closed the door. "She's feeling much better than she did yesterday. Let's let her rest for the remainder of this evening. Jack, how about if I call your parents and ask them if you can stay the night? We can go and get something to eat, and then stop by your house to get you a change of clothes."

Keith's head bobbed up and down, while Jack's eyes grew large with excitement. "Can I?"

"Sure, I don't see why not. I'll have to call your mom and dad, but I'm sure it won't be a problem."

Wade looked over at Keith and Jack, as he drove from the grocery store back to Terry's house. He listened to the chatter between the boys, only half paying attention as they tried to include him in their conversation.

"Do you think so, Mr. Wade?" Keith had asked.

"What's that, buddy?"

"Jack said that last year his mommy and daddy let him get a puppy for his birthday. Do you think Mommy would let me get a puppy? I can ask when we get home."

"Uh," Wade looked from Keith to Jack, who both looked at him expectantly. He turned, focusing on the road. "I don't know. Right now your mother has a lot going on with starting a new business and caring for all of those kids. Having a puppy is a really big responsibility."

"I can take care of it. I'm big enough." Keith puffed up his chest.

Wade glanced at him again, "I know you are, buddy, but why not let your mom get used to things the way they are first, before you add a pet into the mix?"

Keith was thoughtful. "So, I should wait until tomorrow to ask her?"

Wade laughed. "I'm thinking you should wait a little longer than that. Maybe you can ask for a puppy for Christmas."

"Christmas? That's a long time from now, that's almost forever."

"It's sooner than you think," Wade said to Keith, and to himself added, "But not long enough for your mother."

# Chapter 38

Several days later, Wade stood in Terry's kitchen, watching her. She was up to something. What, Wade didn't know, but she was jumpier than Marilyn Manson at a Baptist revival meeting.

Wade watched her as she looked at the clock for the fifth time in ten minutes. She nervously fluttered around the kitchen, aimlessly wiping and sweeping the already clean room.

Wade stepped in front of her blocking her path to the counter. "All right, spill it."

"What?" Terry took a step back, looking up at him. "What are you talking about?"

"You know what I'm talking about, what did you do?"

Terry frowned and walked past him. "I didn't do anything."

Wade slipped his arms around her waist, pulling her back around to face him. "Whatever it is, you know I'm going to find out. So you may as well tell me what the hell is going on."

Terry looked up into his piercing eyes and then bit her lip. "Give me a minute to come up with something." Wade released her and folded his arms, waiting. "Okay, okay," she finally sighed. "I'm working on this case.

There's this guy who's cheating on his wife, and I'm trying to catch him."

"Catch him?"

She rolled her eyes. "Yeah, you—know—catch—him... as in, with another woman," she said to him, as if he were a bit slow.

He blinked at her for a moment. "Terry, you're not a private investigator."

"I know." She waved her arms. "And, therein lies the problem. Dee won't let me work with her, and so I'm trying to prove that I can do the work, that with her help I can be a good PI."

"You can't do that!" Wade said his tone scolding. "You can't just follow people around; you could get into some serious trouble. Anything could happen to you."

"No, nothing is going to happen to me, and I won't get into trouble. It's not like the guy is a criminal or anything."

Wade leaned against the counter running his hands through his hair. "Terry, what are you doing, trying to give me a heart attack? What do you think is going to be going through my mind while I picture you, an untrained civilian, following some strange man around?"

Terry stepped close to him running her hand from his chest to his belly. "You'll be worried about me?" she grinned. "That's so sweet." Her grin faded when Wade's pissed expression became more intense. "Come on, I'm just following the guy, and trying to get pictures of him with his girlfriend. It'll be okay. I'll get the pictures, write up the report, and send it to the wife. When the wife contacts Dee and pays for the service of the investigation, I'll tell Dee that I was the one who solved the case, and she'll have to give me a try."

Of course, Wade looked at her as if she was clueless. He sighed. "Is this what you really want? Are you willing to go through all of this to be a PI? What if Dee doesn't see things the way you're hoping? Are you willing to take the chance? Are you willing to accept the disappointment of her turning you down?"

"Yes?" Terry said, without hesitation.

"I'm assuming that the incident at the park and the restaurant were when you were following your guy, right?"

Terry sighed. "Yeah… well, things didn't go as well as I had hoped."

***

He smiled. "Obviously."

Terry looked up at him, scrunching up her nose. With his arms still folded, Wade ran the index finger of his right hand back and forth across his lips as he watched her. He knew that there was no way he could keep her from going out and following this guy. No way, short of tying her up, or telling Dee. Tying her up might be fun, but that would only work for a few hours. She would be okay while he had her in his bed. He could use his imagination and come up with some creative ways to keep her occupied. But, as soon as he let her go, even if it was just so she could use the bathroom, she would probably shimmy her naked ass out the window, highjack a car and go follow this guy just to piss Wade off. Telling Dee was not an option. If he did, Terry would never forgive him. All she needed was some photos of this guy with his mistress, she could give them to Dee and Dee would make sure that Terry had the proper training before she turned her loose on the unsuspecting world.

"Lady, I truly don't know what I'm going to do with you!" he scolded. "Honestly, sometimes you have the maturity of one of my students. You break into my apartment, bite me when I'm trying to help you, and now you want to play Private Dic'. What am I going to do with you?"

Terry bit her lip, hung her head, and sighed. "So… what are you going to… do?"

"I'm going to help you," Wade said sighing as well.

Terry's head shot up, a look of total shock on her face. "Huh… why?"

"Because… I'm a world-class dope who just happens to completely in love with you, and I don't want to see you get hurt. So, okay; tell me what you have on this guy."

***

"I don't understand why we couldn't drive the van; it's more comfortable." Terry asked as she kicked off her shoes, wiggled her toes, and brought her feet up, tucking them under her rump.

"Because, you've been following this guy for… how long?"

"A little more than a month."

"I'm sure he's bound to notice your van eventually, if he hasn't noticed it already." Terry looked at him for a moment, nodded, and then looked out the windshield. "And you've only followed him from his place of work and his girlfriend's home?"

Terry nodded again. She looked at the plush two-story house that they sat half a block from, and then back at Wade. "So, why are we at his house?"

"Well, you've followed him from work and from the girlfriend's home. Of course he goes other places. Maybe he meets her at a bar or restaurant. Plus, he might not be as nervous when he leaves home. If he is, he'll likely be looking for the wife, and he won't be looking for my truck."

Terry grinned. "Good thinking."

At 7:15 pm, Henderson's Lexus backed out of his garage and onto the street. Wade waited until the car was half a block away before he started his truck and followed. They followed the car through the east side of town to the business district. Wade switched off his headlights, when they reached the corner of the lot that Henderson turned in to. Henderson reached out his arm and swiped a key card in front of a sensor. The gate opened, allowing him to pull into a self-storage facility.

"Wonder what he's doing here?" Terry said.

They peered through the window, watching as Henderson parked in front of one of the storage rooms. He got out of the car and, using a key, he unlocked a padlock, dropping it on the ground. He turned, looked left to right, and then rolled up the sliding door and went inside. He closed the door. After twenty minutes, the door slid open, and Henderson walked out of the room carrying two large cases. He stowed them in the trunk of his car, and made two more trips inside the room to bring out two more cases and a large box.

Wade started the truck and quickly backed up, made a left, and backed down the street far enough so that Henderson couldn't see them sitting there. When Henderson pulled out of the lot, Wade waited a reasonable amount of time before he followed. Henderson drove five minutes to an office complex. He got out, opened the trunk, and carried the items that he took from the storage room inside.

"What do you think he's doing?" Terry questioned.

"I don't know." Wade reached for the door handle. "Sit tight. I'll be back in a sec…"

"Oh, hell no. This is my case."

"Terry!"

"No, I'm serious. This is my thing. I need to do this."

He gave her a peeved looked, but nodded. They got out of the car and walked quietly in the direction of the office. The door of the office that Henderson had entered opened, and he emerged. Wade quickly stepped back in a doorway a few offices down, pulling Terry's back against his front. She could hear him inhale deeply, obviously smelling the fresh intoxication of her hair. Wade clearly couldn't help himself; his nose brushed her hair.

Terry leaned to her left, looked up at him, and mouthed, "Did you just smell me?"

"Yeah," he said, his voice ragged; as they heard the bang of what was probably Henderson closing the door to the office.

"And is that your…?"

"Don't pay that any mind," He leaned close, whispering in her ear. "It's always like that, whenever you're around."

She elbowed him, grinned, and moved closer to him. She enjoyed his body pressed against hers; the feel of his erection pressed against her back and knowing that she was the cause. She imagined that thick long shaft slipping inside her. She moaned inwardly and shook her head.

*Focus girl, focus*. She quickly gave Wade another elbow jab in the gut. "Come on."

***

They crept to the office and peered inside. They didn't see anything at first, and then Wade saw a familiar face exit one of the rooms on the right side of the office: Chad Odell, one of the gym teachers from Jefferson.

"Son of a bitch," Wade whispered.

Another man joined him who was just as familiar as his companion, but this one looked nervous and scared: Jason Bleeker, Chelsea's fiancé.

"Hey," Jason said shoving his hands in his pockets. "I'm all for the selling of a little smack, some weed, but I don't want to get hooked up with no heat."

Odell looked Jason up and down, glowering. He opened his mouth to speak, but Henderson shook his head and stepped in front of Jason, blocking Odell's view of him. "Chad, let me talk to him a minute."

Odell glared at Henderson, and then at Jason. "Dude, you better get your nephew in line." He turned and stormed into one of the side rooms.

Henderson turned to Jason. "Look, you said you wanted in on this."

"Yeah I do…" Jason said slowly.

"Well then, what the hell are you doing?"

"I don't know, something doesn't feel right."

"Come on, Jas, everything's cool. You just need to put in your part of the… capital. Once we get the payoff, you run it through your institution, set up our accounts, and we're all good, just like it's been before."

Henderson raised his hands in a fashion that Wade was sure was meant to pacify Jason, but it only seemed to make him more agitated. Jason fidgeted with something in his pocket as he looked around the office nervously.

"Mom said Aunt Pauline was complaining about you, said that you were being secretive." Jason looked back at Henderson. "She's becoming suspicious."

Don't worry about your Aunt Pauline, I can handle her."

"I don't know, like I said, I got a bad feeling. This time something just doesn't feel right." Jason let out a heavy breath. "All right, let's just finish up and get the hell out of here. We can come back in a few days and go over things thoroughly."

Wade stood, pulling Terry with him.

"Hey!" she whispered.

He put his hand on the small of her back and nearly pushed her as they walked in the direction of the truck. Terry tried to push his hand away, but he moved her hand, hustling her toward the truck as fast as humanly possible.

Terry turned around, quickly poking a finger in Wade's chest. "Okay, the pushing thing. Not working."

Wade grabbed her hand, turning her around and pushed her again. "If you don't behave, pushing will be the least of what I do to you!"

"Stop it," Terry whispered, and turned, pushing him back.

Wade had had enough. He practically lifted Terry off of her feet as he hauled her toward his truck. He opened the door and forced her inside, and then went to the driver's side. Slipping behind the wheel, he started the truck before he even got the door closed. He shifted into drive and pulled out of the lot.

"Terry, what the hell have you gotten yourself in to?"

"What?"

"This guy is not just your average Joe cheating on his wife."

"Yes he is; his wife said so."

"No, he isn't. The wife may not know this, but this guy is into some real nasty shit." Wade dug into his pocket as he pulled out his cellphone.

## Chapter 38

When Wade finished his call, he clicked it closed. He glanced at Terry. "I don't suppose I can convince you not to follow this guy anymore.

She folded her arms, glaring at him. "What do you think?"

He sighed and silently counted to ten. "I thought not." Using the heel of his hand, he hit the steering wheel. "Damn it! Okay, this is what we're going to do…"

# Chapter 39

"Shareese, I'm working late tonight. I don't know what time I'll be home, probably not until 6:30."

She paused and then asked, "Are you sure you're not going anywhere else?"

David fought the urge to sigh. "Come on, Shareese, I don't want to do this again."

"Do what?"

"You know what. I'm working late because I got off early last Thursday and Friday, when I went to your doctor's appointment and Lamaze class. I did that because you said you needed me to be there. You said you wanted my support, and I understand that. Now I have to work late so that I can catch some things up."

She remained silent, but he could picture her pacing across the kitchen floor and pausing to step across the toys that little Davie had dropped at every available space inside. David scrubbed his hand across his close-cropped hair, and closed his eyes. The house was pretty much a mess most of the time, not to mention the boys. Shareese wasn't much of a housekeeper, or cook or caregiver for that matter. She usually let the kids do whatever they wanted, while she was either talking on the phone with one of her many friends, doing something that he thought was totally useless on the internet, or watching television.

## Chapter 39

"I've been trying to get Davie to go to the bathroom, and he won't," she finally said.

When Shareese had their first child, she insisted on naming him David Junior. For the life of him, David didn't know why he didn't argue with that. At the time, he was totally caught up in Shareese, and their relationship was still new. David knew that he and Shareese naming their child David hurt DJ. DJ wouldn't admit it, he was stubborn like his mother in that way, but David knew that it had.

"Did you hear me, David? I said your son won't go to the bathroom for me. If you don't want him to be in diapers when he's four, I'd advise you to help me."

David laughed. Shareese never tried to teach the boy how to use the bathroom. A few months ago, David had started taking Davie to the bathroom with him, with the intention of showing him how a big-boy used the toilet. The boy had immediately developed a fixation with the white throne. Every chance he got, he was in there, flushing it, which wouldn't be so bad if he didn't want to drop things in it when he did. A couple of times it was a sock, one day, a truck, on several occasions it was different toy dinosaurs. Even one of David's shoes took a swim with the Tidy Bowl man, and Shareese couldn't care less.

When David would say something to her about it, she would grab the boy up, fish out whatever didn't go down with the flush, pop the boy's behind, and go on about her business. The only time she ever really paid any attention to the children was when they were going out as a family, and then she dressed herself and the boys as if they were headed to Washington DC to meet the President and First Lady.

"So, you're not meeting someone before you come home, not making a quick stop?" Shareese asked with that sweet tone that David recognized as the calm before the storm.

David rubbed his tired eyes with the heels of his hand. "Come on, Shareese, I have work to do, and I don't have time for this."

"David, I'm not going to sit at home while you're out running around with some other woman," she started in.

David tuned out her words, and she went on about not being like his stupid-assed first wife, and how he wasn't going to cheat on her. How she would go and leave his damned kids in the damned house by their damned selves. That was one major difference between Shareese and Terry. Shareese was jealous and possessive, where Terry was possessive, yeah, but jealous? Not hardly. He didn't think Terry had a jealous bone in her body. If she did, he never saw it.

When he'd started seeing Shareese, seven months before he left Terry, he and Terry had been preparing for bed. He had told her that one of his co-worker's had been left by her husband, and that she said she hadn't seen the signs of him cheating until it was too late. That this woman said that her husband was always going out and had changed the way he dressed, and she hadn't even picked up on it. Terry had only said that it was awful and she felt for the other woman, and asked if David wanted her to talk to her. She said that she could take her out to lunch, and offer a shoulder to lean on, if it was needed.

"Naw, she's all right, I think she was just venting. She seems over it. I think she's seeing someone new anyhow," he'd said.

There hadn't been anyone on his job that told him that her husband had left her. David just wanted to set her up for the next question. "She, Marla, was just telling me how her husband was always going out alone and that she didn't think anything of it, until she found out about the other woman." He had looked at Terry, watching her reaction. "I told her that I go out a lot, and you don't have a problem with it."

Terry hadn't said anything, she'd just nodded and kept applying lotion to her legs.

"Why is that?" David asked. Terry just hunched her shoulders. "Marla said that most of her friends told her that if their men went out constantly, they would be upset, jealous even, but you're not."

Terry had turned to him then. "I don't want to keep you locked in the house like you're a child. You're not my child, you're my husband. I don't think you'd cheat on me, but if you have a mind to, you're going to cheat anyway, and there's nothing that I can do to stop you."

Thinking back, David tried to convince himself that if Terry had been the jealous clinging type of woman, they might still be together. He sighed. Maybe, or maybe not. Shareese was both jealous and clingy, and David didn't know how long he could deal with it.

John Baxter, one of David's co-workers, stuck his head inside David's office, and David felt relief spread though him. "Shareese, I have to go, someone just walked into my office." He said a quick, 'I love you,' followed by an even quicker, 'I miss you,' before he hung up.

John walked into the office, dropping down in the chair across from David's desk. "Hey, David, we still on for lunch?"

David nodded. "I'll be ready to go in about ten minutes. Let me just finish this up," David said.

John slouched down in the chair. "Sure, I'll just hang out here 'til you're finished; I don't want to go back down to my office until after lunch. Mildred keeps giving me extra things to do. As if I didn't have enough on my plate as it is." David just nodded again, not really paying much attention to what his friend and co-worker was saying. "…with her new boyfriend."

David looked up from his work. "What?"

"I said, I saw Terry last week. She was at the movies with her new boyfriend. She's still a good looking woman-"

"What boyfriend? Terry doesn't have a boyfriend. What did this guy look like?"

John clasped his fingers, putting them behind his head, and impatiently shook his foot. "Man, I don't know, some big Asian guy."

"That's not her boyfriend. I asked DJ about him and he said that this dude was his English teacher, and that his mother and him were just hanging out together."

"It looked a hell of a lot more than two friends just hanging out together to me. The kiss this guy planted one on Terry before the theater turned the light out that had everyone around them watching them like it was the best romance scene since *Titanic*. Hell, man, I thought he was going to strip her and take her right there," John huffed and squirmed in his chair. "Damn, man, are you almost done? I'm starving."

David stared at John for a moment, feeling the tension that had eased when he hung up from talking to Shareese return.

# Chapter 40

Wade walked into his parents' house to the smell of roasted turkey and homemade apple pie. "Hello, Nenek, happy Thanksgiving."

"Happy Thanksgiving, happy Thanksgiving," she said, leaning into his hug as she turned up her face for him to plant a kiss on her cheek.

Wade walked through the house to the living room. He greeted Adam and his father before he walked into the dining room to meet his mother. She moved the flower arrangement from the center of the table to make way for the serving platters, and what he was sure to be an enormous turkey. She looked up at Wade as he entered the room, smiling at him. Wade walked to the china hutch to take out the dinner plates for his mother, and began to set them on the table as she folded the napkins.

"What's wrong?" She asked.

"Mamma, I won't be staying until the end of dinner. Jennifer is in town, and I'm going to meet her later."

"I know she doesn't have any family here, why didn't you bring her with you?"

"She didn't want to impose and..."

"It wouldn't have been an imposition. It's Thanksgiving, and she should not be alone."

“She’s not. Well, she won’t be.” Wade hesitated. “I have a friend.”

“A woman?”

“Yes.”

His mother smiled. “You could have brought her, too.”

“Yes I know, but she has children, two boys, and we’ve just started seeing one another and...”

“I understand. You go and spend time with your lady.”

“The family?”

“Don’t worry; I’ll explain everything to them.”

Wade looked down, hoping he wasn’t looking too hesitantly, and then back up at her.

“Don’t worry about it.” she reached across the table, patting his hand. “So, tell me about your lady friend.”

“Her name is Terry, and she’s funny, witty, beautiful, and intelligent.”

“If she can put that sparkle in your eyes, I like her already. And her sons?”

“They’re good kids. Keith is seven and DJ is fourteen. I’m a little concerned about how he’s handling me seeing his mother.”

“It can be hard for a young man, knowing that another man will take his mother’s heart. Right now, he’s the man of the house. You’re a good man, and he’ll soon see it. Just give him time.”

Wade and Jennifer stood on the front porch of the Harrison’s home. When they’d driven up the half-mile drive, Jennifer asked Wade at least twice if he was sure they were at the correct house. Wade had assured her that he hadn’t gotten the address wrong. When they pulled up in front of a house that looked something that should be on the front of a magazine, the only thing Jennifer had said was, “Wooow.”

Now they stood on the porch, Wade casually leaning against one of four columns, as he surveyed the circular driveway. There were four other vehicles in the driveway, besides Jennifer’s: a black SUV, a white Mercedes, a Toyota Highlander hybrid, and Terry’s minivan. He turned at the sound of the front door being opened to see a forty-ish six-foot male coming out. He had dark hair that was almost black, with slight graying at the temples, and friendly eyes that were as green as emeralds.

“Happy Thanksgiving. Come on in.” he stepped to the side, allowing them access. “I’m Ben Harrison, Dee’s husband. You must be Wade.”

“Wade Nelson,” Wade said, reaching for Ben’s extended hand. “This is my friend Jennifer Jenkins.”

“Hello, Jennifer, happy Thanksgiving and welcome to our home.”

“Hi, nice to meet you, you have a lovely home,” Jennifer said, shaking Ben’s hand as well.

Ben led them from the foyer to a large room just off to the left. Tyler was sitting on the sofa, DJ sat on the floor, his back against the sofa. The two of them were intently watching the football game.

“Tyler, this is Wade Nelson, and Jennifer Jenkins. Wade, Jennifer, Tyler Green.”

Tyler leaned forward, clasping Wade’s offered hand. “Hey, man, how’s it going?”

“Good,” Wade said.

“Jennifer,” Tyler greeted her, shaking her hand.

“Hello, happy Thanksgiving.”

“You too,” Tyler said, glancing at the television when he heard a roar.

“And you know DJ,” Ben said.

"Hey, DJ," Wade said.

DJ stared at the television intently. Tyler glanced down at DJ, and reached for him, giving him a subtle smack on the back of his head.

"Oow!" DJ all but cried, flinching away.

"Boy, don't you hear Wade speaking to you?" Tyler shook his head. "Teenagers, you can't live with 'em, you can't kill 'em, 'cause you need them to cut the grass."

Both Wade and Jennifer laughed.

"Let's go back in the kitchen, that's where the women are hiding out," Ben said, leading Wade and Jennifer to the kitchen.

"I see you and DJ get along well," Ben said, his voice thick with sarcasm.

"Yeah, well, me being his teacher is bad, me dating his mother makes things terrible."

"You have to give DJ a little time," Ben said. "I think he believes he has to look out for his mother; he was there when his father brought his new girlfriend home to confront Terry. I think it made more of an impact on DJ than he's willing to admit."

Wade nodded. "Most kids will go through a lot to protect their mothers."

"Yeah, Terry portrays herself as this really tough lady, but inside, she's a softy," Ben said.

"Yeah," Tyler added. "When Holly first met me, she had reservations about dating me. But she and I are sure Terry was working behind the scenes to get us together."

Tyler went on to tell Wade some of the things that Terry did to bring Holly and him together. Over the course of the… stories, the guys settled in, and resumed watching the game.

## Chapter 40

"I know she'd never admit it, though." Tyler checked his watch and then stretched lazily. "Man, its 3:30, we're running late. Beer, anyone?"

"Sure, I'll have one," Wade said.

"Yeah, that sounds good, I'll have one too," Ben agreed stretching his arm along the back of the sofa and propping his feet on the coffee table.

"Wade, you have to get the beers," Tyler said quickly and then folded his arms across his chest, smiling.

"Hey, I'm a guest," Wade reminded them, looking from Tyler to Ben.

"Nope, you're Terry's boyfriend; officially, that makes you family, and negates all guest status," Ben stated, grinning.

"Yeah, and you're the new guy, so today you have to do the beer runs," Tyler added.

"If my younger brother, Kyle were here, he'd be the runner because he's the youngest."

"I don't know," Tyler said slowly, eyeing Wade. "Doesn't beauty come before age when it comes to the beer runs? Wade's kind of cute with that glossy hair and those girly lashes." Tyler held up his hand as Ben busted out laughing. "Not that I would notice such things; I heard the women say it once, but since that's the case, shouldn't his running status be below Kyle's?"

"Hmm… maybe," Ben said as both he and Tyler studied Wade, wearing huge grins on their faces.

Wade shook his head rising from the couch. "Am I going to be getting conned like this whenever we're watching a game together?"

Tyler laughed. "Pretty much."

"Unless the kid's here," Ben injected.

"The kid?" Wade asked.

"Yeah, DJ," Tyler said. "When he's around, he's the designated slave."

Wade shook his head and laughed as he headed for the kitchen.

Terry was standing next to Jennifer, and they were both leaning on the counter, watching Ben's mother, Natalie Harrison, fold the dinner napkins. Holly was basting the turkey, Dee and Keisha were peeling sweet potatoes, and Lisa, Ben's sister, was mixing up a pitcher of fruit punch. Wade crossed the room to the refrigerator as Lisa opened the door, putting the pitcher of juice inside.

"I'm here on a beer run," Wade announced.

Lisa reached inside, taking three beers from the fridge to pass to Wade.

"Dee, you know your husband and Tyler are conmen? They're taking complete advantage of me," Wade pretended to complain.

"Ben?" Dee called into the living room, using a mock chastising tone.

"He's the new guy, sweetheart," Ben called back.

"Sorry, new guy," Dee apologized, laughing.

"Ah," Holly said, closing the oven door. "I remember last year, Kyle was the designated beer runner. I believe he made about twenty runs."

"Twenty beer runs?" Wade said, surprise in his voice. "There's no way those guys could drink twenty beers combined, let alone twenty each."

"No, not just beer," Dee said. "Chips, cookies, water, you know, different things. I don't think they even used most of the stuff they sent Kyle in here for. I think Ben and Tyler were just messing with him."

"Oh yeah?" Wade asked, giving Dee an odd smile.

## Chapter 40

She smiled back, clearly wondering what he had in mind, and then laughed, turning away.

Wade shifted the beers to his left hand and walked to the counter to stand behind both Jennifer and Terry. He leaned over their shoulders and looked at the artwork that Natalie was making with the napkins. With his right hand, she felt him casually brush her bottom. She glanced up at him and smiled.

"Nice," Wade said, and then glanced at Terry.

Natalie beamed at him. "Thank you," She said, obviously thinking that he was complementing her decorating skills.

"You're welcome," Wade said, his eyes still on Terry. He glanced around the kitchen, his eyes focusing on an unopened bag of pretzels on the counter. "Do you mind if I take those?"

"Sure," Dee said.

Holly handed him the bag. "Dinner won't be for another hour."

Wade nodded and left the kitchen, carrying the beer and pretzels. Terry watched his khaki-clad bottom saunter out of the kitchen. She suppressed a moan, looking to her left to meet a grinning Jennifer's gaze. "What?"

"Nothing," Jennifer said, a shit-eating grin on her face.

"Wade seems like a nice young man," Natalie commented, just before they heard Tyler say, "Damn it!" followed by Ben's laughter and him saying, "That was a good one."

A moment later, Tyler entered the kitchen, crossing the room and entered the pantry. He exited a moment later, carrying a broom, dustpan, and small garbage bag.

Tyler looked up, seeing all of the women staring at him. "Wasted the pretzels," he murmured.

"Baby, I'm guessing Wade isn't as easy to fool as Kyle is, uh?" Holly asked him, as he headed back toward the living room.

Tyler grinned at her, wiggling his brows. "We're not finished with him yet. Time will tell; time-will-tell."

The women laughed as Tyler left the kitchen. "When they get together, those two are worse than the kids," Dee said.

"Well then, Wade will fit in perfectly." Jennifer laughed.

***

"I'm glad Dee asked the kids to spend the night," Terry said as they walked up the steps to Wade's apartment.

Terry stood to the side, allowing Wade to unlock the door. He stuck the key in the lock and leaned close to Terry, caging her small body between him and the door.

He brushed a gentle kiss against her brow. "I was hoping they would. I think Jennifer might have made the suggestion."

He opened the door, and Terry backed inside. Keeping her eyes on Wade, she backed across the living room, dropped her purse on the sofa and backed down the hallway to the bedroom. When she reached the bedroom, she turned around and froze. The quilt was a champagne-colored silk with champagne, green and brown-colored throw pillows. In the center of the bed sat a wooden antique serving tray with two Champagne flutes, a bottle of Champagne, and a long-stemmed rose. A dozen candles were placed throughout the room, and they glowed warmly.

## Chapter 40

"Wow, this is beautiful," she said, looking over her shoulder at Wade.

He grinned. "I'm glad you like it. Jennifer helped me pick out the bedding; she also beat us here and lit the candles."

"You'll have to thank her for me." Terry turned to him, standing on her toes and giving him a soft peck on his lips.

"I've been waiting for this moment all day. I hope you can do better than that," he said grinning down at her.

Terry bit her lip. Taking his hand, she led him to the bed and pushed his chest lightly. He sat down and looked up at her. Leaning forward, she began to unbutton his shirt as she pressed a row of kisses along the line of buttons that she unhooked. She pushed the shirt from his shoulders and down his arms while she pressed kisses along his collar bone to his chest, her tongue sliding around his nipple before she gave it little tug. A rippling sensation went through Wade, and he groaned reaching for her arms to pull her up so that her mouth met his. He allowed his teeth to nip her lower lip before sucking it into his mouth, and then released it before devouring her mouth. Terry pulled back, and grasped the hem of her blouse to pull it off.

Wade grasped her hips, drawing her to him. He nipped her taunt nipples through the lace of her blue bra and sucked one of the peaks into his mouth; she shuddered and moaned. Drawing back, he pushed her slacks and panties down her hips and off in one motion. Seeing the bare skin at the apex of her thighs, Wade looked up at her and grinned. He leaned forward and gave her a long, slow lick. Terry braced herself using his shoulders as she felt her knees buckle.

Wade quickly stood and strode across the room to close the door. He turned and reached for Terry. Pulling her to him, he slipped behind her, and turned her to face the mirror that hung behind the door. Tilting her face up toward him, he took her lips in a gentle kiss. He turned her face so she could see them in the mirror. Gently resting his hands on her hips for a moment, he began sliding them up her sides and around to her lush, round breasts, and then unhooked the clasp to her bra. He brushed it aside, as the tips of his fingers grazed the peak of each nipple.

Terry moaned as she ground her hips back against him. Wade leaned down to nip her shoulder. She watched as he slid his hands across her belly and down to the swell of her hips; the stroke of his fingers sent pleasant jolts of heat through her. He took her hands and encouraged her to explore her own body, until her body arched toward him.

Placing his hand over hers, he guided one hand to her mound while he led the other to her breasts. His hand covered hers as he tugged at the taut peaks. He led her right hand to the moistness of her heat and guided one of her fingers, along with his own, inside of her. She gasped as her body tightened, clamping around their fingers. Her eyes fluttered closed.

"No," he whispered. "Keep watching." She caught her lip between her teeth as her body began to move. "That's it, babe," Wade whispered as he moved their hands deeper and faster.

"Oh God," Terry moaned.

"That's it," He whispered again, just as her body trembled and exploded.

## Chapter 40

Wade walked her toward the bed and eased her down on the mattress. “Don’t move. Stay there, just like that."

He moved away from her. A few seconds later, Terry heard the rustling of the rest of his clothes and the quick tear of foil. When she felt him behind her with his arms around her, Terry felt the jump and pulse of his shaft against her thigh. She reached for him and he grabbed her wrist.

"No, none of that; not this time." He raised her arm, placing it next to her head. "First, I'm going to take you, fast and hard. Then, after I make you scream my name, I’m going to take my time and do things to you that you've never dreamt.”

Terry looked over her shoulder to meet his hungry gaze, and bit her lip in anticipation. He grabbed her lip, sucking it between his teeth and gently nipped it as he brought her right knee up toward her body. His right hand lightly brushed the tip of her left nipple. She moaned again as her hips thrust back to meet his. He slid his hand down her body and his finger massaged her tight nub before sliding into her tight wet opening. He slipped one finger inside and listened to her moan before he added another with the first.

“Oh shit!” Terry groaned as she bucked against his hand.

He quickly substituted his shaft and thrust it inside her, and paused to rest his forehead against her shoulder while she adjusted to him. After a moment he drew back, Terry looked over her shoulder giving him a wicked smile, and pushed her hips back.

He felt an unexpected tightness and she cried out his name just as he lost control. His body shattered and he roared as felt his climax release.

***

Terry moaned as she drifted back to awareness. "Wake up, sleepy head." He whispered, catching the lobe of her ear between his teeth. Terry moaned again came fully awake to the delicious feeling of Wade easing inside her inch by slow inch.

He moved slowly gently stroking and she groaned drawing her lip between her teeth. "How long do you think this is going to last?"

Wade grinned leaning forwards and nipped her lip. "For a couple of hours at least."

Terry moaned shifting her hips and thrusting upwards meeting his strokes. "No. I mean this. You and me. When it comes to relationships, I don't seem to be able to get it right."

"Babe, there's no right or wrong in a relationship, only what works."

"It didn't work with David. And in other relationships I cut and ran before things could go bad. Before they could see who I really was, before they decided to leave."

"I'm sorry they hurt you." He said looking down into to her eyes. "I would never hurt you. Could never hurt you." His movements slowed even more as he swerved his hips.

"Never?" She asked.

"Only if it brought you pleasure." he leaned down drawing her nipple into his mouth and giving it a gentle nip before letting it pop out. Terry squeaked as his tongue gently lapped at the sting and her squeak turned onto a moan. Terry brought her legs up wrapping them around his back as he picked up the pace of his thrusts.

"You don't know, do you?"

She moaned again arching her back. "Know what?"

## Chapter 40

"How much I love you?" Terry paused looking into his intense gaze. "I've never felt this way about anyone. Ever. I love everything about you, your quick wit, and sharp tongue. How life gives you clay and you turn it into rich soil. The way you moan when I make love to you." He leaned down gently sucking her lower lip and sucking it between his lips before deepening the kiss. Her eyes fluttered closed and she felt his kiss seep through her to her very soul. "I love you babe."

Terry felt tears slip from her eyes and run a trail to her hairline. Opening her eyes, she pulled her right hand free from his and traced her finger along the edge of his mouth "I love you too."

# Chapter 41

The next day, Dee called Terry to tell her that she would keep the boys for the day. She said that since it was Black Friday, Terry could go shopping for holiday gifts for the boys, and that hopefully she and Wade could spend the day together.

Terry laughed as they walked onto the front porch. Wade took the bag from Terry's hand and, using her keys, she opened the front door.

"No, I think we should…" Terry's comment died in mid sentence, and she froze, staring at the sight in the middle of her living room.

Standing with his arms folded was her ex-husband, David, wearing an extra large, bright red Christmas ribbon, a red Santa hat, a big grin, and nothing else. The sound of David's swearing, and the snickers coming from her right, brought Terry out of her stunned state. Shaking her head, she turned around, pushed Wade out of the door. She was right behind him.

Terry leaned against the porch columns, glaring at Wade. After five minutes, he was still trying to get a handle on his laughter and, for the life of her, Terry didn't see what he thought was so funny. "I don't get it. If I walked into your apartment to find a naked woman standing in your living room, I don't think that I could laugh about it. And here you are, practically busting a gut."

"You have to admit, it is as funny as hell."

"But a naked man in my living room? That doesn't bother you?"

"No, it doesn't. I don't feel insecure."

Terry rolled her eyes. "That's because you're arrogant."

"No, that's because I'm sure of your feelings for me." Wade stepped closer to Terry, pulling her into his arms and dropping a kiss on her lips.

"You're still arrogant," she said when he drew back, looking into her eyes.

"Well, maybe about the knowledge that I know how to make you scream."

Both Terry and Wade looked up when David finally opened the front door.

He stared at Wade's arms around Terry. Reluctantly, he stepped out onto the front porch, "Terry, why is he here?"

"That is none of your business; I don't have to answer to you, but you do need to tell me why the hell you were in my house, naked!"

David took a step in her direction. "Terry, we need to talk, in private."

"No, we don't, David. And I really don't care why you're here. All I want to know is that it'll never happen again."

David glanced at Wade and then back at Terry. He ran his tongue across his teeth, his eyes shifting slightly. "Terry, I've made a terrible mistake."

"Yeah you did, you shouldn't have brought your ass here today…"

"No, I mean, I never should have left you."

"David, what the hell are you talking about?" Terry frowned.

Wade folded his arms across his chest and leaned against the rail as he watched David.

David fidgeted for a moment; he didn't want to speak in front of Wade, but he was determined to have his say. David steeled himself for what might come. He'd come this far. He'd embarrassed and humiliated himself in front of some damned man who thought that he could have his wife and kids. There was no turning back. Straightening his shoulders, he kept his eyes on Terry.

"Terry, I'm sorry. I made a mistake. I messed up. Please forgive me." Terry remained silent just watching him. "I never should have left you and the boys; I was a fool who was going through a mid-life crisis."

Terry looked up at him. "You..."

"I'm sorry, baby. Please. Let me come home."

Terry looked in Wade's direction. He couldn't read her expression. She turned back to David. "David, what about Shareese?"

"I can't do it anymore. I can't deal with her, she's young and immature. We have nothing in common except the children. We have nothing."

Wade watched as tears sprang to Terry's eyes, and he immediately felt a moment of uncertainty. He stood straighter, looking from Terry to David and then back again, trying to decide if he should leave. Seeing a tear travel down Terry's cheek, Wade's jaw clinched. Okay, if she wanted to be with his guy, that was fine. But there was no way he was going to voluntarily leave her with this jerk.

## Chapter 41

"David," Terry said slowly, brushing the unchecked tear from her cheek, and then took a step close to him. She placed her palm against his chest. "I should knock you on your ass!" He blinked at her, clearly stunned. "So you're going to leave this girl with three babies and think you can just come running back to me? No, buddy, that shit is not happening!"

"Terry…"

"No! You need to stop right there. I can't believe you would try this shit. No, actually, I *can* believe it. You are so sorry; you need to go home to your woman and your children, and beg her to stay with you. Does she know you're here? What did you tell her?"

David looked uncomfortable, but only briefly. "Shareese doesn't know I'm here. She doesn't know I want you back. Terry, this is my home."

"No, it isn't, not anymore, mister, and I have the papers to prove it." Terry frowned up at him. "You mean to tell me that that girl doesn't even know that you're thinking about leaving her?" David didn't answer. "God! You are such a loser; I should call her right now and tell her what you're doing. She probably wouldn't believe me, but I'd be doing her a favor by letting her know just what kind of asshole you are."

"Terry, I'm not staying with Shareese," David said. Terry remained silent and when he realized that she wasn't going to comment, he took a quick step back. His expression grew angry. He glared at Wade and thrust his chin up as he spoke. "I don't like you having strange men around our sons."

Terry looked at him and shook her head. It was clear that she didn't feel anger toward David. Hell, if Wade was any judge of her character, she didn't even feel vindicated. After all, this was DJ's and Keith's father, and he was about to ruin his life. From the expression on her face, she just felt sorry for him.

Terry sighed. "David, go home."

# Chapter 42

"How did everything go on Thanksgiving? Did you have a good time?" Nurjahan asked Wade the following Saturday. Wade glanced in his father's direction. "He knows, I explained everything to him."

He looked at his mother, his eyes saying that he wished she had not, but either she couldn't, or didn't want to understand. "Everything went well."

"Your mother told me about your problems with this woman's son," his dad said. "You know how these teens are nowadays. The two of you need to put your foot down and tell him to stop being a baby and deal with it."

Wade looked away from his father for a moment, and then turned back to him. "It's not that easy, dad."

"How is it not easy? That's the problem with these kids nowadays; the parents let them rule everything. That's the way I raised you, your brother, and your sister. And that's what you need to do with these kids, if you're going to be a part of their lives. You need to go in there and take charge."

Wade glared at his father. "I don't need you telling me how to live my life!"

"I'm just telling you how to deal with teenagers. I know what I'm talking about. I raised you right, and you need to do the same thing. You need to have a firm hand with them and let them know who's the boss," Wade Sr. snorted. "You need to toughen up. Don't let these kids walk all over you. I didn't let you-"

"No!"

"What the hell do you mean; no?"

"I don't need you telling me how to deal with my woman and her children, when it took you close to fifteen fucking years to figure out how to deal with your own."

Wade Sr. glared at him. "Don't you dare talk to me like that!"

Nurjahan took a step closer to her husband, resting a hand on his shoulder. "Why don't you both just calm down?"

"That's right, boy; you need to calm your ass the hell down."

"Don't tell me to calm the fuck down," Wade yelled at his father.

"I'm your father. I'm trying to tell you something that obviously you need to learn. I raised three children, you didn't."

"Bullshit," Wade bellowed. "You don't know the first thing about children. You don't even know about being a man. A man doesn't put his hands on his woman."

His father reeled, clearly appalled. "I never did that. I never touched your mother. I was a good provider, and a good husband to your mother. I was a good man, and you know it."

"Yes, you did, you beat the shit out of Mamma, and you beat the shit out of me!"

"Wade!" his mother rounded the table, placing what she hoped was a calming hand on Wade's chest.

"You liar! I did no such thing. I was a good father and a good husband. I did everything for you, gave up everything for you." Wade Sr. shook visibly, but not from fear or sorrow.

Wade could see that, he could see the hatred burning in the steel gray eyes staring back at him. Wade was so angry, his temples pounded thickly and his throat was tight. Was this man insane, or was the sinister bastard just pretending, because he didn't want to face what he did to his family? Wade suppressed the urge to drive his fist into his face. Eyes narrowed, Wade uttered a low growl.

"Why are you here?" Wade Sr. said, sarcasm creeping in his voice, hatred piercing his eyes.

"I'm here to see my mother and grandmother," Wade said just as hotly.

"Well, you're not wanted here. This is my house."

Wade slid the chair back from the table. "You know, you're a very lucky man. You're lucky that my mother loves you as much as she does or you wouldn't be here today. You need to thank her for your life, because if it weren't for her, I would have killed you long ago. She saved your worthless life, the woman that loves you and would do anything for you. Even after you beat her until she was black and blue, kicking her while she covered my body with hers. Do you know that that night, I wanted you dead? I lay in my bed, and I thought and plotted, and if it wasn't for mama, I would have killed you in your sleep!"

Wade watched his father as the depth of his son's hatred registered. Wade turned and left the house without a second glance.

# Chapter 43

When DJ walked downstairs, Wade rose from his place on the sofa. DJ froze when he saw him and then turned as if to head back upstairs.

"Hey, DJ, why don't we go for a walk?" Wade suggested.

DJ stopped and turned to look at Wade, and then he shook his head. "I don't want to."

"I think it would be a good idea," Terry said, picking up DJ's jacket and holding it out to him. "Dinner will be ready when you get back."

Wade picked up his jacket and slipped it on. "We'll just take a walk over to the park."

DJ heaved a weighty sigh and glanced in Terry's direction. She looked at him expectantly. He crossed the room, took his jacket from his mother, and slipped it on. Grabbing his basketball, he reluctantly followed Wade out the front door.

Terry rushed to the door. "Hey." DJ turned as Terry walked to the top steps. She straightened the collar of his jacket and patted his chest whispering, "Behave."

Wade and DJ walked in silence until they reached the park. Wade took off his jacket and took the ball from DJ to bounce it as he walked toward the empty basketball court. DJ watched Wade dribble the ball a few times before dunking the ball. Wade retrieved it, bounced it and then dunked it several more times before DJ entered the court.

Wade bounced the ball to DJ, and he bounced it, ran to the hoop, jumped, and dunked the ball.

"I know you don't like me," Wade finally said. "And I'm wondering if you can tell me what the problem is?"

DJ hunched his shoulders. "You're all right," He said, his eyes never leaving the ball as he bounced it.

Wade walked in front of him and DJ looked up. Wade held up his hands and DJ passed him the ball and watched as Wade effortlessly jumped and dunked the ball.

"Are you worried about your mom?" DJ looked away. "I know how it is to be your age and worry about your mother."

"Did your parents get divorced?"

"I wish," Wade muttered. He bounced the ball a few times and then stopped, catching the ball, and held it under his arm. "Look, I'm going to tell you something that I have only confided to two people, my best friend, and your mother." DJ fidgeted uneasily, looking around. Wade waited until he was sure that he had DJ's undivided attention. "My dad was a pig, and he treated my mother like crap."

DJ watched Wade for a moment. "He cheated on her?"

"Yes, but he used to beat her as well."

DJ shoved his hands into his pockets and looked down. "My dad cheated on my mom, but he never hit her."

"I know. My dad really hurt my mom, he broke her body, but worse, he tried to break her spirit."

"Why did he do that?"

Wade looked around the empty basketball court, and then back at DJ. "I honestly don't know. But I can tell you that I love you mother. And I'll never intentionally hurt her, ever."

"My mom likes you a lot too. But…"

"But, what?" DJ held his hands up and Wade threw the ball. He caught it and threw the ball into the hoop.

"When my dad got with Shareese, he didn't want to have anything to do with Keith." Wade noticed that DJ didn't mention himself, but he could also see the pain that his father not wanting to spend time with him had caused as well. "Keith is just a little kid, and my dad just forgot about him. If you and my mom get together, what will happen to Keith? Who's going to take care of him?"

"Your mother will. She would never forget you guys just because she's dating me. She loves you more than anything in this world and that will never change. And I care about you. I know it's hard for you to believe, but I do."

DJ shuffled from foot to foot. "I don't want a new father."

"I'm not trying to be a father; I only want to be your friend, if I can." DJ remained silent. "One day, your mother and I may decide to get married, and if we do, I'll be your step-father, but I'll never try to take your father's place. And, as far as your having a problem with me telling you what to do…well, I'm going to always do that, that's just who I am. Even if I wasn't seeing your mother, I would tell you what to do. That's part of being a teacher and a responsible adult."

They played one-on-one for about forty-five minutes, and then Wade walked from the court grabbing their jackets.

"Let's get back to the house, your mother's cooked dinner, and she's probably waiting for us."

## Chapter 43

DJ put on his jacket, picking up the ball, and dribbled it as they walked from the park. He glanced at Wade. "Maybe we should go out to eat?"

"Your mom went through a lot of trouble preparing a special dinner for us. I think she'd be really disappointed if we suggested going out to dinner."

DJ laughed and playfully pushed Wade's arm. "I guess you've never tasted my mom's cooking before, have you?"

When they entered the house, Wade went in search of Terry, while DJ went up to his bedroom. Wade stopped in the kitchen doorway and leaned against the doorjamb, watching as Terry danced around the kitchen, her hips swaying seductively as she sang off key to *Marvin Gaye's, Let's Get It On*. Wade grinned and pushed himself from the wall to walk up behind her and slip his arms around her waist.

She jumped slightly and then laughed. "Hey. How did things go?"

"Good." He leaned over her shoulder, looking into one of the pots. What are you making?"

"Onion Chicken in Balsamic sauce."

He kissed her cheek. "Point me in the right direction, and I'll set the table."

They were seated around the table. Wade sat at one end with Terry across from him. DJ sat to Wade's right, and Keith was to his left. Terry walked from the kitchen carry a serving platter with steaming plump chicken breast, surrounded by onions, peppers and red potatoes, smothered in a brown sauce.

"Wow, looks delicious, babe."

Terry grinned as she sat down and placed her napkin across her lap. She passed the serving plate to DJ to put a chicken breast and potatoes on his plate, before passing the platter to Wade. Wade put food on his plate and served Keith before passing the platter to Terry.

While Wade was spooning food onto Keith's plate, DJ rose and went to the kitchen before he quickly returned to his seat. Grinning at his mother, he sat a bottle of hot sauce in the center of the table. "Keisha says that hot sauce makes everything taste good."

Wade coughed on a laugh, and Terry glowered at him. He met her gaze and kept a straight face, but she probably saw the corner of his mouth twitch as he was fighting to hold back a smile. She rolled her eyes and then glared at DJ.

She snatched the bottle of hot sauce from the table, putting it on the floor next to her chair. "Eat."

Wade laughed then, and when Terry glowered at him, he put a spoonful of food in his mouth. He chewed for a moment and then frowned. He chewed a few more times, and then smiled at Terry before reluctantly scooping another spoonful into his mouth. Terry beamed proudly before digging into her meal.

DJ laughed, leaned toward Wade, and whispered. "I warned you."

# Chapter 44

It was a week after Thanksgiving, twelve days since Terry and Wade had followed Henderson to that warehouse. Every day Terry had asked, "Wade, when are we going in? When are we going to bust that dirt bag, Henderson?"

Wade would always tell her, "Don't worry, Babe, I have it under control."

She didn't know it, but *she* wasn't doing anything. He was not taking a chance of having anything happen to her. His team was able to get someone inside the warehouse during the middle of the night to plant a few listening devices. Everything was set, and a raid was scheduled for the next three nights. Wade dropped his head back on the headrest. If he didn't get those pictures of Henderson with his mistress she would be really upset.

After initially following Henderson, Wade investigated and found out that Henderson's girlfriend, Lauren Parker, didn't have a record, no parking tickets, nothing. She did have a knack for picking men who had long criminal records. Her last three boyfriends had spent time in prison; the most recent one was serving fifteen years for armed robbery. The two before him had records connected to drugs. To Wade's surprise, Lauren was the mother of Lindsey, DJ's friend. The investigation further showed that Chad Odell and Lauren had had a relationship, years before, and were still acquainted. Evidently, Lauren introduced Odell to Henderson, or vice versa. Either way, the two men set up shop, and brought Jason in. Lindsey, who was a busy little girl, transported marijuana for distribution and went completely undetected.

Terry raced down the driveway to Wade's truck. She popped the door open and slid inside leaning over and giving him a quick kiss. "Hi."

"Hey, babe."

Despite his misgivings, he couldn't help but smile at her eagerness. He pulled from the curb.

"What are we going to do?"

"We're headed down to West Randolph. Your guy and his girlfriend are meeting at Blackbird's."

Terry glanced at him. "How did you find that out?"

He didn't answer, just smiled. They pulled into the parking lot, and Wade turned around to reach into the backseat and grab his camera. "Sit tight, babe, I'll be right back."

"Where the hell do you think you're going?"

"I'm going to get your pictures."

"No, you're not." Terry pulled her digital camera from her pocket. "This is my case; I want to do this myself."

He moaned, "Terry…"

She met his gaze. "No. I'm going. You wait here. If I can't at least take a picture, then I don't deserve to have Dee train me as an investigator."

Wade groaned and then nodded reluctantly. He watched Terry get out of the car and cross the parking lot.

## Chapter 44

Ten minutes later, Terry came rushing out of Blackbird's. She ran across the parking lot, her coat billowing behind her. In one hand, she clutched the camera, while her other hand waved frantically in the air as she yelled, "Start the truck! Start the truck!"

## Chapter 45

I'll get the coffee and meet you at the desk," Holly's partner said, as they walked into the squad room.

"Hey, Lawson, someone's here to see you; she's waiting for you at your desk," One of the other officers called to Holly.

She waved to him, and walked along the row of desks, wiggling out of her jacket as she moved. Halfway toward the end of the row, her pace slowed and she saw Terry sitting in one of the chairs a few desks away from her own. Holly shook her head when their gazes meet. She bit the inside of her mouth to stop the curse that she felt forming. Instead of slowing her pace, she shifted her gaze and walked past Terry.

Terry rose from her chair, following Holly to her desk. "Hey, you'll never guess what happened. I just left the office of the FBI."

"I knew it. I just knew it. Ain't this a mother…?" Holly growled, not bothering to look at Terry as she opened the top left hand drawer of her desk and dropped her purse inside.

"Oooh, the take out jar," Terry said in a singsong voice.

She grinned at Holly when she received a murderous glare and tapped the jar that sat on the corner of Holly's desk. Holly glared at her more intently, and then, digging into her pocket, she pulled out a five-dollar bill, shoved it into the jar, and let it rip – she gave Terry a full five dollars' worth!

"Wow," Terry grinned again. "I didn't know you knew all those words, and you put them together so well." Holly let off another string of curses. "You done? You feel better now?"

"I can't believe you; you promised me that you wouldn't get into any more trouble. What the hell are you doing here?"

"I didn't get in trouble."

"Why would the FBI pick you up? I'm sure you're not here on a social visit."

Terry sat down in the chair across from Holly's desk, leaning forward. "Guess what happened."

Holly sat down and put her forehead in her hands. "I'm afraid to ask."

Terry looked around them, and then back at Holly. "The guy that I was following, the case that I was working on. Well, turns out that he has been running this drug and arms ring."

"What?"

"Yep, Wade was investigating him, and he didn't know that his guy was my guy."

"How the hell did you…? What do you mean, Wade is investigating? You got him involved in this mess?"

"Yeah. I mean, no. Well, technically I didn't get him involved, even though he is, since he's FBI, and it was his case."

"He's what? Wait a minute, Terry, start at the beginning."

"Okay, listen," Terry started from the beginning or the beginning of where Wade had decided to help her, as she put it, finish her mission. "And guess what else? DJ's friend, Lindsey, is Henderson's girlfriend's daughter. She and a few of the kids at school are involved, as well as one of the gym teachers." Terry grinned. "I got the pictures of this guy cheating with his mistress slash business partner. Mr. home-wrecker-dirt-bag also got busted for running drugs and arms. Oh, yeah, you remember when DJ got in trouble at the beginning of the school year; you know when he was trying to cut out early? Well, that kid. Remember when DJ's friend Micah, Dennis, or whatever his name was, they found some drugs in his backpack? Well, guess who he got it from?" Holly waited expectantly. "Ms. Lindsey herself." Terry shook her head. "Man, talk about lowlifes. This guy and his loser skank girlfriend were using her daughter and friends to distribute drugs at the school."

"Geez."

"So," Terry spread her arms wide and threw them in the air. "I solved the case."

Holly watched her in amazement for a moment. "Well, I'll be damned."

Terry bit her lip and slid to the end of her seat. "Holly…" *Oh shit.* Terry never called her Holly and warning bells went off in her head. "I need a favor."

"What?" Holly asked reluctantly.

"I need you to tell Dee about me working as a PI."

"Nope," Holly answered before Terry could finish asking.

"Come on."

"Nope!"

"Please…" Terry said, including a little whine.

"When Dee finds out what you did, she's going to be livid. I don't even want to be the one to tell her."

Terry sighed. "Is that your final answer?"

"Yep."

"Damn."

# Chapter 46

The next evening, Abby opened the front door of the home before Terry had a chance to knock.

"Hey, kiddo," Terry said, putting her arm around Abby and kissing the top of her head. "Where's your mama?"

"In the kitchen, talking to Aunt Dee."

Terry walked toward the kitchen, slowing, when she heard Dee's voice.

"I didn't know what to say to her, she was going on and on about the photos that she received from us about her husband." Terry heard Dee say as she walked into the kitchen. She froze in the doorway and debated if she should slip out and hope that she could do it unnoticed. "I didn't even know what the hell she was talking about."

Out of the corner of her eye, Holly saw Terry enter the kitchen and she knew from the look on Terry's face that she was contemplating a quick getaway. "Terry did you hear that?" she spoke up, before Terry could sneak out.

Terry's back was to the kitchen and she was tiptoeing in the opposite direction by the time Holly finished her question. *Damn, busted.* She turned back to the kitchen doorway and groaned inwardly. "Uh, what? Oh you know what? I forgot that I was supposed to…"

Holly gestured toward the chair next to Dee, indicating that she wanted Terry to sit down, and quickly spoke, cutting off Terry's excuse. "Dee said that she just had one of their clients call her about a case that was closed, and they don't know how that happened."

Terry looked first at Dee, and then Holly, before grudgingly sitting down. Holly turned back to Dee asking, "So, everything turned out okay?"

"Well, kind of. Yeah, the client is glad that she found out her husband was cheating, but she freaked out because he was busted for some drug thing. I didn't get all the details, but the gist of the story is that he and the woman that he was cheating with were running some drug and gun dealing thing."

"But, your case turned out okay. You got all the information that you needed?" Holly asked.

"Yeah, some of the photos were a little shoddy, and the report wasn't in the style and format that we use, but it was okay. I don't understand what's going on, I've asked Chris and Blaine. They swear they don't know anything about it. If I find out that they do and they're messing with me, I'm going to rip them a new one. All I've been doing today is trying to figure out what the hell is going on, and it's really starting to piss me off."

"Well, damn," Terry tugged her purse up her shoulder. "You guys seem to have this all under control." She slid from her chair. "Let me just get out of your hair."

"Sit down, Terry." Holly demanded.

"Okay," Terry said sitting back down, but keeping her purse on her lap as a sort of barrier between her and Dee.

Holly sighed. "Dee, I have to tell you something; but, before I do, you need to remember that I'm a cop, and as much as I love you, if you commit murder, I'm going to have to arrest you."

"What the hell are you talking…" she glanced from Holly to Terry, obviously seeing the guilty look Terry was trying to hide. "You didn't?"

"Before you freak out on her," Holly said. "Let her explain."

Dee turned back to Holly. "You knew this?"

Holly's brows rose in guilt. "Well. Um… I did, but I didn't find out until a couple of weeks ago."

"A couple of weeks ago? And you didn't tell me?"

"I made her promise not to tell you," Terry said quickly.

"That doesn't matter, you still should have told me," Dee yelled at Holly, completely ignoring Terry.

"I'm sorry, I know I should…"

"Don't yell at her," Terry snapped. "You don't have a right to get mad at Red. She's always been there for you. It's not her fault anyway, it's mine. I never should have put her in this position. I'm sorry, Holly."

Both Holly and Dee stared at Terry for a moment, complete looks of surprise on their faces at her fierce defense of Holly. Holly smiled at her and nodded.

"Look, Dee, I just wanted to prove that I could be a PI. I really wanted this, and I just thought that if I could solve one of your cases, you would see how serious I was."

"Terry…" Dee said, as she shook her head.

"I did everything the way I thought you would, um…well, everything except getting stuck in that drain and losing my Cole Haan's when I was chasing some junkie bitch who stole my thirty bucks."

"You lost your Cole Haan's?" Dee asked.

"You got stuck in a drain pipe?" Holly asked at the same time.

Terry signed. "I just wanted to show you that I'm not worthless and that I could be of some help."

Dee looked at the dejected expression that Terry was giving her, and sighed. "Okay, Terry, I can see you're serious about this investigation thing, and I think it's a good thing. I honestly hope I don't live to regret this…" She paused. "I'll let you come to work with me and teach you as much as I can."

Terry grinned at Dee. "Thanks. Um… but, I don't know if I want to be a PI now. Um, I sort of like working with the kids. They sort of grow on you, you know?"

"Hold on. Are you serious? After everything you've done?" Holly asked.

Terry nodded, "I mean, don't get me wrong, they still drive me crazy sometimes, but I've finally found something that I'm good at. And, I do like doing it, for the most part. And it's a business that I can honestly say that I started on my own."

Dee and Holly both smiled at her.

"I'm proud of you," Dee said.

"Me too," Holly added. "Plus, if Abby couldn't come to your house every day after school, I don't know what she'd do. Tyler or myself for that matter, she'd drive us crazy. 'Mommy, can I go to Aunt Terry's house', 'Mommy what is Aunt Terry doing and why can't she watch us anymore?' " Holly said, doing an excellent imitation of her daughter. "She would have me calling you every day and begging you to come and get her. I'd probably end up paying you to take her to work with you just so I can have some peace."

Terry laughed. "I'd miss her too. Plus, if I ever want some adventure, I can always help Wade with one of his cases."

"Hmm, have you discussed this with Wade yet?" Dee asked.

"Yeah, I'd like to be a fly on the wall when you bring that subject up," Holly said.

"I did a good job with his thing. He'll value my experience," Terry said proudly.

Both Dee and Holly looked at each other before they burst out laughing.

Terry laughed again. "It won't be that bad. I've already helped him with the Henderson case."

Dee's brows rose and Terry proceeded to tell her how she and Wade followed Henderson to the warehouse and found out about the drug ring.

"Wow, you've been rather busy," Dee said.

Holly leaned across the table toward Terry. "What I want to know is, did you really get stuck in a drain pipe?"

"Yeah."

Holly grinned. "Man, I bet that was priceless; I would loved to have been there to see that."

"You would," Terry laughed as she told Holly and Dee about her adventures as a PI.

# Chapter 47

"Hey, Happy New Year," Dee said, opening the front door. She was nearly bowled over by Keith as he raced past her. "Hey, watch the baby bump." Dee laughed knowing that Keith was in a hurry to find Abby.

"Hi, Aunt Dee," DJ greeted her, as he passed her heading in the direction that Keith had disappeared.

"Hi, sweetie," she said to DJ, as she leaned close to Terry, embraced her, and stepped back to allow them to enter the house. She gave Wade a brief hug as well. "We're all in the kitchen." Dee said, leading Terry and Wade down the hallway.

When they entered the kitchen, Terry and Wade greeted everyone.

"Hey," Terry said hugging Jennifer. "I didn't know you'd be here. After last night, I thought you'd be too tired to go out."

Terry and Wade had gone to the New Year's Eve party that Jennifer had invited them to. They had left a little after midnight, but Jennifer had decided to stay.

"Wade asked Dee if it was okay if I spent the day with you guys." She smiled up at Wade and gave him a quick wink.

"Hey, Terry Ann," Keisha greeted her from her perch on the tall stool at the counter.

## Chapter 47

"Hey," Terry said, stopping at Keisha's side and snatching up a celery stick from the platter in the center of the table. Terry eyed the man sitting next to Keisha, who absolutely was *not* Deion.

"Hey, Hugo," Wade greeted the other man.

He reached around Terry to clasp his hand. Terry's brows rose. She looked back and forth from Keisha and Hugo. Keisha grinned at her.

"Hi, Wade, I didn't know that you knew Keisha."

"Ooh," Wade said. "Hostess."

Hugo glanced at Keisha, adoringly and nodded. Terry noticed the look that passed between Hugo and Wade.

"Hugo," Keisha said. "This is my cousin, Terry, and you seem to know Wade, he's her boyfriend." Keisha bit her lip giving Terry a small smile.

"No, I'm not," Wade quickly said. Terry looked up at him, her eyes large. "You said that you didn't want anything serious. You said no boyfriend."

Terry looked around the kitchen, all eyes were on her. She glared up at Wade. "So, what are you trying to say?"

"I'm saying that we're not official."

Terry sucked her teeth, propping her hands on her hips. "All right, Wade, will you be my boyfriend?"

Wade looked down at her, looked around at the people gathered around them, then turned back to Terry. "No, Terry, I don't want to be your boyfriend."

Terry felt hot tears burn the back of her throat. She swallowed hard. "Okay, no problem."

"I don't want to be your boyfriend." Reaching inside his pants pocket, he pulled out a small blue box. "But I'll settle for being your fiancé."

# Epilogue

Terry smiled, inhaling the scent of roses. She looked to her left at Dee and Holly, each dressed in soft peach silk gowns. Both gave her a tearful smile. She looked to her right at Wade; he bought her hand to his lips, kissing her knuckles.

He mouthed, 'I love you,' and then aloud said, "I do."

"Do you, Terry Ann Meyers, take Wade Nelson to be your wedded husband," the minister said. "To have and to hold from this day forward, for better for worse, for richer for poorer, in sickness and in health, to love, cherish, and to obey…?"

Terry's lips formed an O-shape as she looked at the man standing in front of her.

Terry looked over her shoulder. Her friends and family were sitting there smiling and happy. She turned back to the minister and slowly raised her hand. He paused and frowned. She stepped close and whispered in his ear, and then reached inside her left satin glove, pulled out a slip of paper and handed it to him. She moved back, taking her place next to Wade, looked up at him and hunched her shoulders. The minister grinned and cleared his throat unfolding the paper.

Terry looked over her shoulder at their guests again. "Sorry, I don't do 'obey' well."

"So I've noticed," Wade said with a grin.

Everyone laughed as the minister started to read from the slip of paper.

"Do you, Ann Meyers, take Wade Nelson, to be your lawfully wedded husband? Will you be his friend, partner, and lover from this day forward? Will you vow to be faithful in sickness and in health, in good times and in bad? Will you support him in his goals, and respect him," The minister paused and looked up at Terry, who gestured for him to keep reading. "As long as he respects you?" Laughter and snickers were heard throughout the church.

"Will you promise to laugh with him, cry with him, cherish him, and learn how to cook for him?" More laughter filled the room. "And love him unconditionally for as long as you both shall live?"

"Absolutely," Terry nodded.

"By the power vested in me, I now pronounce you man and wife. Wade, you may kiss your bride."

Cheers rang through the room as he did so.

"Please stand and allow me to introduce Mr. and Mrs. Wade Nelson," The minister said, as Wade and Terry turned and walked hand in hand down the aisle.

A few hours later, Wade felt his breast pocket, feeling the two tickets he had stuck there early that morning. In four hours, he and Terry would be on a plane headed to their honeymoon in Malaysia. Holly and Dee had agreed to take care of the boys. Terry had found someone who was willing to accept her kids from the daycare during the honeymoon, and he had two weeks off. Seated next to him was his new wife, dressed in the most beautiful gown he'd ever seen. The halter-top ecru gown had a plunging neckline that revealed Terry's voluptuous cleavage and held Wade completely captivated.

He smiled, and fantasized about all the things he wanted to do with those gorgeous breasts, while he sipped from his champagne flute.

Wade suddenly coughed, nearly choking on the champagne. "What?"

Holly's eyes sparkled as she noticed the look on Wade's face. "Terry was just telling us that she was sure she was going to be able to keep the daycare going and work with you simultaneously."

"Yeah?"

Dee's eyes held as much mischief as Holly's did. "She was saying how easy it would be for her to juggle both careers, seeing how she did it while she solved that case for me. You know, the case that you helped her with."

Dee then gave Wade a huge smile and he groaned. He looked at Terry. "Um, work with me how, babe?"

"You know, I'll be helping you with some of the cases that you'll be investigating. We are partners after all."

He glanced at everyone sitting around the table; Holly's lips twitched as she tried to suppress her laughter. Dee's smile grew larger, while Ben and Tyler merely grinned.

"You did promise to be my partner in our vows…" Terry said, before Wade laughed and pulled her close, capturing her lips. She moaned melting into him, and slipped her arms around his neck. If nothing else, his beautiful wife was going to keep him on his toes for the next fifty or sixty years.

## If you enjoyed reading *Until Now...*, you'll also like Denise Skelton's other novels.

**My Everything**

At the age of 20, Benjamin Harrison's father dies, leaving him to provide for his mother and sister. Years later, his sister is in need of a bone marrow transplant, and Ben seeks the help of Meyer's Investigations to find an unknown sibling to save her. His immediate attraction to the sexy female P.I. sets things in motion, and their relationship blossoms.

Adventuresome private investigator Deanna Meyers senses her attraction toward Ben, but she is reluctant to date him after seeing what her best friends go through with their own interracial relationships.

Ben's ex-girlfriend Janet and Dee's cousin Terry have one thing in common. They both want Dee out of the picture. But only one will go to any lengths to make that happen. Even kill.

**My Angel**

Simone Porter, an inner city youth-center director, has lived her whole life being dominated by her over-controlling mother, yet she retains her romantic nature and idealistic views about life and love. Matthew Turner, however, has been hurt by a materialistic wife who used his kindness and affection and threw it away for another man. Now his heart is hardened and he feels he will never love again the way he once loved his wife.

Brought together by an almost deadly "accident," Simone and Matthew develop a bond that becomes the basis for a fantastic friendship. Despite the extreme disapproval of Simone's mother and Matt's father, they become best friends. But is friendship alone enough to heal Matt's broken heart? And is Simone capable of going against her mother's wishes and standing for up for what she wants?

As they juggle work, family conflicts, and their own conflicting feelings, the passion and attraction between them becomes too great to ignore. However, Simone is torn between Alan, the man her mom wants for her, and Matt, the man her heart wants for her. Matt must decide between the ex-wife that used to be his everything, and Simone, his "Angel." However, in this battle between true love and family influence, Simone and Matt learn that it is sometimes harder than it should be for best friends to become lovers. And Matt's relationship with his ex-wife proves to be more dangerous to them than anyone could have imagined …

**Forgotten Promises**

True Love Comes Along Once in a Lifetime….

That's what Detective Holly Lawson James believed. Her husband and co-worker Edmond was everything a woman could want in a man and a partner; strong, warm and romantic, he filled her life and her heart with passion and joy - until a police sting went terribly wrong and abruptly took him from her and their little girl, Abby. On that day her life changed forever. Now five years later Holly has grown accustomed to being alone, a state that suits her perfectly well, because she's sure that true love comes along only once in a lifetime…

Despite promising his wife otherwise, Tyler Green knew he would never find love again. He had watched powerlessly as cancer ravaged his beautiful Felicia. Day by day, moment by moment, the illness, like a thief, dragged her closer toward death and tore away big chunks of his heart. When it was finally over he was left empty and cold, but it doesn't matter to Tyler because he's sure that true love will never head his way again…

Still, love has a way of getting through to the stoniest of hearts and all it takes is one mischievous little girl and an unlikely meddling angel to prove them both wrong. But there is danger lurking in the shadows of their new beginning and one person's obsession may well cause Holly to lose the most important thing in her life…her daughter!